Five

What *not* to do at IIT

Chetan Bhagat is the author of two blockbuster novels – *Five Point Someone* (2004) and *One Night @ The Call Center* (2005) – which continue to top bestseller lists. In March 2008, the *New York Times* called him the 'biggest-selling English-language novelist in India's history'. Both his books have inspired major Bollywood films.

Seen more as the voice of a generation than just an author, this IIT/IIM-A graduate is making India read like never before. *The 3 Mistakes of My Life* is his third novel.

After eleven years in Hong Kong, the author relocated to Mumbai in 2008, where he works as an investment banker. Apart from books, the author has a keen interest in screenplays and spirituality. Chetan is married to Anusha, his classmate from IIM-A, and has twin boys – Ishaan and Shyam.

Praise for
Five Point Someone
and
one night @ the call center

Five Point Someone

What *not* to do at IIT

A Novel

by

CHETAN BHAGAT

Rupa . Co

For my mother

For IIT, my alma mater

Contents

Acknowledgements

Well, to say this is my book would be totally untrue. At best, this was my dream. There are people in this world, some of them so wonderful, that made this dream become a product that you are holding in your hand. I would like to thank all of them, and in particular:

Shinie Antony — mentor, guru and friend, who taught me the basics of telling a story and stayed with me right till the end. If she hadn't encouraged and harassed me all the way, I would have given this up a long time ago.

James Turner, Gaurav Malik, Jessica Rosenberg, Ritu Malik, Tracie Ang, Angela Wang and Rimjhim Chattopadhya — amazing friends who read the manuscript and gave honest comments. All of them also stayed with me in the process, and handled me and my sometimes out-of-control emotions so well.

Anusha Bhagat — a wife who was once a classmate, and was the first reader of the draft. Apart from being shocked by some of the incidents in the book, she kept her calm as she had to face the tough job of improving the product and not upsetting her husband.

My mom Rekha Bhagat and brother Ketan, two people with an irrational, unbreakable belief in me that bordered on craziness at times. My relationship with them goes beyond the common genes we share, and I, like every author, needed their irrational support for me.

My IIT friends Ashish (Golu), Johri, VK, Manu, Shanky, Pappu, Manhar, VP, Rahul, Mehta, Pago, Assem, Rajeev G., Rahul, Lavmeet,Puneet, Chapar and all others. This is a work of fiction, but fiction needs real inspiration. I love them all so much that I could literally write a book on them. Hey wait, have I?

My friends in Hong Kong, my work colleagues, my yoga teachers and others that surround me, love me and make life fun.

The editor and the entire team at Rupa for being so professional and friendly through the process.

And lastly, it is only when one writes a book that one realizes the true power of MSWord, from grammar checks to replace-alls. It is simple — without this software, this book would not be written. Thank you Mr Bill Gates and Microsoft Corp!

Prologue

I had never been inside an ambulance before. It was kind of creepy. Like a hospital was suddenly asked to pack up and move. Instruments, catheters, drips and a medicine box surrounded two beds. There was hardly any space for me and Ryan to stand even as Alok got to sprawl out. I guess with thirteen fractures you kind of deserve a bed. The sheets were originally white, which was hard to tell now as Alok's blood covered every square inch of them. Alok lay there unrecognizable, his eyeballs rolled up and his tongue collapsed outside his mouth like an old man without dentures. Four front teeth gone, the doctor later told us.

His limbs were motionless, just like his father's right side, the right knee bent in a way that would make you think Alok was boneless. He was still, and if I had to bet my money, I'd have said he was dead.

"If Alok makes it through this, I will write a book about our crazy days. I really will," I swore. It is the kind of absurd promise you make to yourself when you are seriously messed up in the head and you haven't slept for fifty hours straight...

1

Bare Beginnings

BEFORE I REALLY BEGIN THIS BOOK, LET ME FIRST TELL you what this book is not. It is not a guide on how to live through college. On the contrary, it is probably an example of how screwed up your college years can get if you don't think straight. But then this is my take on it, you're free to agree or disagree. I expect Ryan and Alok, psychos both of them, will probably kill me after this but I don't really care. I mean, if they wanted their version out there, they could have written one themselves. But Alok cannot write for nuts, and Ryan, even though he could really do whatever he wants, is too lazy to put his bum to the chair and type. So stuff it boys – it is my story, I am the one writing it and I get to tell it the way I want it.

Also, let me tell you one more thing this book is certainly not. This book will not help you get into IIT. I think half the trees in the world are felled to make up the IIT entrance exam guides. Most of them are crap, but they might help you more than this one will.

Ryan, Alok and I are probably the last people on earth you want to ask about getting into IIT. All we would say as advice is, if you can lock yourself in a room with books for two years and throw away the key, you can probably make it here. And if your high school days were half as miserable as mine, disappearing behind a pile of books will not seem like such a bad idea. My last two years in school were living hell, and unless you captained the basketball team or played the electric guitar since age six, probably yours were too. But I don't really want to get into all that.

I think I have made my disclaimers, and it is time for me to commence.

Well, I have to start somewhere, and what better than the day I joined the Indian Institute of Technology and met Ryan and Alok for the first time; we had adjacent rooms on the second floor of the Kumaon hostel. As per tradition, seniors rounded us up on the balcony for ragging at midnight. I was still rubbing my eyes as the three of us stood to attention and three seniors faced us. A senior named Anurag leaned against a wall. Another senior, to my nervous eye, looked like a demon from cheap mythological TV shows — six feet tall, over a hundred kilos, dark, hairy, and huge teeth that were ten years late meeting an orthodontist. Although he inspired terror, he spoke little and was busy providing background for the boss, Baku, a lungi-clad human toothpick, and just as smelly is my guess.

"You bloody freshers, dozing away eh? Rascals, who will give an introduction?" he screamed.

"I am Hari Kumar sir, Mechanical Engineering student, All India Rank 326." I was nothing if not honest under pressure.

"I am Alok Gupta sir, Mechanical Engineering, Rank 453," Alok said as I looked at him for the first time. He was my height, five feet five inches – in short, very short – and had these thick, chunky glasses on. His portly frame was covered in neatly ironed white kurta-pajamas.

"Ryan Oberoi, Mechanical Engineering, Rank 91, sir," Ryan said in a deep husky voice and all eyes swung to him.

Ryan Oberoi, I repeated his name again mentally. Now here was a guy you don't see in IIT too often; tall, with spare height, purposefully lean and unfairly handsome. A loose gray T-shirt proclaimed 'GAP' in big blue letters on his chest and shiny black shorts reached his knees. Relatives abroad for sure, I thought. Nobody wears GAP to bed otherwise.

"You bastards," Baku was shrieking, "Off with your clothes."

"Aw Baku, let us talk to them a bit first," protested Anurag, leaning against the wall, sucking a cigarette butt.

"No talking!" Baku said, one scrawny hand up. "No talking, just remove those damn clothes."

Another demon grinned at us, slapping his bare stomach every few seconds. There seemed to be no choice so we surrendered every item of our clothing, shivering at the unholy glee in Baku's face as he walked by each of us, checking us out and grinning.

Nakedness made the difference between our bodies more stark as Alok and me drew figures on the floor with deeply embarrassed toes, trying to be casual about our twisted balloon figures. Ryan's body was flawless, man, he was a hunk; muscles that cut at the right places and a body frame that for once resembled the human body shown in biology books. You could describe his body as sculpture. Alok and I, on the other hand, weren't exactly what you'd call art.

Baku told Alok and me to step forward, so the seniors could have better view and a bigger laugh.

"Look at them, mothers fed them until they are ready to explode, little Farex babies," Baku cackled.

The demon joined him in laughter. Anurag smiled behind a burst of smoke as he extinguished another cigarette, creating his own special effects.

"Sir, please sir, let us go sir," Alok pleaded to Baku as he came closer.

"What? Let you go? We haven't even done anything yet to you beauties. C'mon bend down on all fours now, you two fatsos."

I looked at Alok's face. His eyes were invisible behind those thick, bulletproof spectacles, but going by his contorted face, I could tell he was as close to tears as I was.

"C'mon, do what he says," the demon admonished. He and Baku seemed to share a symbiotic relationship; Baku needed him for brute strength, while the servile demon needed him for directions.

Alok and I bent down on all fours. More laughter, this time from above our heads, ensued. The demon suggested racing both of us, his first original opinion in a while but Baku over-rode him.

"No racing-vacing, I have a better idea. Just wait, I have to go to my room. And you naked cows, don't lóok up."

Baku raced up the corridor as we waited for twenty tense seconds, gazing at the floor. I glanced sideways and noticed a small water puddle adjacent to Alok's head, droplets falling from his eye.

Meanwhile, the demon made Ryan flex his muscles and make warrior poses. I am sure he looked photogenic, but didn't dare look up to verify.

Our ears picked up Baku's hurried steps as he returned.

"Look what I got," he said, holding up his hands.

"Baku, what the hell is that for...?" Anurag enquired as we turned our heads up.

In each of his hands, Baku held an empty Coke bottle. "Take a wild guess," he said as he clanged the bottles together, making suggestive gestures.

Face turning harder, arms still in modelling pose, Ryan spoke abruptly, "Sir, what exactly are you trying to do?"

"What, isn't it obvious? And who the hell are you to ask me?" choked Baku.

"Sir, stop," Ryan said, in a louder voice.

"Fuck off," Baku dismissed, disbelief writ large in his widened eyes at this blatant rebellion against his age-old authority.

As Baku put the bottles in position, Ryan abandoned his pin-up pose and jumped. Catching him unawares, he grabbed the two bottles and stamped hard on Baku's feet. Baku released his hands and the bottles were with Ryan, James Bond style.

We knew that stomp hurt since Baku's scream was ultrasonic.

"Get this bastard," Baku shrieked in agony.

The demon's IQ was clouded by the events but his ears registered the command for action and he had just collected himself in response when Ryan smashed the two Coke bottles on the balcony parapet. Each bottle now was butt-broken, and he waved the jagged ends in air.

"Come, you bastards," Ryan swore, his face scarlet like a watermelon slice. Baku and the demon retreated a few paces. Anurag, who had been smouldering in the backdrop, snapped to attention. "Hey, cool it everyone here. How did this happen? What is your name - Ryan, take it easy man. This is just fun."

"It's not fun for me," growled Ryan, "Just get the hell out of here."

Alok and I looked at each other. I was hoping Ryan knew what he was doing. I mean sure, he was saving our ass from a Coke bottle, but broken Coke bottles could be a lot worse.

"Listen yaar," Anurag started as Ryan cut him short.

"Just get lost," Ryan shouted so hard that Baku seemed to blow away just from the impact. Actually, he was shuffling backward slowly and steadily till he was almost flying in his haste to get away, the demon following suit. Anurag stood there gaping at Ryan for a while and then looked at us.

"Tell him to control himself. Or one day he will take you guys down too," Anurag said.

Alok and I got up and wore our clothes.

"Thanks Ryan, I was really scared," Alok said, as he removed his spectacles to wipe snot and tears, face to face with his hero at last.

There is a reason why they say men should not cry, they just look so, like, ugly. Alok's spectacles were sad enough, but his baby-wet blubbery eyes were enough to depress you into suicide.

"Yes, thanks Ryan, some risk you took there. That Baku guy is sick. Though you think they would have done anything?" I said, striving for a cool I did not feel.

"Who knows? Maybe not," Ryan rotated a shoulder, "But you can never tell when guys get into mob mentality. Trust me, I have lived in enough boarding schools."

Ryan's heroics were enough to make us all bond faster than Fevicol. Besides, we were hostelite neighbours and in the same engineering department. They say you should not get into a relationship with people you sleep with on the first date. Well, though we hadn't slept together, we had seen each other naked at primary meet, so perhaps we should have refrained from striking up a friendship. But our troika was kind of inevitable.

"M-A-C-H-I-N-E," the blackboard proclaimed in big bold letters.

As we entered the amphitheatre-shaped lecture room, we grabbed a pile of handouts each. The instructor sat next to the blackboard like a bloated beetle, watching us settle down, waiting for the huddled murmurs to cease.

He appeared around forty years of age, with gray hair incandescent from three tablespoons of coconut oil, wore an un-tucked light blue shirt and had positioned three pens in his front pocket, along with chalks, like an array of bullets.

"Welcome everyone. I am Professor Dubey, Mechanical Engineering department...so, first day in college. Do you feel special?" he said in a monotone.

The class remained silent. We were busy scanning our handouts and feeling like a herd.

The course was Manufacturing Processes, often shortened to ManPro for easier pronunciation. The handouts consisted of the course outline. Contents covered the basic techniques of manufacturing – such as welding, machining, casting, bending and shaping. Along with the outline, the handout contained the grading pattern of the course.

Majors – 40%
Minors – 20%
Practicals – 20%
Assignments (6-8) and Surprise Quizzes (3-4) – 20%

Prof Dubey noticed the limp response to his greeting and made his voice more exuberant. "Look at the handout later. Don't worry, you will get enough of these, one for every course. Put them aside now," he said as he stood up and walked toward the blackboard.

He took out a chalk from his pocket with a flourish celluloid-terrorists reserved for hand-grenades and underlined the word 'machine' approximately six times. Then he turned to us. "Machine, the basic reason for existence of any mechanical engineer. Everything you learn finds application in machines. Now, can anyone tell me what a machine is?"

The class fell even more silent. That's the first lesson: various degrees of silence.

"Anyone?" the professor asked again as he started walking through the rows of students. As the students on the aisles felt even more stalked and avoided eye contact, I turned around to study my new classmates. There must have been seventy of us in this class, three hundred of us in a batch. I noticed a boy in front of me staring at the instructor intently, his head moving to and fro, mouth ajar; a timid sort, whom Baku could polish off for snack any given day.

"You," Prof Dubey chose me as his first casualty.

It was the first time *the* condition struck me, where tongue cleaves unto dental roof, body freezes, blood vessels rupture and sweat bursts out in buckets.

"You, I am talking to you," the professor clarified.

"Hari, Hari.." somebody inside me called but could only get my answering machine. I could have attempted an answer, or at least a silly 'I don't know' but it was as if my mouth was AWOL.

"Strange," surmised Prof Dubey dubiously as he moved to another student.

"You in the check shirt. What do you think?"

Check Shirt had hitherto been pretending to take notes to escape the professor's glance. "Sir, Machine sir...is a device...like big parts...sir like big gears and all..."

"What?" Prof Dubey's disgust fell like spit on Check Shirt. "See, the standard just keeps falling every year. Our admission criteria are just not strict enough." He shook his oiled skull, the one that contained all the information in this planet, including the definition of machines.

"Yeah, right. Busted my butt for two years for this damn place. One in hundred is not good enough for them," Ryan whispered to me.

"Shshh," ordered Prof Dubey, looking at the three of us, "anyway, the definition of a machine is simple. It is anything that reduces human effort. Anything. So, see the world around you and it is full of machines."

Anything that reduces human effort, I repeated in my head. Well, that sounded simple enough.

"So, from huge steel mills, to simple brooms, man has invented so much to reduce human effort," the professor continued, as he noticed the class was mesmerized by his simple clarification.

"Airplane?" said one student in the front row.

"Machine," instructor said.

"Stapler," suggested another.

"Machine."

It really was amazing. A spoon, car, blender, knife, chair — students threw examples at the professor and there was only one answer — machine.

"Fall in love with the world around you," Prof Dubey smiled for the first time, "for you will become the masters of machines."

A feeling of collective joy darted through the class for having managed to convert Prof Dubey's sour expression into smiles.

"Sir, what about a gym machine, like a bench press or something?" Ryan interrupted the bonhomie.

"What about it?" Prof Dubey stopped beaming.

"That doesn't reduce human effort. In fact, it increases it."

The class fell silent again.

"Well, I mean…" Prof Dubey said as he scouted for arguments.

Boy, did Ryan really have a point?

"Perhaps it is too simple a definition then?" Ryan said in a pseudo-helpful voice.

"What are you trying to do?" the professor asked tight-lipped as he came close to us again, "Are you saying that I am wrong?"

"No sir, I'm just..."

"Watch it son. In my class, just watch it," was all Prof Dubey said as he moved to the front.

"Okay, enough fun. Now, let us focus on ManPro," he said as he rubbed off the word 'machine' from the blackboard and the six underlines below it, "my course is very important. I am sure many professors will tell you about their courses. But I care about ManPro. So, don't miss class, finish your assignments and be prepared, a surprise quiz can drop from the sky at any time."

He went on to tackle casting, one of the oldest methods of working with metal. After an hour on how iron melts and foundry workers pour it into sand moulds, he ended the session.

"That is it for today. Best of luck once again for your stay here. Remember, as your head of department Prof Cherian says, the tough workload is by design, to keep you on your toes. And respect the grading system. You get bad grades, and I assure you – you get no job, no school and no future. If you do well, the world is your oyster. So, don't slip, not even once, or there will be no oyster, just slush."

A shiver ran through all of us as with that quote the professor slammed the duster on the desk and walked away in a cloud of chalk.

2

Terminator

THEY SAY TIME FLIES WHEN YOU ARE HAVING FUN. IN THE first semester alone, with six courses, four of them with practical classes, time dragged so slow and comatose, fun was conspicuous by its absence. Every day, from eight to five, we were locked in the eight-storey insti-building with lectures, tutorials and labs. The next few hours of the evening were spent in the library or in our rooms as we prepared reports and finished assignments. And this did not even include the tests! Each subject had two minor tests, one major and three surprise quizzes; seven tests for six courses meant forty-two tests per semester, mathematically speaking. Luckily, the professors spared us surprise quizzes in the first month, citing ragging season and the settling-in period of course; but the ragging season ended soon and it meant a quiz could happen any time. In every class we had to look out for instructor's subtle hints about a possible quiz in the next class.

Meanwhile, I got better acquainted with Ryan and Alok. Ryan's dad had this handicraft business that was essentially a sweatshop for potters that made vases for the European market. Ryan's father and mother were both intimately involved in the business and their regular travel meant Ryan stayed in boarding school, a plush colonial one in hill-town Mussoorie.

Alok's family, I guess, was of limited means, which is just a polite way of saying he was poor. His mother was the only earning member, and last I heard, schoolteachers didn't exactly hit dirt on pay-day. Besides, half her salary regularly went to support her husband's medical treatment. At the same time, Alok's elder sister was getting near what he mournfully called 'marriageable age', another cause of major worry for his household. Going by Alok's looks I guess she wasn't breathtakingly beautiful either.

I also got familiar with Kumaon and other wing-mates. I won't go into all of them, but in one corner there was Sukhwinder or the 'Happy Surd' since his face broke into sunny smiles at proximity with anything remotely human. Next to him was the studious Venkat, who coated his windows with thick black paper and stayed locked inside alone. There was 'Itchy' Rajesh whose hands were always scratching some part of his body, sometimes in objectionable places. On the other side of the hallway were seniors' rooms, including Baku, Anurag and other animals.

Ryan, Alok and I often studied together in the evenings. One month into the first semester, we were sitting in my room chasing a quanto-physics assignment deadline.

"Damn," Ryan said as he got up his easy chair to stretch his spectacular spine. "What a crazy week; classes, assignments, more classes, assignments and not to mention the coming-attraction quizzes. You call this a life?"

Alok sat on the study desk, focused on the physics assignment, head bent down and sideways, just two inches above his sheet. He always writes this way, head near the sheet, pen pressed tight between his fingers, his white worksheets reflected on his thick glasses.

"Wha..." Alok looked up, sounding retarded.

"I said you call this a life?" Ryan asked, this time looking at me.

I was sitting on the bed cross-legged, attempting the assignment on a drawing board. I needed a break, so I put my pen down.

"Call it what you want," I said, words stifled by a Titanic yawn, "but that is not going to change it."

"I think this is jail. It really is. Damn jail," Ryan said, hitting the peeling wall with a fist.

"Maybe you're forgetting that you're in IIT, the best college in the country," Alok said, cracking knuckles.

"So? You put students in jail?" Ryan asked, hands on hips.

"No. But you expect a certain standard," Alok said, putting his hand up to indicate height.

"This is high standard? Working away like moronic drones until midnight. ManPro yesterday, ApMech day before, Quanto today...it never ends," Ryan grumbled. "I need a break, man. Anyone for a movie?"

"And what about the assignment?" Alok blinked.

"Priya has *Terminator* on," Ryan beguiled.

"Then when will we sleep?" Alok said.

"You are one real *muggu* eh?" Ryan said indulgently to him.

"I'll go," I said, keeping my drawing board aside, "come Alok, we'll do it later."

"It will get late, man," Alok warned half-heartedly.

I stood up and took his pen, put it into his geometry box. Yes, Alok had a geometry box, like he was about twelve years old.

"Come get up," I said when I noticed two paintbrushes in his box. "Hey, what are the paintbrushes for?"

"Nothing," Alok mumbled.

I lifted the brushes, painting imaginary arcs in air. "Then why do you have them? To give colour to your circuit diagrams?" I laughed at my own joke, waving the brushes in the air. "Or to express your soul in the ManPro class? To draw Prof Dubey's frowny face?"

"No. Actually, they are my father's. He was an artist, but he's paralyzed now."

There are times in life you wish dinosaurs weren't extinct and could be whistled to come and gulp you down. I went motionless, fingers in mid-air.

Ryan saw my face and pressed his teeth together to be simultaneously tch-tch sympathetic to Alok and stop laughing at me. "Really Alok? That's really sad. I'm sorry man," he said, putting his hand around Alok's shoulder. The bastard, scoring over me for no fault of mine.

"It's okay. It was a long while ago. We are used to him like that now," Alok said, finally getting up for the movie while I was still hoping I'd evaporate.

When we walked out, Ryan was with Alok, me trailing six steps behind.

"Well, I have lived in boarding school all my life, so I can't really understand. But it must be pretty difficult for you. I mean how did you manage?" Ryan continued.

"Barely managed actually. My mother is a biology teacher. That was the only income. Elder sister is still in college."

I nodded my head, trying desperately to evince how empathetic to his cause I was, too.

"How do you think I got into IIT? I was taking care of him for the past two years," Alok said.

"Really?" I said, finally getting my chance to get into the conversation.

"Yes, every day after school I was nursing him and reading my books."

Ryan had a scooter, which made it easy for us to get to Priya. It was illegal for three people to ride together in a triple sandwich, but cops rarely demanded more than twenty bucks if they stopped you. Chances of getting caught were less than one in ten, so Ryan said it was still cheap on a probability weighted basis.

Priya cinema at night was a completely different world from our quiet campus. Families, couples and groups of young people lined up to catch the hit movie of the season. We bought front row tickets, as Alok did not want to spend too much. Personally, I think he was just too blind to sit far away. In any case, the movie was science fiction, which I should have guessed given Ryan's choice; he always picked sci-fi movies. I hate sci-fi movies, but who asks me? This one had time travel, human robots, laser guns, the works, presented in an unfunny way. In ten minutes, the obscenely muscular hero's heroics looked too silly to even smirk at, and I was yawning uncontrollably.

"Wow!" Ryan said, bringing his hand to his face as the villain launched a torpedo from his backpack.

"What the hell do you see in these movies?" I whispered, just to jack his trip.

"Man, look at all those gadgets."

"But they're all fake. It is fiction."

"Yes, but we could have them one day."

"Time travel? You really think we could have time travel?" Ryan's ridiculous when he gets excited.

"Hush, it's hard enough to understand the accent guys," Alok objected.

When we returned to Kumaon at midnight, our asses were set on fire, I mean not literally, but everyone from Venkat to Sukhwinder were running around with notepads and textbooks.

"Surprise quiz. Strong rumour of one in ApMech," Happy Surd explained as he furiously riffled through his notes, for once not electrified at our company.

ApMech was Applied Mechanics, and apparently, some student in Nilgiri hostel had visited the professor's office in the evening to submit a late assignment. The professor had sinisterly advised to "keep revising your notes", waggling left eyebrow at the same time. Enough to ring the alarm as news travelled through the campus like wildfire.

"Damn. Now we have to study for ApMech. It will take hours," Alok said morosely.

"And we have the Quanto assignment to finish as well," I reminded.

Everyone gathered in my room to study. It was at two in the morning that Alok spoke. "This whole movie thing was a dumb idea, I told you."

"How was I to know? Anyway, why are you taking arbit tension?" Ryan took offence.

"It is not arbit. It's relative grading here, so if we don't study and others do, we are screwed," Alok said, stressing the last word so hard even Ryan was startled.

Just then, a mouse darted out from under my bed.

"Did you see that?" Ryan said, eager to change the topic. He removed his slippers, hoping to take aim and strike the rodent down. However, the rodent had other ideas on his own demise and dived diplomatically back under the bed.

"Yes, there are these creepy mice in my room. Little bastards," I said, almost affectionately.

"You want me to kill them for you?" Ryan offered.

"It's not that easy. They are too smart and quick," I said.

"Challenge?" Ryan said.

"I beg you brothel-borns, not now. Can we please study?" Alok said, literally folding his hands. The guy is too dramatic.

Ryan eased back into the chair and wore his footwear. He opened the ApMech book and exhaled deep through his mouth.

"Yes sir, let us mug and cram. Otherwise, how will we become great engineers of this great country," Ryan mock-sighed.

"Shut up," Alok said, his face already immersed in his workbook.

Ryan did shut up after that, even though he kept bending to look under the bed from time to time. I was sure he wanted to get at least one mouse, but the little creatures smartly maintained a low profile. We finished our Quanto assignment in an hour and then revised the ApMech notes until five, by which time Ryan was snoring soundly, I was struggling to stay awake and even Alok's eyes had started watering. We still had around a third of the course left, but it was necessary to catch some sleep. Besides, the quiz was only a rumour, we did not know if it would actually materialize.

But rumours, especially ugly ones, have a way of coming true. Thirty minutes into the ApMech class, Prof Sen locked the door and opened his black briefcase. "Time for some fun. Here is a quickie quiz of multiple choice questions," he said.

Prof Sen passed the handouts to the front row students, who in turn cascaded them backward. Everyone in class knew about the rumour, and the quiz was as much a surprise as snow in Siberia. I took the question sheet and glanced over the questions. Most of them were from recent lectures, the part of the course we could not revise.

"Crap. We never got to the lectures for question five onward," I whispered to Alok.

"We are screwed. Let's get screwed in silence at least," he said as he placed his head in his 'study' position, left cheek almost touching the answer sheet.

We never discussed the quiz upon our return to Kumaon that day. Other students were talking animatedly about some questions being out of course. Obviously, we never finished the course, so we did not know better. We did not have to wait for results too long either. Prof Sen distributed the answer sheets in class two days later.

"Five? I got a five out of twenty," I said to Alok, who sat next to me in class.

"I got seven. Damn it, seven," Alok said.

"I have three. How about that? One, two, three," Ryan said, counting on his fingers.

Prof Sen wrote the customary summary scores on the blackboard.

Average: 11/20
High: 17/20
Low: 3/20

He kept those written for a few minutes, before proceeding with his lecture on cantilever beams.

"I have the lowest. Did you see that?" Ryan whispered to me, unmoved by cantilever beams. It was hard to figure out what he was feeling at this point. Even though he was trying to stay calm and expressionless, I could tell he was having trouble digesting his result. He re-read his quiz, it did not change the score.

Alok was in a different orbit. His face looked like it had on ragging day. He viewed the answer sheet like he had the coke bottle, an expression of anxiety mixed with sadness. It's in these moments that Alok is most vulnerable, you nudge him just a little bit and you know he'd cry. But for now, the quiz results were a repulsive enough sight.

I saw my own answer sheet. The instructor had written my score in big but careless letters, like graffiti written with contempt. Now I am no Einstein or anything, but this never happened to me in school. My score was five on twenty, or twenty-five per cent; I had never in my life scored less than three times as much. Ouch, the first quiz in IIT hurt.

But take Ryan's scores. I wondered if it had been worth it for him to even study last night. I was two points ahead of him, or wait a minute, sixty-six per cent ahead of him, that made me feel better. Thank god for relative misery!

Alok had the highest percentage amongst the three of us, but I could tell he did not find solace in our misery. He saw his score, and he saw the average on the board. I saw his face, twisting every time he saw his wrong answers.

We kept our answer sheets, the proof of our underperformance, in our bags and strolled back to Kumaon. We met at dinner in the mess. The food was insipid as usual, and Alok wrinkled his pug nose as he dispiritedly plopped a thick blob of green substance mess-workers called *bhindi masala* into his plate. He slammed two rotis on his stainless steel plate and ignored the rest of the semi-solid substances like dal, raita and pulao. Ryan and I took everything; though everything tasted the same, we could at least have some variety of colors on our plate.

Alok finally brought up the topic of the quiz at the dinner table.

"So, now you don't have anything to say?"

Ryan and I looked at each other.

"Say what?" I said.

"That how crap this is," Alok said.

"The food?" I said, fully aware Alok meant otherwise.

"No damn it! Not the damn food," Alok said, "The ApMech quiz." His expression changed from the usual tragic one to a livelier angry one. I found that expression marginally more pleasant to look at and easier to deal with.

"What about the quiz? We're screwed. What is to discuss in that?" Ryan simplified.

"Oh really. We are screwed, no damn doubt in that," Alok said.

I think Alok picks up a word and uses it too much, which ruins the effect. There were too many 'damns' in his dialogue.

"Then drop it. Anyway, you got the highest amongst us. So, be happy."

"Happy? Yes, I am happy. The average is eleven, and someone got seventeen. And here I am, at damn seven. Yes, I am happy my damn *Terminator* ass," Alok scoffed.

I told you, Alok ruins the effect. I wanted to tell him that he should stop 'damn' right now but something told me he would not appreciate the subtleties of cursing right now.

"What? What did you just say?" Ryan said, keeping his spoon down on the plate, "Did you say *Terminator*?"

"Yes. It was a stupid idea. *Your* stupid damn idea," Alok said.

Ryan froze. He looked at Alok as if he was speaking in foreign tongue. Then he turned toward me. "You heard what he said? Hari, you heard? This is unbelievable man."

I had heard Alok, nothing being the matter with my eardrums but I wasn't paying attention to anything apart from keeping count of the 'damns'.

"Hari, you think I screwed up the quiz?" Ryan asked slowly.

I looked at Alok's and Ryan's faces in quick succession. "Ryan, you got three. You still need me to tell you that you screwed up?" I counter-questioned, mediating on something I did not understand yet.

"No. I mean Alok is saying I screwed up the quiz for both of you because I took you to the movie. You think so or...?"

"That is not what I said..." Alok interrupted even as Ryan raised his hand to indicate silence.

I understood Ryan's question now, but I did not know how to answer it, without taking sides.

"But how does that...."

"No, Hari tell me. Is that what you expect your best friends to say?" Ryan asked.

"It is not important. And besides, you did not drag us forcibly to see that crap movie," I said, reminding myself to never see sci-fi again.

Ryan was satisfied with the answer. He relaxed his raised hand and smiled, "See, there you go."

"But Alok is right too. We should have a limit on the fun factor. You can't screw with the system too much, it comes back to screw you — the quiz is an example."

"Thank you sir," Alok said, "That is exactly what I am saying."

Cool, I had managed to come out clean in this one. Sometimes, if you just paraphrase everyone's arguments, you get to be the good guy.

3

Barefoot on Metal

THE QUIZ MISHAP REINVIGORATED OUR COMMITMENT TO studies for a while. Ryan was quieter when we studied in the rooms, controlling his urge to discuss emergency topics ranging from movies to food to new sci-fi movies, leading to more productive study sessions. Though our scores moved closer to class average, assignments can get dull as hell after a while, and you need a break. Ryan often dozed off between assignments, or stared unseeingly at the wall, whispering curses frequently every time he opened a new book.

"Okay then," he sighed one day, stapling his assignment. "I have finished today's crap. You guys going to mug more or what?"

"Why are you always calling this crap?" Alok asked, perplexed.

"Take a wild guess," Ryan said, tossing his assignment on the table like a used tissue.

"But why?" Alok said, "I mean, surely you studied a lot to get into IIT right?"

"Yes, but frankly, this place has let me down. This isn't exactly the cutting edge of science and technology as they describe themselves, is it?"

I closed my book to join in the conversation. "Boss, mugging is the price one pays to get the IIT tag. You mug, you pass and you get job. What let-down are you talking about?"

"That is the problem, there is this stupid system and there are stupid people like you."

I hate Ryan. When he is on his own trip, we all turn stupid.

"Continuous mugging, testing and assignments. Where is the time to try out new ideas? Just sit all day and get fat like Hari."

Ryan doesn't like mugging, therefore, I am stupid and fat. People like him think they are god's gifts to the world. What's worse, they are.

"I don't have any new ideas. And I am not that fat, am I?" I said turning to Alok. Looking at him I instantly felt better.

"Fatso, look into a mirror. You should do something about it."

"It is genetic, saw a TV documentary once," I defended weakly.

"Genetic, my ass. I can make you lose ten kilos like that." He snapped his fingers.

I did not know where Ryan was going with this, but it could not have been pleasant for me. Being fat was more appealing to me than running behind the insti bus or climbing the stairs of these buildings fifty times a day. "Ryan, forget about me. If you don't want to mug, should we go to the canteen for a parantha?"

"Boss, this is the problem — all food and no exercise. I've decided, Hari has to go on an exercise routine," Ryan said, jumping up. "We start tomorrow morning then."

Ryan decided for other people. I don't know if it was his good looks or just his good-natured vanity that you didn't want to prick, but mostly he got away with it.

"Wait Ryan, what the..." I began.

"Actually, Alok you should come, too. Interested?"

"Go to hell," Alok muttered as he dived back into his books like a squirrel with a nut.

I thought about losing ten kilos. All my life people had called me Fat-Man, to the point where plumpness was part of my identity now. Of course, I hated that part of my identity and Ryan did seem to know what he was doing, and his own body was great. Heck, I thought, it was worth a try.

"What do I have to do?" I capitulated.

"Early morning jogs around the whole campus, around four kilometers."

"No way, I can't even walk four kilometers," I dismissed.

"You wimp, at least try. You'll feel great afterwards," Ryan said.

Sure enough, Ryan mercilessly kicked at my door at five a.m. sharp the next morning. I hate Ryan. Anyway, I opened the door and he stood there waiting for me to change into T-shirt and shorts.

"Four kilometers?" I was drowsy and pitiful at the same time.

"Try, just try," Ryan enthused.

It was still dark outside when I left Kumaon. I was happy for that small mercy — no one would see an eighty-kilo globe-shaped creature bouncing along the road. To do the four-kilometer route meant reaching the other end of campus, past the hostels, sports grounds, insti building and the faculty housing. I thought I could cheat and cut corners, but I wanted to give Ryan a chance, not that I hated him any less for it.

My entire body groaned as muscles I never knew existed made themselves known. In ten minutes, I was panting like a trekker on Mount Everest without oxygen, and in fifteen, I felt a heart attack coming on. I panted for a few minutes and started again till I passed the insti building and was in the faculty-housing colony.

Dawn broke, revealing manicured lawns and picture postcard bungalows of our tormentors in class. I passed Prof Dubey's house. It was hard to imagine this man out of class, living in a home, watching TV, peeing, eating at a dining table. By now, I was wet with sweat and my face beyond red, reaching rare shades of purple.

I stopped, huffing and puffing, when I went bump at the knees. Stumbling at the unexpected impact, I kind of whooshed forward, extending my hands just in time to save myself from a bad fall. I sat stunned on the road, recovering from the shock and breathlessness, and then turned around.

A red Maruti car was the culprit! I continued panting as I squinted my eyes to see the driver through the windscreen. *Who was trying to kill me when I was already dying?* I wondered, waiting for my breath to return to normal.

"I am so-so sorry," a female voice announced. A young girl, around my age, in a loose T-shirt and knee-length shorts, clothes that one usually wore at home. She skipped forward in a silly way, which was probably her attempt to run toward me. I noticed she was barefoot.

"I am so sorry. Are you all right?" she enquired, tucking her hair behind an ear.

I was not all right, and it was her damn fault. But when a young girl asks a guy if he is all right, he can never admit he is not.

"Yeah. I guess," I said, flexing my palms.

"Can I give you a lift?" she asked nervously, extending a hand to help me up.

I looked at her carefully as she came closer. Maybe I was seeing a female after a long time or something, but I thought she was really pretty. And the whole just-out-of-the-bed look blew me. Only girls can look hot in their nightclothes: Alok, for instance, looks like a terminally ill patient in his torn vest and pajamas.

"I was actually jogging," I said, holding her hand and getting up as slowly as I could without being obvious. Who wants to abandon a pretty girl's hand? Anyway, I had to after I was standing up.

"Hi. I am Neha by the way. Listen, I am really sorry," she said, adjusting her hair again with the hand I had just held.

"Hi. I am Hari, still alive so it is okay," I grinned.

"Yeah, you see I am learning to drive," she said pointing to the 'L' sign on the windscreen. That is understandable, I thought, you are allowed to hit people if you are learning to drive, especially if you are eye-candy.

Now to be very frank, I wasn't hurt or anything. For one thing, she was driving at like two kilometers an hour, and I think my adipose tissues absorb bumps better than most people's. Still, I wanted to milk this moment.

"You sure you don't need a lift? I feel really bad," she said, wringing her hands.

"Actually, I am sort of tempted to get a drop back to Kumaon," I said.

"Sure. Please come in," she said and chuckled, "if you trust my driving, that is."

We got into the car. I saw her sit carefully in the driver's seat, as if she was running the starship Enterprise or something. Then she placed her bare foot on the accelerator. Now maybe it is because I am an engineer, but that was hot. Bare female skin on metal is enormously sexy. There was dark red nail polish on her toenails, with one or two toes encircled in weird squiggly silver ringlets that only girls can justify wearing. I just wanted to keep looking at her feet but she started to talk.

"Kumaon hostel, so a student, eh?"

"Yes. First year, mechanical engineering."

"Cool. So how are you finding it, college and everything? Fun?"

"Nothing much, just running around to keep up all the time."

"So you have to study a lot? What do guys call it — mugging."

"Yeah, we have to mug. Some damn profs get this vicious joy driving students nuts...."

"My dad is a prof," Neha said.

"Really?" I said and almost jumped in my seat. I was lucky I did not fully express my insightful views on professors and I was hoping she was not Prof Dubey's daughter.

"Yes, I live in faculty housing," she said. The car had passed the housing blocks now, and we were nearing the insti building.

"And that is my dad's office," she said, pointing to one of the dozens of rooms.

"Really?" I said again, my mind racing flashback to gauge if I had done anything that could get me into trouble. "What's his name?" I asked casually.

"Prof Cherian. You probably don't know him, he won't take a course until your third year."

I shook my head. I had heard the name, but never seen Prof Cherian. Then I remembered our first class. "Is he the head of the Mechanical Engineering department?" I said, looking austerely away from her feet.

Sensing my anxiety, she patted my arm while shifting into third gear. "Yes, he is. But don't be tense, he is the prof, not me. So relax." She burst out laughing as if she knew of my fascination with her feet.

We chatted for a few more minutes along the insti-hostel road. She told me about her college, where she was studying fashion design. She had lived in this campus for over ten years and knew most of the professors.

She apologized again when we came near Kumaon, and asked if she could do anything for me.

"No, it is all fine really," I reassured her.

"Sure Hari? So will I see you again when you jog?"

"I guess," I said, dreading another round of Ryan's training.

"Great. Maybe sometime, I can drive you to the deer park outside campus, lots of joggers there. And you get excellent morning tea snacks there. I owe you a treat," she said.

I was nervous at meeting the daughter of my head of department again. But her offer, and mostly she herself, was too irresistible.

"That sounds great," I said leaping out of the car, "free food is always welcome. Keep bumping me."

She smiled, waved and the little red car disappeared from sight. Her image still floated in my head as I reached the Kumaon lawns. Ryan was already waiting there, doing push-ups or pull-downs or something. He had seen me get out of the car and demanded full explanation. I had to then repeat it to Alok. Though they exhibited appropriate excitement, asking me how she looked and everything, they also told me to stay away from her, given she was a prof's offspring.

But they had neither seen her nor talked to her. I was dying to meet her again, was waiting for the next time I bumped into her and could feast silly at the sight of those two bare-naked feet!

4

Line Drawing

Bang in the middle of the first semester came
Ryan's scooter. His parents sent him a dollar cheque as a
Christmas gift as everybody else around them was doing in
Europe. Ryan was not a Christian and cared two hoots about
Christmas, but loved the cheque and cashed it; *voila* scooter –
a beautiful Kinetic Honda in gleaming metallic blue.

When Ryan got it to Kumaon, all the students gathered
around it to pay homage, but only Alok and I got to park our
butts on it. It was for two people, but Ryan carried both of
us; we went to class, canteen and on rare occasions to movies
like the *Terminator* zipping away on Ryan's Kinetic, letting the
world watch us in envy and the scooter in probable pity,
groaning as it was under our combined weight.

Meanwhile, classes got worse. The professors kept up the
pressure and the overworked students worked even harder to

beat the average, thereby pushing the average higher. We still studied together, but the resolve to concentrate was breaking down. We had managed to reach average grades in a few assignments, but in physics we had messed up.

One night Alok got a call from home. His father had had a seizure or something and someone had to take him to the hospital pronto. Alok's mother had never done this alone and she sounded hysterical enough to warrant a trip for herself to the hospital.

There was a strong rumour of a physics quiz circulating but Alok had no choice. Ryan offered his scooter, which Alok couldn't drive for nuts. Hence Ryan had to go as well. I did not want to be alone, so I went along.

It was the first time I'd seen Alok's home. I told you he was kind of poor, I mean not World Bank ads type starving poor or anything, but his home had the barest minimum one would need for existence. There was light, but no lampshades, there was a living room, but no couches, there was a TV, but not a colour one. The living room was where lived Alok's father, entertaining himself with one of the two TV channels, close to unconscious by the time we reached. Alok's mother was already waiting, using her sari edge to wipe her tears.

"Alok, my son, look what happens when you are not here," she said in a pathetic voice that would make even Hitler cry. Man, I could totally see where Alok got his whining talent. Anyway, I hired an auto and Ryan and Alok lifted the patient into it. We then went to the hospital, checked him in and waited until a doctor, unfortunate enough to work in an overcrowded free government hospital, saw Alok's father. We returned to Kumaon at three in the morning exhausted and nauseated by hospital smells.

Of course, you can imagine what happened the next day, the physics quiz, that's what happened and we screwed up big time. We got like two on twenty or some such miserable score. Alok tried to ask the professor for a re-quiz, who stared back as if he had been asked for both his kidneys.

That physics quiz episode broke Alok a bit. Now he was less vigilant when Ryan distracted us from studies.

"You know guys, this whole IIT system is sick," Ryan declared.

"There he goes again," I rolled my eyes. We were in my room.

I expected Alok to ignore Ryan, but this time he led him on with a monosyllable. "Why?"

"Because, tell me, how many great engineers or scientists have come out of IIT?"

"What do you mean? Many CEOs and entrepreneurs have," I said, a mistake as Ryan had not finished yet.

"I mean this is supposed to be the best college in India, the best technology institute for a country of a billion. But has IIT ever invented anything? Or made any technical contribution to India?"

"Doesn't it contribute in making engineers?" Alok asked, snapping shut his book. I knew that with Alok not keeping us in check, we were not going to study any more that day. I suggested we go out to Sasi's for paranthas and skip the mess dinner. Everyone agreed.

Ryan continued to muse. "Over thirty years of IITs, yet, all it does is train some bright kids to work in multinationals. I mean look at MIT in the USA."

"This is not the USA," I said, signalling Sasi's minions to bring three plates of paranthas. "MITs have budgets of millions of dollars."

"And anyway, who cares, I want to get the degree and land a good job," Alok said.

Sasi's was a ramshackle, illegal roadside establishment right outside the IIT hostel gates. Using tents and stools, the alfresco dining menu included paranthas, lemonade and cigarettes. At two rupees each, the butter paranthas were a bargain, even by student standards. Proprietor Sasi knew the quality of food in the mess and did a voluminous business serving dozens of students each day from every hostel. We got three plates of paranthas, and the dollop of butter on top melted and produced a delicious aroma.

"See, it is not always the money," Ryan said, flicking ash. "So IITs cannot do space research, but we surely can make some cheaper products? And frankly, money is just an excuse. If there is value, the industry will pay for research even at IIT."

"So what the hell is wrong then?" I was irritated. I seriously wanted Ryan to shut up, now that the food was here. I mean, if he did not want to study, fine, but spare us the bloody lecture, it wreaks havoc on digestion.

"What is wrong is the system," Ryan denounced soundly, sounding like a local politician. Blame the whole damn system if you can't figure anything out.

But Ryan had more. "This system of relative grading and overburdening the students. I mean it kills the best fun years of your life. But it kills something else. Where is the room for original thought? Where is the time for creativity? It is not fair."

"What about it is not fair? It gets me work, that's all I care," Alok shrugged, taking a break from devouring his rations.

"Wow, that rhymes," I said.

"See your attitude is another problem. You won't get it, forget it," Ryan said.

"That rhymes too," I said and Alok and I broke into giggles. I knew I was annoying Ryan like hell, but I really wanted him to shut up or at least change the topic. That lazy bastard would find any reason to goof off.

"Screw you," Ryan gestured, diving back to his plate.

"Anyway," I said, "so what is the plan for the weekend?"

"Nothing, why?" Alok looked up.

"Well, we have the scooter now."

Ryan stayed silent.

"Hey, stop sulking like a woman." I nudged his elbow until he had to laugh.

"Yes, we can go, you dope. Connaught Place?"

"Why?" Alok repeated.

"Well, they have this cheap dhabha there with the best butter chicken and we can catch a good Hindi movie. And then maybe check out some girls in the market." Ryan's eyes were exaggeratedly lecherous.

"Sounds good," I said, the mention of girls making me think of Neha. I had not bumped into her again, maybe I should go jogging again.

"Alok, you'll come too, right? Or will you mug all day?"

"Uh..there is this ApMech worksheet...anyway, screw it man...yes, I will come," Alok capitulated.

We did go to Connaught Place that weekend and had quite a blast. The movie was what every Hindi movie is like – regular boy meets girl, boy is poor and honest, girl's dad is rich and a crook. However, the heroine was new and eager to please the crowds so she bathed in the rain, played tennis in mini-skirts and wore sequined negligees to discos. Since all her hobbies involved wearing less or transparent clothing, the audience loved her. The girl's father damn near killed the boy who flirted with his hot daughter, but ultimately the hero's love and lust prevailed. The hero had no damn assignments to finish and no freaky profs breathing down his neck. I know, these Hindi movies are all crap, but they do kind of take your mind away from the crap of real life like nothing else.

After movie came lunch. The dhabha was great as Ryan is never wrong about these things. He ordered for everyone, which he always does. And he orders big – right from boneless butter chicken to daal to paranthas to raita. The spoilt brat even orders the overpriced Coke, I mean, which student orders Coke in restaurants? Anyway, the meal was great, and an overactive desert-cooler sprayed water on our faces and kept the ambience cool.

Tearing his rotis like a famished Unicef kid, Alok got chatty. "This is too good man, the chicken is fundoo here."

"So tell me, Fatso, did you have fun today or not?" Ryan asked.

"Uh-huh," said Alok, mouth too stuffed with food, but he meant yes.

"Then tell me, why the hell do you want to kill yourself with books?"

"Aw, don't you guys start arguing again," I groaned. I had enjoyed my day so far and watching these jokers go at it is really not funny after a while.

"We are not arguing," Ryan said, in a tone that sounded like he was arguing with me now. He took a deep breath. "Okay, here is the thing. I have been thinking."

Oh please, spare us, I thought. But it was too late.

"Guys, these are the best years of our life. They really are. I mean, especially for someone like Alok."

"What, why specially me?" Alok was baffled, nibbling at a chilli from the salad bowl.

"It brings out the amino acids in your eyes," I joked, when he coughed at the tangy spiciness.

"Because," Ryan told Alok, "look at your life before this. I mean, I know you love your dad and everything. But like, you were just nursing him and studying for the past two years. And after college, you'll probably have to live with them again, right?"

"I'll take up a job in Delhi," Alok nodded, a bit more serious now, though his mind was still preoccupied with chicken breast.

"Exactly, so it is back to the same responsibility again. I mean, you will earn and everything, and maybe hire a servant. But still, would you be able to have this kind of fun?"

"I love my parents, Ryan, it is not a responsibility," Alok said and stopped eating. Boy, this must have affected him. Usually, the Fatso will not leave chicken for his life.

"Of course, you love them," Ryan waved a hand. "I mean, I can understand that even though I don't love my parents."

"What?" I said, though I had not wanted to be part of their argument.

"I said I don't love my parents. Is that a big deal?"

Alok raised his eyebrows at me. I mean, if Alok could love his dad, who if you think about it, is no more than a vegetable with vision, how could this brat not love his parents? And his parents were nice, I mean they gave him everything - the blue scooter, clothes from Gap and money for the damn colas at restaurants. His parents had worked their asses off all their lives, started selling flower pots with two potters, and then moved all over India to make a name until two years ago when they went overseas. They weren't making any big money out there yet but wanted to keep sonny boy happy, this spoilt, pig-headed, marginally good-looking ass who did not love them!

"Screw you," I blessed.

"Screw you! You don't even listen to me," Ryan said.

Yeah right, that when I listened to this idiot all the time.

"Why?" Alok said, getting back to his food.

"I don't know why. I mean, I have been in boarding school when I was six. Of course, like every kid I hated it and cried when they left me. But then, it was at boarding school I got everything. I did well in studies, got noticed in sports, learnt how to have fun and live well and made my best friends. So, somewhere down the line, I don't miss them anymore. Just kind of outgrew them. Sure, we meet at vacation time and they send letters, cash. and everything but..."

"But?"

"But I don't miss them."

"So you don't think that is wrong?" Alok picked teeth.

"Heck, no. I mean, for me my friends are everything, they are my family. Mom and Dad are nice, but I don't love them the way I love my friends. I mean, I don't love them, but I love my friends."

"So you *love* us then Ryan aah? *I love you*," Alok said in a falsetto; he was obviously satiated, his lighter mood a proof of his post-gluttony bonhomie.

"Up yours, Fatso, love you my ass," Ryan said and some heads turned to look at us.

Ryan, however, came back to his earlier theory.

"Anyway, my point is, these are our best years. So either we can mug ourselves to death, or tell the system to stuff it."

"And how exactly do we tell the system to stuff it?" I enquired.

"I mean, not like stop mugging completely or something, but like, let us draw a line. We can study two-three hours a day, but do other stuff, say sports, have you guys ever played squash? Or taken part in events – debates, scrabble and stuff, an odd movie or something sometimes. We can do so much at the insti."

"Yeah, but very few people do it. And they are the ones with pretty bad GPAs," Alok said.

"See, I am not saying we stop mugging. We just draw the line. A day of classes, then three hours a day of studies and the rest is our time. Let's just try, just one semester. Isn't it fair? A kind of decentralization of education."

Alok and I looked at each other. Ryan had a point. If I never played squash in college, I'd probably never play it again. If I did not take part in Scrabble now, I'd never do it when I had a job.

"I can try," I said, mostly to agree with Ryan. He would not have stopped otherwise anyway.

"Three hours is not enough." Alok was doubtful.

"Okay, three and a half for our super-mugger," Ryan said, "Okay?"

Alok agreed, but his voice was so meek, it sounded like the chicken he just ate speaking from within.

Ryan was elated, and he drove us back to Kumaon at speeds that made the traffic police dizzy. No one stopped us, or rather, we didn't stop. I covered the number plate with my foot, so that cops could not take it down. After all, this was a celebration of drawing the line.

Meanwhile, I ran into Neha at the campus bookstore. I had not met her since she had tried to kill me and it wasn't anyone's fault. Mostly that whole jogging plan was a bad idea. Even with the prospect of meeting Neha, I just could not wake up. I did try once again, but I was late and did not see her car. After that, all my motivation dropped and Ryan gave up on waking me up. He had to, cause I kind of threatened to withdraw from his draw-the-line study plan. So, what I'm trying to say is, when I saw Neha again, it was a nice surprise.

"Hi," I said, raising my hand to catch her attention.

She looked at me, and then kept looking, her face expressionless. She acted as if she did not recognize me. Then she went back to flipping pages of the notebooks she had just bought. Now that was hell, I mean, if you are in a public place and say 'hi' to a girl, all beaming and everything and she's like 'have we been introduced?'

The shopkeeper looked at me, as did a few other customers, and I felt like low-life though I gave it another try. I mean, just a few weeks ago she was all sympathetic and friendly, so maybe she just couldn't place me.

"Neha, it's me! Remember the car accident in the morning?" I said.

"Excuse me," she said huffily and departed.

This time the shopkeeper looked at me like I was a regular sex-offender. The girl bumped me and gave me a lift and all dammit, I wanted to scream, even as I bought my pencils and loose sheets. So I am not that attractive and that is reason enough not to recognize someone in public because I guess being friends with ugly people kind of rubs off badly on you. I had been some sort of a loser in school as well, so this was not a total shock. I mean what happened to me once in my school, I don't even want to get into all that but somehow, I felt strange. I don't know, Neha did not look like that kind of girl.

I walked out of the shop as quickly as possible to get away from the humiliation. I was feeling crap. I mean, she could have at least said "hi," I thought. I know I am fat and if I were a girl, I'd probably not talk to me either. I was walking alone on a narrow path connecting the bookshop to the hostel, when someone tapped my shoulder. I turned around and guess who?

"Hi," said Neha.

Go to hell, was my instant mental reflex. But I turned to look at her and damn, she was pretty. And with that one tiny dimple on her right cheek flashing every time she smiled... Now try saying 'go to hell' to that!

"Hi. Neha, right?" I said, this time really careful and slow.

"Of course. Hey, I am really, really, really sorry, I could not reply to you properly there. There's a reason," she divulged.

Now, girls do this all the time, they think repeating an adjective makes it more effective; the three 'reallys' were supposed to constitute an apology.

"What reason?" I said.

"It is just that, I mean...can we just forget it?"

"No, tell me why?" I insisted.

"The shopkeeper there knows me and my dad for the last ten years and they talk regularly."

"So?"

"My dad is really strict about me talking to boys and he will totally flip out if he hears I am friends with a student."

"Really? Just greeting someone?"

"He is like that. And campus rumours always get blown out of proportion. Please, I am sorry."

She was being a bit ridiculous, I thought, but I kind of knew where she was coming from. Some girls' dads are a bit touchy, and with over a thousand boys with their proportional quota of hormones on campus he would be worried.

"Well, I can't see you then anyway, right?"

"You can as long as it is out of campus."

"We live here!"

"Yes, but there is a world outside. We can go to the Hauz Khas market. Do you feel like some ice-cream?"

It is hard enough to say no to pretty girls or to ice-cream but when it's offered together, it is well nigh impossible. I said yes, and she instructed me to walk out the campus gate and walk two blocks to an ice-cream parlour. She would come there as well, but gave me a five-minute headstart, walking sedately behind me.

It was completely weird to walk alone that way, and I kept thinking how stupid I'd look in the parlour if she did not show up. At least I'd have ice-cream, I thought. Food is almost as good as girls.

But Neha did show up and inside the Cadbury's ice-cream parlour she was a different person.

"So, Mr Jogger, did not see much of you after that day. Did I scare you off?" She began to giggle. Girls do this all the time, say something half-funny, and laugh at it themselves.

"No, it's just a pain to wake up."

"Well, I was kind of hoping to see you," she confessed.

"Yeah, looked like it at the bookshop."

"I said I am sorry, Hari," she said, and touched my arm again like she had earlier. I kind of liked that, I mean, which guy wouldn't. You have this pretty girl all smiley and sorry and touching your arm; better than ice-cream I tell you.

There are two kinds of pretty girls in Delhi. One is the modern type, girls who cut their hair short, wear jeans or skirts, and tiny earrings. The second is the traditional type who wears salwar-kameez, multi-coloured bindi and large earrings. Neha was more the second type, and she wore a light-blue *chikan* suit with matching earrings. However, she was not a forced traditional type, like fat girls who have no choice but to wear Indian clothes. Neha was just fine, and actually way out of my league, with her long light brown hair, which she mostly left open, a curl catapulting carelessly on to her forehead. Her face was completely round, but not because she was fat or anything, just a natural cute shape. I just kept looking at her as my strawberry ice-cream melted.

"Friends?"

"I guess so. You know, when you ignored me there, I first thought it was because of the way I am."

"What way are you?"

"Never mind," I said.

I told Neha about our harebrained scholastic plan.

"Three hours? Pretty brave I must say. Guess you are underestimating the profs and their love for assignments," she said, scraping up whatever remained in her cup.

I shrugged my shoulders. "Anyway, you tell me about yourself. Learnt driving now?"

"Yes, I even got a licence," she chirped and opened her bag to show it to me. She started taking stuff out of her handbag and a million things came out – lipsticks, lip balms, creams, bindis, earrings, pens, mirrors, wet tissues and other stuff that one can live without. She found what she was looking for eventually.

"Wow. Neha Samir Cherian, female, 18 years," I read her name aloud.

"Hey, stop it. You are not supposed to notice ladies' ages."

"That is for sixty-year-old women, you are young." I returned her licence.

"Still, I like chivalrous men," she said, repacking her bag and the million belongings.

I did not know if it meant something. I mean, did she want me to know what kind of men she liked, or did she want me to be like the men she liked, or did she like me. Who knows? Figuring out women is harder than topping a ManPro quiz.

"Samir, isn't that a guy's name?"

"It is my brother's. I decided to keep it when I got this licence made."

"Really? What does your brother do?"

"Not much," she shrugged. "He's dead."

Now this was unexpected. I mean, I just thought I'd tease her on a mannish middle name and everything but this was turning heavy. "Oh!" I said.

"It's fine, really, he died one year ago. We were just two years apart, so you can imagine how close I was to him."

I nodded my head. Her beautiful face was turning sad and I wished I could do something clownish to change subjects.

"How did it happen?" I asked, for it seemed the polite thing to do.

"A freak accident. He was crossing the rail-tracks and got hit by a train."

I wondered if I could take a chance and hold her arm like she had a few minutes ago. I mean, that is how shallow I was. She was all choked up and everything, but all I could think of was if I could make my move.

I shifted my hand closer, but she startled me by talking again. "Life goes on, you know. He was my only sibling, so that is kind of tough. But life goes on," she repeated, more to herself than to me.

I pulled my hand back. I sensed this was not the best moment.

"Ice-cream? C'mon let us do round two," she said brightly and went up to the counter without waiting for me. She returned with these two big sundaes, and she was smiling again.

"So he had a train accident? In Delhi?"

"Yes. You don't think that can happen?" she asked challengingly.

"No....o."

"C'mon, tell me something cheerful about your hostel."

I told her about Ryan's scooter and how we over-speed on it and things. It was hardly interesting, but it changed the topic. We talked about other things until dusk and Neha's internal clock went off.

"Have to go," she jumped up. "Shall we walk back?"

"Yeah. Separately though right?" I was catching on fast.

"Yes, sorry please," she said in a mock-baby tone that girls lapse into at the slightest provocation.

I stood up, too.

"So, Hari?"

"So what?"

"Aren't you going to ask me out or what?"

That stumped me. I mean, of course I'd wanted to but thought she'd say no for sure and then I'd have felt crap all night. I would have been satisfied with the ice-cream and everything but this was kind of neat, and now I had no choice anyway.

"Huh? Sure. Neha, would you like to go out...with me?"

She had made it pretty safe for me, but I tell you, the first time you ask a girl for a date, it is like the hardest thing. Almost as stressful as vivas.

"Yes, of course I will. Meet me at this parlour next Saturday, same time as today."

I nodded.

"And next time, don't be this shy IIT boy, just ask."

I smiled.

"So, what are you waiting for? Leave now."

A demure five minutes ahead of her, I pleasantly dwelt on the mechanics of the female mind, waddling back into hostel.

5

Make Notes not War

U.S. WAS GUNNING FOR IRAQ, TAKING AS ITS FIRST CASUALTY our majors, or end-semester exams. Thousands of kilometres from our campus, a despotic dictator annexed another smaller despotic dictator's country. It just so happened that both countries had heaps of oil and that made the whole world take notice. Next, the world's most powerful country asked the dictator to get the hell out. Big dictator refused and very soon it became clear that he would be attacked.

So, what the hell did this have to do with the three of us at IIT, you'd think. If this was one of Ryan's stupid sci-fi movies, the three of us could be like involved in a conspiracy, using the IIT lab to provide superior weapons to the CIA or something. But this was not sci-fi, and the three of us considered ourselves lucky to complete the ManPro welding assignment on time, let alone provide superior war technology.

No, the Gulf war did not personally invite our involvement but it was a big bang that swallowed our first semester majors, a catalyst for all our competitive, macho instincts.

But before that let me tell you of the glory days of the short-lived 'draw-the-line' policy. As per plan we studied for three exact hours every day, mostly late unto night, which meant we had the evenings free for fun.

"The best game ever invented," Ryan said as he took us to the squash courts despite Alok and me looking like guys who never came near a mile of a squash court.

"This game will rest your mind, and burn some of that fat off." Ryan, who had been the squash captain in his school, tossed warm-up shots in the court.

Unless you are like a champion or something, you probably know how difficult the damn game is. The rubber ball jumps around like a frog high on uppers, and you jump around it to try and connect it to your racket. Ryan had played it for years and Alok and I were hopeless at it. I missed connecting the ball to the racket five times in a row, and Alok did not even try moving from his place. After a while, even I gave up. Ryan tried to keep the game going as we stood like extra pillars on court.

"C'mon guys, try at least," Ryan called out.

"I can't do this," Alok said and sat down on the court. The guy is such a loser. I mean, I could not play squash for nuts, but at least I won't sit down on the court.

"Let us try again tomorrow," Ryan said, optimistic to say the least.

He dragged us to court for ten days in a row, but Alok and I got no better. We found it hard enough to even spot where the ball had gone, let alone chase it.

"Ryan, we can't do this man," Alok said plaintively, panting uncontrollably. "If you really want to play this, why don't you find other partners?"

"Why? You guys are getting better," Ryan said.

Yeah right, maybe in thirty years, I thought grimly.

"So you don't enjoy this?"

What was Ryan thinking? Enjoy? *Enjoy?* I was in danger of tearing that ball into roughly fifty pieces.

"Not really," I ventured mildly.

"Fine then, we don't have to do this. I mean, I can give up squash," Ryan said.

"No, that is not..." Alok said.

Ryan had already decided, no point arguing with him. It was his whole 'where my friends go, I go' stand, though I kind of felt bad making him give up his favourite sport.

"You can play with others," I suggested.

"Others aren't my friends," Ryan said in a firm voice that sounded like the final word. Alok and I shrugged and we left the court.

After squash came something tamer and less active, chess. Alok and I felt somewhat up to this one, for, unlike squash, we could at least touch and move the game pieces. But Ryan usually won, and I would never be passionate about bumping off plastic pieces like him.

Apart from chess, we spent our free time riding Ryan's scooter, feeling the fierce wind whistle through our hair. We caught every new movie, visited every tourist destination in Delhi, did everything, went everywhere.

For the most part, we managed fine within the three hours assigned to studies. Sometimes assignments took longer, leaving no time for revision. That worried Alok, especially when the end-semester exams edged closer, and he suggested increasing the limit. And we would have if it hadn't been for one thing – the afore-mentioned Gulf war.

Now wars happen all the time and India alone has fought more than it can afford. But the Gulf war was different, as it came right on TV. CNN, an American news channel, had just opened shop in India and brought the deserts of Iraq right into our TV room.

"This is CNN reporting live from the streets of Baghdad. The sky is lit up with the first air raid," a well-groomed person told us.

Alok, Ryan and I looked up from our chess game. It was sensational, spectacular and unlike anything we had ever seen on TV. To put it in context, this was before cable or any private channels came to India. Until then we had two crummy government channels in which women played obsolete instruments and dull men read news for insomniacs and retards. Colour had only arrived two years ago, and most programs were still black and white. Then, in one quick week, we had the glitzy, jazzy and live – CNN.

"Is this real? I mean is this happening?" Alok looked dazed.

"Of course, Fatso. You think this is a play?" Ryan scoffed as two American pilots hi-fived themselves after hours of pounding a perfectly real city. A CNN reporter asked them questions about their mission. The soldiers told about bombing a godown, and taking down a power station that gave electricity to Baghdad.

"Wow, the Americans are going to win this," Alok said.

"Don't underestimate the Iraqis, who have fought wars for ten years. Americans are just pounding from the air," Ryan said.

"Yes, but America is too powerful. Saddam hasn't a clue."

"He does, wait till a land battle happens," Ryan defended.

The war sucked us in like quicksand, Alok and Ryan got really into 'who is going to win this' kind of crap. I mean, you stop doing that when you are twelve I think (Superman or Batman?), but there was no stopping them. I liked watching the war as well, though I primly took no sides.

Iraq was kind of anonymous then, and we unabashedly cheered on America. IIT cared about America. Most of our foreign aid came from rich American firms and quite a large percentage of our alumni went on scholarship there and for jobs, constituting a chunk of the brain drain. So, unsurprisingly, our heart bled for the US.

At the same time, the war visuals became more gruesome. Americans pounded Baghdad non-stop, and Saddam hid himself deep in one of his oil wells I think. Many times, Americans hit civilian targets and people died and everything, and that was crap. I mean, the aid to IIT was fine, but how can you justify bombing kids? But then, Saddam was kind of this loser General anyway, and apparently shot his own people when he was grumpy. Oh, it was impossible to take sides in the Gulf war. And it was all pointless for us anyway. These guys would realize this soon.

"Man, the majors are eight days away," Alok finally said one day. "We've got to switch off the TV."

"We still study three hours though." Ryan quirked an eyebrow.

"Screw three hours! It's not enough," I contributed.

"I think Iraq will win," Ryan said.

"Drop it, man, America has busted him," Alok said, "so please I beg you Ryan, let's study before we're busted too."

"Not yet, ground battle not done yet," he said righteously.

Luckily, the war ended five days before the majors. America won big-time, and Iraqis ate crow before ground battle. Saddam left Kuwait alone and Americans were happy all the oil in the world was theirs to burn and Ryan did not eat for a day or so.

"This is not fair. Real wars are fought on the ground," he wailed as we started revisions for the final tests in our room.

"Shut up, Ryan. Americans got what they wanted. Now can we study?" I said.

"Unfair man. US is a schoolroom bully."

"ApMech, ApMech" Alok muttered like a mantra.

Squash, chess and the war — all ate into our studying hours. In the five days before exams, we dropped the three-hour rule, well we had to; the heaps of course material was un-doable even if we studied thirty hours a day. It was important to clamp down on Ryan and we studied until three in the morning every day and passionately prayed India would go to war on the morning of our first majors.

A day before the majors were practical tests. It was the only part of the course Ryan enjoyed, and he dragged us early to the physics lab. We were in the same group and had to conduct an electrical setup and then answer questions in a viva-voce. We got a resistance-voltage relationship testing experiment.

I hated practical tests. Most of all, I dreaded the viva-voce. I don't know if I told you about my condition; it strikes me whenever someone looks me in the eye and asks me a question. My body freezes, sweat beads cover me brow to groin, and I lose my sense of voice. How I hated vivas and when Ryan was all excited assembling the circuit for the experiment, I hated him too.

"Hey guys, watch this," Ryan said, holding the circuit components in his hand.

Alok looked up from his notebook.

Ryan spent the next ten minutes connecting resistors, capacitors, switches and cables to each other. It was completely unconnected to our experiment and Alok was seriously getting worried.

"Ryan, can you please connect the resistor-voltage setup so we can start our experiment?" Alok said.

"Wait Fatso, we have two hours to do the experiment. Do they have a small speaker here?" Ryan fumbled through the component box.

"What do you need a speaker for?" I said even as Ryan found one and made the final connection.

"For this," Ryan said and switched his circuit on. He moved a few connections, and soon Hindi music came from the speaker.

"*Ghar aaya mera pardesi...*"

"What the hell!" Alok jumped as if a ghost had shimmered into the lab.

"It is a radio, stupid," Ryan said, eyes all lit up, "I knew we had all the parts to make one."

"Ryan," I said, as firmly as possible.

"What?"

"We are having a damn major here," I said.

That is Ryan. The guy will do clever things but only at the wrong time and wrong place.

Alok panicked, too. "The viva is in twenty minutes, boss."

Ryan ripped off his circuit and looked at us in disdain as if we were tone-deaf listeners who had rejected live Mozart.

We just about managed to finish the circuit on time when Prof Goyal walked in.

"Hmm…," the Prof said tugging at the circuit wires. Ryan had made the circuit; he was good at this, we trusted him.

"So, Ryan what will happen if I change the 100-ohm resistor with a 500-ohm resistor?"

"Sir, we would have higher voltage across, though there would be a higher heat loss as well."

"Hmm…" Prof Goyal scratched his chin in response, which meant Ryan was right.

"So Alok, how do you read the stripes on this resistor to get the ohm resistance?"

"Sir, the red stripe is a 100-ohm, then 10 for the blue, implying 110 ohm."

Our group was doing well. But Prof Goyal was not done. Despite my frantic hopes, he turned to me.

"So Hari, if I add another resistor on top of the 110 ohm resistor, what happens to the current flow?"

A trick question. The current flow depends on how one connects the new resistor, in series or parallel. In series, the current would drop. In parallel, it would increase. Yes, this was the answer. I think so, right?

I had recited the answer in my mind. But Prof Goyal stared at me and me alone while asking the question, not surprising since he prefixed the question with what was a good facsimile of my name.

"Sir..." I quivered as my hand started to shiver. My condition was upon me.

"What will happen to the current flow?"

"Sir..I...sir," I said, inexorably tumbling toward total paralysis. I mean, I totally knew the answer but what if it was wrong? I tried articulating, but the thoughts did not cash into words.

"Sir, the current flow depen..." Ryan intervened, trying to save the situation.

Prof Goyal raised his forefinger.

"Quiet, I am asking your group member, not you."

I shook my head and lowered it. There was no use, I had given up.

"Hmm..." Prof Goyal said, not scratching any part of his face. "The standard of this institute is going down day by day. What are you, commerce students?"

Calling an IIT-ian a commerce student was one of the worst insults the profs could accord to us, like a prostitute calling her client a eunuch. The institute was the temple of science and anyone below standards was an outcaste or a commerce student.

Prof Goyal scribbled a C+ on our group experiment sheet, and tossed it at us. Ryan caught it, I think.

We did not have much of a chance to discuss the physics practicals, as the majors started the next day. I had even postponed my next rendezvous with Neha until after the exams. I had called her once, getting her number from the faculty's internal directory. She freaked out, telling me not to call home without notice. How the hell was I supposed to give her notice? Anyway, we had fixed to meet the day after my majors.

Majors were when everyone studied in Kumaon, lights remained on in rooms until dawn, people rarely spoke – and then only on matters of life or death – and consumed endless cups of tea in the all-night mess. Ryan, Alok and I scrambled to revise our six courses. The exams schedule was three continuous days, leaving little time to discuss the tests. I knew I had done fine in some tests and screwed up some. Alok had developed a permanent scowl and Ryan could maintain his laid-back air only with the utmost effort; no jokes, majors blow the wind out of anyone. ManPro, ApMech, physics, mathematics, chemistry and computing. One by one, we finished them. When majors ended, it did seem like the worst was over though the results come only after two weeks.

Those two weeks between the end of majors and the results were bliss. Even though the second semester began, no one really got into the new courses until they knew how they'd done in the first semester. The profs were busy evaluating tests, going easy on new assignments, giving us plenty of time to kill. Ryan upgraded us from chess to crossword puzzles, taking us from cryptic clues to rhyme words to anagrams.

Meanwhile, I met Neha again on a summery evening early into the second semester even though she had short-circuited when I called her. It was the same ice-cream parlour.

"God, are you crazy or what, calling at home?" she greeted.

I didn't know what to say. I thought I'd been pretty cool to think of getting the number from the profs directory and everything.

"How else am I to reach you?

"My parents are very strict about me getting calls from boys."

I couldn't tell her, "Your parents sound like regular psychos," so in *non-sequitur*, I asked, "Strawberry?"

She was wearing a demure white salwar-kameez that day. She held my hand as she took the cone from me. God, she is beautiful, I tell you.

"So how am I supposed to reach you?"

"Call me on the 11th."

A pink tongue darting out to catch some melted cream from reaching the ground had disoriented me. "Huh?"

"Just call me on the 11th of any month."

Now Neha is beautiful and everything, but she can be pretty loony at times.

"What? Why 11th?"

"Because no one is at home that day. You see, my brother died on 11th May. So on every 11th my parents go to this temple near the rail-tracks where he died. They are gone most of the day."

"Really? And you don't go?"

"I used to. But it used to remind me of Samir a lot. I'd be depressed for days afterward and the doctor told me not to go."

She said it matter of factly, as if she were choosing an ice-cream flavour. It was strange, but a hell of a lot better than her gearing up to cry or something; I can't stand people who cry in public.

"Only on 11th?"

"Well for now, that is the only safe date," she said and laughed, "why? You want to talk more often?"

I did nót answer her. I mean, I just thought it weird that I could call her only on that one day a month, like I had a dental appointment or something. But girls are weird, I was learning.

"So tell me," she said tapping my hand again to change the topic, "how were the majors?"

I loved it when she touched me in any way, that's how deprived or depraved I was; I almost forgot her question in the aftermath of the tiny localized tremors exploding on my skin's surface.

"Uh majors...nothing great. Results come in one week or so."

"Did well?"

"Not really."

"You want me to put in a word to Dad to increase your grades?" she said.

"Can you?" The pinkness enveloped me.

"I'm kidding."

Of course. She giggled as if she had got me. Like I thought I believed she could help me with my grades or something. Girls love laughing at their own jokes but Neha amused is better than Neha looking around furtively.

I suddenly leaned forward, bringing my face close to hers. Catching her breath, stifling that laugh and pink tongue, she watched me wide-eyed. I removed the wallet from my back pocket and sat down casually again.

"What happened?" I asked idly.

"I thought...never mind." She blinked.

Ha, gotcha.

6

Five-point Something

"THEY'RE OUT!" ALOK SAID, SHAKING RYAN'S SHOULDER
on a Saturday morning as if India had won the World Cup or
nude women were rolling on the grass outside. "The major
results are out!"

"I want to sleep," Ryan said, burrowing deeper under the
quilt that Alok eventually succeeded in tugging off.

We reached the insti where a crowd of students had
gathered to see their first set of grades. From these one could
determine their first grade point average, or GPA, on the 10-
point scale. The topper would be close to 10.00, while the
average would be around 6.50. We, however, were closer to
the bottom. Clicking through the scientific calculator, Alok
calculated our scores.

"Ok, Hari is at 5.46 and... Ryan is at 5.01 and I ...I'm
at 5.88," Alok said.

"So all of us are five-pointers," I said, as if making a particulary insightful comment.

"Congrats Alok, you have topped amongst us," Ryan said.

Topped amongst us, I thought. As if we were the high-brain society or something. These were pathetic grades: we ranked in the high 200s in a class of 300 students. Alok recalculated his score, hoping for some miracle to happen on the calculator. But miracles never happen in IIT, only crap grades do.

"Screw that. Bloody hell, I am just a 5.88. This is so below average."

"We knew that, right?" Ryan said, "Whatever. Alok, let's celebrate this over chicken."

"Celebrate!" Alok spluttered. "I have just screwed up any chance of getting a US scholarship or a good job and you want to bloody celebrate?"

"Grow up, Fatso. What do you want to do? Mug more in mourning?" Ryan was calm.

"Fuck you," Alok said.

It was the first time he had used the 'F' word. From him, it sounded peculiar, I mean he is still a kid.

Ryan's calmness vanished faster than a prof's smile. "What did you say?" he turned toward me, "What did the Fatso say?"

Why was the bastard dragging me into this? Ryan had damn well heard what Alok said. In fact, all the twittering students around us had heard it too.

"C'mon guys, let's take the show to the hostel," I pleaded. I don't care if they kill each other, but privacy I insist on. They were in no mood to let go and for a moment I thought they were going to ignore me and have a fisticuff right there. Somehow, I knew this wasn't one of the regular Ryan-Alok arguments; this had, at its core, their basic character contrasts.

"Let's go," I said again and they dragged their feet back to the scooter. Ryan rode us back to the hostel as rashly as he possibly could, intentionally going over every bump on the road. He has his own strange way of sulking I tell you.

We sat in Ryan's room after dinner, we had not spoken a word since the insti. I had thought a little about my little GPA. Yes, a five-pointer was pretty crap. From now on, every prof would know that I was a below average student and that would influence my grade in future courses. I knew a few five-pointers who were panned at campus recruitment last year. This was crap, how did I get into this situation? Was I just not smart enough? At the dinner table, other students were either plain morose or extremely excited. There was the studious Venkat, who never left his room and was always quiet at meals. Today, he was smiling. He had a nine point five. He sat next to Alok, and told his stories of topping in four out of six courses. Alok was talking only to him and totally ignoring us. There were others too. Even the Smiling Surd in our wing had managed a respectable seven point three. I think the three of us were the lowest in Kumaon or something. I could have mulled more over my future, or rather the lack of it, but Ryan and Alok's swollen faces filled my immediate vision.

We trooped into Ryan's room and sat quietly for half an hour or so. Nobody opened a book, looked at each other or said a word. I wondered if we were going to stay quiet forever. I mean, that couldn't be such a bad thing. We could attend class, study together and eat together, quiet as mice. Maybe our grades would improve as well. It really isn't that important for people to talk.

But my rosy fantasy of silence was finally broken by Ryan.

"So, you are not going to apologize?" he asked belligerently.

"Apologize? Me? It is *you* who should apologize Ryan," Alok said.

"You are the one who said 'fuck you' in front of the whole damn insti," Ryan said, "and I should apologize? Hari, can you believe this? *I should apologize.*"

Now this had nothing to do with me, so I ignored Ryan. Let the two nuts figure it out amongst themselves.

"You just don't fucking get it do you?" Alok said, going the 'damn' way with 'fuck'.

Ryan kept silent.

"Get what?" I said. I mean, I really wanted to know what I was missing in this moronic conversation.

"Get this. Today I got a GPA of 5.88. Damn it, a 5.88. Over 200 students have done better. Do you know in my twelve years in school I never even got a second rank."

In most parts of the world, that would be a pretty loser statement to make. To announce that you were like this nerd in school is hardly something to be proud of. But that is Alok for you.

"So?" Ryan said, "your insti grades are bad. And who cares about how much you mugged. Why the hell should *I* apologize?"

"Because damn it…because it is *your* damn fault," Alok said and stood up.

Now that was whacko. Poor Ryan had just managed to scrape a five, and now he was getting crap from Alok.

"*My* fault?" Ryan said and started laughing. "Hari, listen to this. Fatso screws up his grades and it is Ryan's fault. *My fault*. Hey Alok, have you gone nuts or something?"

"Say something," Alok beseeched me.

"Say what?' I looked away from both of them.

"It is okay. If Hari does not have the guts to say it, I can. *You* and *your* ideas, Ryan. Study less, draw the line, enjoy the best years, this system is a machine, crap, crap and more crap all the time."

Ryan stood up from his chair as well; I think it gives you an edge in the argument if you stand up, kind of more serious and purposeful.

"I know you are upset and everything but there is no need to overreact. Just some stupid grades..."

"I am not overreacting," Alok said and sat back down. "And it is not just stupid grades for me. I don't have my parents earning dollars like yours. I came to this institute with a purpose. To do well, get a good job and look after my parents. And you have fucked it up."

Another F-word; Alok was still upset I guess.

"Stop saying fuck all the time," Ryan said.

"I will say whatever I want. That is the problem. No one can say anything to you. You propose something, Hari blindly agrees and we all end up doing it. You are just a spoilt brat. Someone who wants to do whatever he wants without caring for his friends."

"What? What did you just say? That I don't care for my friends?" Ryan said. Though his voice was notched at a menacing pitch, I noticed his hands starting to shiver a little bit.

"No. You don't care about anything – not studies, not the insti, not your parents and not your friends. You just want to have your fun."

"You're crossing the line here," Ryan warned.

"I am drawing the line for a change. From now on, I am not going to hang out with you anymore, it is official."

Now it was pretty clear that Alok was overreacting. "What are you saying, man?" I said.

"No drop-shrop it. I have listened to you guys for the entire first semester and screwed up everything," Alok said.

"So what are you going to do?"

"Like I said, no more hanging out with Ryan. From now on, I am going to be with Venkat. He has agreed to let me study with him. He got a nine point five you know?"

I felt disgusted. Nobody in Kumaon talked to Venkat; given a choice he wouldn't talk to himself. He had a good GPA and everything, but he was hardly human. Venkat woke up at four in the morning to squeeze in four hours of muggins before classes. Every evening he spent three hours in the library before dinner. Then after dinner, he studied on his bed for another couple of hours until he went to sleep. Who on earth would want to be with him?

"You are sick Alok," Ryan said, "you are just one sick person."

"My grades are important to me. My future is important to me. Does that make me sick?"

I went to Alok and put my arm around his shoulder; kind of felt he needed comfort during insanity. "C'mon Alok, we can study more..."

"Stop c'mon-Aloking me, will you?" Alok pushed my arm away, voice all wobbly. "Enough is enough," he said, his face contorted exactly like his mother's.

This heredity factor fascinated me; was there a how-to-cry gene? Or was this something he had picked up while growing up? Maybe Alok's family all cried together sometimes; mother, sister and himself bawling away with his father, who could still produce tears from one eye.

"You don't understand that I have responsibilities. I have to do well to support my family. Half my mother's salary goes for my father's medicine. She has not bought a new sari for herself in five years," Alok said as he choked on his tears. He needed to blow his nose.

Ryan sat down to watch Alok, intrigued. He could take 'fuck yous' ten a minute, but crying was a different game altogether. And the whole one-saree-in-five-years was tough to argue against. I mean, how do you argue with that? How many sarees a year is reasonable? I don't know, and Ryan for sure had no damn clue.

"And my sister needs to be married," Alok went on, "everyone is counting on me. And you guys don't understand. Ryan wants to play chess, see TV, enjoy his years. I hate enjoyment."

"Will it make it better if I say sorry? I mean, you aren't making any sense. And this whole parents deal — you know I don't understand that." Ryan was gentling, I could see.

But this shifted Alok into higher gear. "Of course, you don't. How could you? You never had them."

"I had them. I mean I still have them. But I don't sit and cry for them."

"Because you don't love them."

"Yes I don't. But at least I am not crying like a baby."

"Shut up!" Alok screamed and continued crying.

"You are a baby. A sissy-fat baby. Sorry sissy baby, now wipe your nose," Ryan said and started laughing. It is something he always does when he can't think of anything else, a kind of conversation filler.

"Shut up you...you..." Alok said.

"I want my mummeeeeee," Ryan said, imitating Alok's choked tones.

"...shut up, you abandoned orphan!"

Silence. Yes, sometimes people say something so messed up that all bets go off. Ryan's laughter vanished in a nanosecond. I sat up straight, confused if I'd heard right. Even Alok noticed the change in expressions and froze. Twenty solid, slow and long seconds of silence followed.

"Orphan. Hari, he called me an orphan," Ryan said.

I stayed silent. Alok stayed silent.

"Just get out. Go to Venkat or whichever prick you want to be with. Just get lost," Ryan said.

"I don't need you to tell me. Hari?" Alok said, not crying anymore.

"Yes?" I said.

"You coming with me?"

"Where?"

"Do you want to be with me or Ryan?"

This was so damn unfair. I had nothing to do with all this. Yet, I had to now choose between my friends.

"Yes, go with this loser Hari, go hold his hand."

"I am not going anywhere," I said.

"So you choose Ryan," Alok said in defeated tones.

"I am not choosing anyone. You are the one who is leaving. Do whatever you want," I said, disgusted with both of them.

There were no more words. Alok got up and left. Ryan shut the door behind him as hard as he could. It was purely symbolic, as we never shut the door in our rooms.

"You saw what he did. And he expected you to go with him, ha!" Ryan said.

"Fuck you," I said.

I met Neha soon after, though I was getting sick of the ice-cream parlour, and of the sickeningly sweet strawberry flavour. Neha still looked beautiful as hell, but I didn't feel like talking to her. In fact, I did not feel like talking to anyone.

"What's wrong?"

"Who said anything was wrong?" I said. I can be quite a prick if I want.

"It is all over your face. Now are you going to tell me or what?"

That is the thing with girls. They are like half your size or something, but if they know you like them, they boss you around. Who the hell did she think she was?

"It is nothing."

She placed her hand over my arm and self-respecting nitwit that I am, I melted faster than the ice-cream; like the bad mood bugs running through me suddenly got Baygon-sprayed.

"Neha, those bloody Alok and Ryan."

"Language!"

"Sorry, I mean my friends, my best friends, they had this massive argument and now our group has split."

"What was the argument about?"

"About grades. Alok said it was Ryan's fault we did badly."

"Really, how badly?"

I told her about our five-pointer grades.

"Damn, did you say five-pointers?" she said.

"Language!" I said.

"Oh sorry. I mean that is kind of low by insti standards."

See that is the thing. Once you get a GPA in IIT, everyone has an opinion about it, about you, even if it's a fashion design student.

"I know," I said, "but that is not what I am upset about. It is this place. I hate it."

Neha started laughing. I told you, didn't I, she can be a bit loony at times. "What is there to laugh about?" I asked, irritated.

"Nothing. Just how people would die to get in here."

"I know," I said, "but it sucks. I have tons to study, my grades are crap, and I don't have friends anymore."

"So Alok wants to mug, and he goes to the mugger," she paraphrased the recent events after I had told her the longhand version, "but how come you chose Ryan?"

"I didn't choose, Alok left," I reminded her.

"What are you going to do?"

I shrugged.

"You know my dad was a 10 when he was a student."

"He was a student?" I had never thought of Cherian as anything less in size or years.

"Yes, a class topper. Guess he wouldn't be too happy to know I am with a five-pointer," she said happily.

"So now you also want to stop talking to me," I said.

"No silly. I am joking," she said and laughed. Why does she do this all the time, tell jokes that are funny to her alone?

"Whatever."

"Come here," she said, tapping the seat next to her in the parlour.

"Why?"

"Just come here."

Like a trained pet, I got up from the seat opposite and sat next to her; pretty girls have this power to turn Mary, making lambs out of people.

She held my hand and turned her face toward me. "I like this five pointer," she said, and kissed my cheek.

"One, two, three, four, five," she listed, smacking my right cheek each time. "See, now that isn't too bad."

Damn, I was melting again. "Can I kiss you back?"

"No, I don't have a GPA," she pointed out.

I loved people who did not have a GPA. I loved anyone who was not at IIT. I did not want to go back. I wondered if I could work at the ice-cream parlour, filling cones all day and never have to worry about classes, courses, grades, and Alok-Ryan arguments.

"Let's see a movie, how about Saturday next?" she asked.

"Sure," I said, snapping out of my fantasy of working in the parlour.

"Great. Gotta go now. I'll pick you up from this parlour at two. Matinee show," she said and left.

I waited for five minutes, read the list of five daily specials and thought about the five kisses. Somehow, it made up for my five-point GPA.

How I wished I had got a higher GPA, if only to get more of those ice-creamy kisses!

7

Alok Speaks

FATSO, CRY-BABY, MUGGER, TRAITOR, SISSY, THAT IS HOW I come across to you. You probably picture me as this boy who refuses to grow up, the perennial prodigy who wants to show his good report card to his parents year after year. You are free to judge me, my whining over grades, my splitting with the group, my reticence to cut apron strings, an umbilical cord that stretches out across Delhi all the way from Rohini Colony to the IIT campus, binding me to mother.

Allow me, however, to tell you this my way, for yes, this is Alok Gupta, and His Highness Hari has given me an itsy-bitsy space here to give vent to my feelings. But before I do that, let me tell you a story.

Once upon a time, there lived a boy in a lower-middle class home in one of the suburbs of Delhi. Let us call this boy Loser — just to make it easier — whose father and mother were schoolteachers, art and biology respectively. Loser grew up in a simple home filled with notebooks and canvases, and learnt how to draw before learning to tie his shoelaces. Loser was good in studies (owing to two teachers looking over him at home), but what he loved most was to paint. Loser took part in every art competition for his age, and won most of them. The prizes kept coming in — and dozens of painting sets, calligraphy sets and stationery coupons later, it was clear Loser was above average at the easel. He wanted to be an artist when he grew up, and of course, this was a silly dream. For in India, there is only room for one or maybe two artists who are ninety years old (or better still, dead) to survive. Yet Loser did not care, he knew he would make it and nothing could stop him from his goal.

But that is when life screws you. Right at moments when you feel you have got it all figured out. Loser's father got this prestigious mural painting job, which for once paid well. The job involved painting the ceiling of the lobby in the education department building. Murals are hard anyway, and painting a ceiling is excruciating work. They put these bamboos upon which the artist lies down and works, and hopes to create that one masterpiece that will make the world crane their necks and take notice.

However, the only time people noticed Loser's father was when he fell down from the bamboo structure, ten meters down, and that was to step out of his way lest they broke his fall.

Right side paralysis, doctors said. Half of Loser's father was gone, but more importantly, the whole of his salary was gone, the right hand that painted was gone and so was Loser's dream.

Loser's father came home bed-ridden and never left it for ten years. His one good eye shed tears every now and then, and the sorrow of never painting again brought one infection after the other.

Soon, the bottles of paint were swapped with bottles of medicine. There was no money to afford a nurse, and Loser was appointed one. He was in class seven then, and for the rest of his school years he sat next to his father's bed after school.

For a while he painted, but soon he realized the family needed money more than landscapes. IIT, the one college in the country that virtually guaranteed a future, caught his eye. Yes, to become an engineer was the only way out of poverty.

Loser's mother used to cry every night. But she could not give up. She had to keep on teaching the digestive system and the endocrine system and reproductive system year after year to go on.

"One day, they will be out of this," Loser vowed to himself as he helped his father change sides at night and studied pulleys, magnetism and calculus for the IIT entrance exam. For two years, Loser did not step out of the house apart from school, gained fifteen kilos and muttered calculations while wiping bed-sores.

And one fine day he made it. He was in the IIT. How happy his mother and half-a-father were. Yes, four more years of discipline and he could emancipate everyone. That is when he met Ryan and Hari. And then, to remain with them, he screwed up his grades to the lowest in the institute.

Ryan, the man who lives for the moment, who does not want to be like him? Rich parents, good looks, smart enough to get into IIT, athletic enough to be good in sports and fun enough to always attract friends. Ryan is infectious, and Hari is a perfect example of this infection. If Ryan wants something, Hari gives it to him. So, if Ryan does not want to study, Hari will close his books. If Ryan thinks GPAs are not important, then Hari stops caring about them. Ryan is Pied Piper....

I remember when he came home once, he lifted my father to carry him out, and kept holding him even in the auto. It was he who argued with the hospital staff to get us a good bed, and then stayed with us until three a.m. Yes, Ryan is good, he is very, very good. For who would have broken Coke bottles for unknown freshers? Or who would have screwed up his new scooter and overloaded it with three people, two of them in possession of large butts?

But there is more to Ryan. Like did you know his parents send him a letter every other week? Or that he never replies to any of them? Yes, he will tell you he doesn't love them or whatever crap he dishes out. But the truth is, he keeps every letter neatly in a file. When he is alone in his room at night, he opens the letters and reads them again. I mean, if he is so cool and everything, why can't he respond to them occasionally? And why does he keep re-reading those letters anyway? I always knew Ryan had issues but Hari is blind.

See, even though I think I have figured out Ryan somewhat, I cannot for the hell of it understand Hari. I mean, he really is like me — ordinary, unattractive, fat and dull. But he wants to be somebody else — someone cool, smart and sharp like Ryan. But deep down, he knows that this is not possible. He will always remain the under-confident kid who turns corpse during viva. The uncool cannot become cool. If only he'd accept that, he would be able to think straight. But he doesn't, and so went along with Operation Pendulum.

When I first split up with them, I was really not sure if I had done the right thing. But after Operation Pendulum, I am not sure if I should have ever come back. Well, that is life. It screws you right when you think you have figured it out.

8

One Year Later

I KNEW 365 DAYS HAD PASSED SINCE ALOK LEFT US BECAUSE third semester results had just come out that day. How irrelevant they seemed now; another five point something, another tattoo stamped on your worth as an individual in IIT society. Ryan and I had gone to the insti to see the results, but that was incidental, the real reason was to chill out on the insti roof.

I don't remember when we first discovered this roof, it must have been soon after we started smoking grass, which was soon after we had started vodka, which was soon after we had started listening to Pink Floyd. Floyd, vodka, grass and the insti roof; finally, we were on to what really mattered in life, the stuff that made IIT life bearable, especially when you were a five-point something.

The giant insti building had nine stories; one had to take the clandestine service stairs on the ninth floor to get to the roof. There was an old lock guarding the entrance to the terrace, but thankfully the bolt was even more ancient. It took Ryan three minutes with a screwdriver to remove the rusted bolt and then we were on cloud nine, the highest point on campus. The bare, rough concrete surface made up the flat patch of terrace, there was no parapet. It was mostly empty, too, apart from the insti-bell tower, and a few dish antennas that helped the computer and telecom networks. After dark, only the stars above were visible. If one stood up and looked down, one could see the street lights on campus roads and distant views of Kumaon and other hostels a kilometre away.

Ryan laid out the vodka, the joints and his small Walkman in autopilot, familiar with our twice a week routine.

We lay down on the concrete, still warm from the sunlight in the day. Ryan divided the pair of earphones, such that we had one earphone each, passed a joint to me, and we kept the vodka bottle in the center. Sip, puff, sip, rewind, stop and play.

The lyrics washed over us and we flew up to the sky as it flew down at us.

"You see all those kids screaming over their GPA," Ryan said, releasing a smoke-ring.

I think smoke is beautiful; weightless and shapeless, it almost appears as deceptively powerless as the person releasing it, yet, it comes from within and rises above us all. Crap, I am talking all artsy stuff, grass does this to me.

"Yes, I saw them. And I see how they look at us," I said.

"How?"

"Like what the hell are we there for? How does our miserable GPA matter anyway? As if we are blocking their view or something."

"Screw them," Ryan said, words of wisdom from the man who knows everything.

"It's true though," I said, "we really serve no purpose here..."

"Of course, we do. We are the under-performers."

"So?"

"So we bring the average down. We make them look better. Hence, we bring happiness in their lives."

"Point," I conceded.

"But it is not the students that bother me. It is the profs."

"You are talking about the design class right?"

"Yes, that Prof Bhatia. I mean you were there, right? I gave him some ideas on how one could design a suspension bridge and he got all excited. He told me to make a scale drawing and submit it, said he would give me a special internship project. Then he asked me my name and found out my GPA. So then he calls me and says to forget about the drawing and internship. Can you believe that scum?" Ryan said.

We had finished one joint each. Ryan sat up to make another one, crushing the grass and tobacco hard, as if it were Prof Bhatia's innards.

"Screw him," I passed the words of wisdom back to Ryan. We refilled our glasses, as it turned dark on the roof.

"Yes, screw all profs," Ryan said.

"Yeah. Though Prof Veera is all right." Prof Veera was our fluid mechanics professor.

"Yes, not him. Though I have heard the worst one is yet to come," Ryan said as he lit up the second joint.

"Who?" I debated whether I should smoke more. Ryan's tolerance was much higher and he could probably make a wholesome meal out of dope but I knew I was getting trippy. For one thing, I felt I was feather-light; up here, it felt like I was floating above the world. Screw all profs, all students and all design assignments.

"Prof Cherian."

"Neha's dad?" I said, somewhat returning to my senses.

"Yes. They say he's a real terror. Like he is the head of the department, and is this total control freak with other profs and students."

I knew Neha's dad was a control freak, at least with his daughter. "Who told you?"

"It is well known, ask any senior. Anyway, for the record, Anurag told me."

"So when does the control freak teach us?"

"Next year. He takes third year courses," Ryan said.

"Next year, too far. Give me another joint."

There were still more than two years to leave this place. And the worst prof was yet to come. I deserved another joint.

"Here," Ryan said, passing me the crude cigarette. He was a good pal, one who rolls joints for you.

"Anyway, I don't want to talk about grades or profs. Talk about something else," I said.

Ryan stayed silent; I guess he was searching for another topic.

"How is your girl?" he asked after straining his brain for twenty seconds.

That is how Ryan addresses Neha. He never says her name, as if her being 'my girl' is more important than her being Neha.

"Neha is great. Going for a movie next week."

"So you guys serious?"

"Serious about what?"

"I don't know, like you love her and everything?"

"I don't know," I said.

That is how men talk about their relationships. Nobody knows anything – neither the questioner nor the answerer.

"Has she said anything?"

"Well, you know how she is. So damn moody all the time. Sometimes she is all cuddly, holds my hand, and acts cozy at the movies. But when I try something, she stops me and gives me these lectures on how she is a decent girl and I should learn to behave."

"What do you do? You are a bastard I know," Ryan said and started laughing. Screw him. That is the thing with people who know you well, they judge you before they hear you out.

"I do nothing. Like I mean, do you know we have not even kissed yet. Like I have met her twenty times, but every time I get the push. She has like this under-the-elbow policy."

"Sounds like a nice girl. You're lucky."

"Screw nice. I don't want nice."

That is true, nice people are completely boring. They don't give you joints, and they don't let you kiss them.

"Talk to her then. Tell her to be naughty. I am sure she wants to be bad," Ryan said.

"Are you crazy? She is a girl; girls never want to be bad."

"They do. Just that they want it a little less than us."

I couldn't imagine Neha wanting to do the same things I wanted to do with her. "I don't believe you. Did you ever have a girlfriend?" I said.

"Then don't believe. Anyway, enough talk about women. Time for another drink and tape," Ryan said.

Ryan never talked much about himself. Sometimes, I wondered if he was gay. But he wasn't, I mean, I would have known. I practically lived with the guy, and unless he found me hideously unattractive, I think I would have known. But he wasn't gay, for he did notice the heroines in movies, whistled at pretty girls on the street. Maybe he just wasn't in the mood for women most of the time.

He changed the tape and put on another Pink Floyd. I saw the levels of the vodka bottle drop and Ryan scraping through his brown bag for the last joint of the day. A half-moon lit up the sky, and bright little stars looked smug, winking down at us like students with higher GPAs.

You know the thing about Floyd? Not only are they damn good, they sound better with every drink, like the singers designed them for alcohol. Like samosas-chutney, idli-sambhar or rajma-chawal, Floyd and vodka are in a combo-class of their own.

"You know what today reminds me of?" Ryan said.

"What?"

"The first sem results. You remember?"

"Yes, I do. The first fiver."

"And after that."

"What?"

"Fatso left us."

Ryan still referred to him as Fatso and even though it is derogatory, it was always laced with indulgence. I know Ryan had not spoken to Alok for the entire past year and he wouldn't let me as well. "Don't go to him. He left us," he said, and I knew Ryan would do some serious sulking if I rebelled.

"How come you thought of Alok today?" I asked, rising to see how much vodka remained. Surely, Ryan had drunk too much to be talking this.

"I just mentioned him today. I think of him more often."

Ryan in a profound mood. Grass and vodka have mixed to optimal levels.

"Screw him," I said as the song reached some of my favourite lines.

"What do you think he is doing right now?" Ryan said.

"Who?" I said, "Alok?"

Ryan nodded.

"Probably mugging away with Venkat. I hear he is a six-pointer now," I said.

"You know Hari, Alok did the right thing."

"Yeah, right."

"No, I am serious. You should have left me too. I am not good for you."

Now what is going on here, I thought. Am I going to have to waste real good dope in making Ryan feel all wanted and better about himself? I have two options: one, to tell him to shut up and enjoy the song, two, do what he wants me to do.

"What is the deal Ryan? Not feeling good?"

"No, I am fine. You should have left me. Everyone leaves me. They must be right."

"What?"

"They do. Dad, Mom, Alok…they all do."

"No need to be senti, Ryan, just enjoy the evening."

"You think Fatso was right? You think I did not care for him?" he demanded.

I hate it when people want to be assured, you have no choice but to play ball.

"No Ryan, Alok was wrong. He will realize it someday. Now just close your eyes and cruise a little," I advised.

I closed my eyes. The grass and vodka were now in complete control of the policeman in me, making me see what I wanted to see. I saw Neha sitting next to me, smiling and embracing me. Her hair, and especially that one soft, floppy lock, brushes me. Her round faces resembles the moon, or is it that I am actually watching the moon? This is trippy and the grass is getting the better of me but I want to be gotten the better of. I continued drifting until Ryan interrupted me.

"You know the best thing about the insti roof?" He stood up, towering over me.

"That no one knows we are here."

"No. The fact that you always have an option."

"What option."

"You can jump over the edge and end it all."

"Shut up, Ryan." I struggled to sit up.

"I'm serious. They can do whatever, but I can still control my options."

"You are too drunk Ryan, I want to go back," I said, sobering up fast. Sometimes, you want your commonsense to get the better of you.

We never missed the fluid mechanics class in the fourth sem and the reason was Prof Veera. That and the fact that the class was at noon and we finally woke up by then. Prof Veera was completely different. For one, he was like twenty years younger than other profs. No more than thirty, he dressed in jeans and T-shirt, which bore his US university logos. He had like five degrees from all the top universities – MIT, Cornell, Princeton etc, and T-shirts from all of them. He carried this CD-man with him, and after class, he would plug it into his ears before he left. Students said Prof Veera had just joined the insti, and was not supposed to be taking a full course so early. However, the prof he was assisting had a heart attack or something, and Prof Veera had to teach us.

"Hi everyone," Prof Veera said as he entered class. He offered chewing gum to the first row students. The front row guys were all mugging nine-pointers, and freaked out at his offer. They declined, and he shrugged and popped a piece in his mouth and turned to the board.

"Turbulent flows," he wrote in big letters on the board.

"Guys, in the first five lectures, we studied simple flows called laminar flows. The shape and direction of these flows are predictable with the help of formulas and equations. You know which equation, right?"

He looked around for answers. Unlike other profs, he did not stick to the first row. In fact, he scavenged at the back. "Okay, I am not going to ask the studious kids all the questions. I want to ask the cool dudes at the back."

Ryan and I were chronic backbenchers; out of sight, this was the most defensive position for the outcaste five-pointers, but Prof Veera did not care.

"Ryan, tell me, which is the first principle equation for laminar flows?"

"Sir, me?" Ryan said, surprised that a Prof would know his name.

"Yes you, Ryan. I know you know the answer."

"The Navier-Stokes equation."

"Right. You want to write it down for the class?"

Ryan ran up to the board and the nine-pointers in the front row smirked at a five-pointer contributing to class. The equation was right though; Ryan doesn't go up to the board unless he knows he's right.

"Perfect, thanks Ryan. By the way, was it you who wrote the impact of lubricant efficiency on scooter fuel consumption in your last term paper?"

"Well, yes sir."

"Is it true you actually tested the data on your scooter?"

"Yes I did, sir. Not accurately though."

"I like that," Prof Veera said, looking at the nine-pointers who were busy taking frantic notes like trained parrots. "I really like that."

Ryan came back to his seat. I could tell he loved fluid mechanics, and most of all, he loved Prof Veera. He never missed FluMech and he would do anything for Prof Veera. Others however – the testy design prof, the painfully dull solid mechanics prof and the assignment-maniac thermodynamics prof – were a different story. Ryan could cut up their guts with a lathe machine in the machining workshop given a chance.

I met Neha at Priya cinema a week after the FluMech class. I would have said I met my girlfriend but the damn problem was I was still not sure. I had known her for over a year, but she called me different things depending on her mood. First, I was just a friend. Then I was a good friend, then a friend who was special, then really-really good and special friends or some such crap. For her, calling someone a boyfriend was a big thing. Her dad had made her promise that she would never have a boyfriend, and she wanted to keep it. Of course, it did not prevent her from watching movies with me hand in hand every two weeks for over a year.

"Late again?" she said. I must have been late by like two minutes.

"Had fluMech class. Prof Veera overshot time and we did not even realize it."

"Prof Veera is that young guy right?"

"Yes, you know him?"

"Not really. Dad mentions him. I think my dad hates him."

"Your dad sounds like a total..."

She raised her eyebrows.

"Let's go in. I don't want to miss the trailers."

The movie was *Total Recall*, another sci-fi action crap. That's the thing about English theatres in Delhi. They either show action or adult movies. I don't mind the latter except that you can't really take a girl to them. Especially these really nice and good-Indian-traditional girls like Neha. So, you have the choice of sci-fi action nonsense or a Hindi movie. No self-respecting girl will watch a Hindi movie on a date. Hence, there I was again, to watch Arnold flex his muscles and blow up planets.

"You like sci-fi," she said as she took her seat.

"I do," I said. What choice did I have anyway?

"Typical IIT engineer."

Yeah right. Typical IIT engineers, my girl, don't skip design class to watch stupid movies.

And then just when I thought it couldn't get worse, it did. Neha and I took our seats in the balcony (Rs 35/ticket, total rip-off) and waited for the trailers to begin. However, according to a new government regulation, the theatre had to screen a 'family planning documentary' first.

Okay, so India has this big population. So maybe people should just use some protection and we would have less new people. Simple enough, right? So you would think. Apparently, nobody wants to use contraception, so the government has to show people a more permanent way to not have kids.

The documentary began; a doctor in a government hospital introduced himself with a beatific smile. He was supposed to be your friend in family planning, though I think he was the angel of death, especially when he recommended one sure shot procedure – vasectomy.

The documentary showed this mill worker who had this idyllic home where he lived with his simple wife (who cooked all the time) and two kids. Then one day he sleeps and has a dream that he has six kids or something (obviously that would have taken a lot of screwing his wife, but they skipped all that). The kids need more food, education, toys and keep asking dad for more. But dad is tired from the mill job (not to mention the screwing) and breaks down. That is when our friend in family planning or angel of death appears.

The doctor had this portable flip-chart with a picture of the male anatomy. He opened it, and the whole theatre, especially the front rows, started hooting. (Theatres are the opposite of class lectures, the front row is where the action is.)

Anyway, so all this is going on when I am on my date. I had never approached the topic of sex (let alone controlling sex) with Neha. But there he was, the angel of death, showing the exact location of the cuts so that the male organ came under control. I was embarrassed like every other man in the balcony.

Neha looked at me, noticing I was shifting around in my seat. "You all right?"

"Don't you think this is too much? Why do they have show this indecent stuff?"

"What? It is educational."

"Yeah, right. I need that when I come to see a movie."

"Oh come on Hari. I actually think it is pretty funny."

The wife on screen listened carefully to the doctor and smiled at the prospect of sex without any consequences. I think the doctor and the wife had a thing going, but that was just my imagination.

To the relief of all, the documentary ended in like half an hour. The mill worker wakes up and realizes how he must control his family and signs his reproductive facilities away. Happy ending, smiling faces of wife and kids which turn into cartoons, and the inverted triangle of the population control department. 'Small Family Happy Family' was the last nugget of wisdom thrown at us before trigger-happy Arnold took over the screen.

Neha held my hand as the movie began. She had grown comfortable with doing this and I could not hope for anything more. I remembered my last conversation with Ryan. Could Neha also secretly want to do more than hold hands? Could I just ask her? Should I just make a bold move?

We went to Nirula's after the movie for a meal. "So, what is Prof Veera like, tell me," Neha said, cutting the pizza we ordered into equal-sized pieces. Girls love organizing food on a table.

"He is really different," I said. "Like he doesn't discriminate between nine-pointers and five-pointers. And he likes original thinking. Even his assignments push you to think more."

"Like how?"

"Like he gave a term paper asking students to think about an engineering problem linked to fluid mechanics. Most profs would have just said, 'do all the numericals at the end of Chapter 10' or something, but Prof Veera invites ideas."

"Sounds cool. Is he good looking?"

"I think so."

"Then I should try to see him. Maybe I'll ask dad to invite him home," she said and laughed.

A surge of jealousy rose within me. Somehow Prof Veera didn't seem so nice anymore. "Go to hell."

"Hey, are you getting jealous?"

"No, why should I get jealous? I'm not your boyfriend."

Neha laughed really hard. Jokes only she finds funny. Stupid woman, I feel like cutting off her cute lock of hair.

"I am just kidding, silly," she said. "In any case my dad will kill me for that. And he hates him anyway. But it is nice to see you all worked up."

"I'm not."

She held my hand, though she hadn't stopped laughing. What is so funny to women all the time? And why do I still find her so beautiful? And why the hell can't I kiss her?

She stopped laughing and got back her composure. "Sorry, Hari. Don't feel bad, you are my sweetest little special friend."

Now what is that? Another title for the fortnight?

She bent forward to kiss my cheek. Now is my chance, I thought. Give her the illusion that you don't care then as soon as her mouth comes to the cheek, jerk once and move your lips there instead. This is the only way to kiss good Indian women, Ryan told me.

"What are you doing?" Neha pulled back.

I tried to look innocent.

"Were you trying to kiss me on the lips?"

"No."

"Hari, you know I am not into that."

Then what the hell are you into? Funny private jokes? Or your stuck-up father?

"Because this is wrong. This spoils everything. Because it feels wrong. You are not a girl, you won't understand."

Yes, I wanted to say, and you are not a guy, so you will not understand. So, should we just eat our pizza and go home? I didn't say anything. I had lost my chance, and right then even my desire. Besides, her face had turned sad. I didn't want her to be upset. Because we fixed our next date at the end of the meal. I didn't want to not fix the next date. "This pizza is good."

"You want to meet next Thursday?"

"Sure."

"I have to buy a gift for a friend's birthday. Will you come to Connaught Place with me?"

I agreed. I was sick of Priya and all the overpriced dating alternatives around it.

"Cool. I'll get the car, and pick you up from the ice-cream parlour," she said.

I scraped through the crumbs on the pizza plate without looking up.

"Venkat, I have certain responsibilities…" Alok said.

"But they aren't my problem are they? This is the third time this month. It is about time I stop listening to this sort of stuff," Venkat said, interrupting him.

It was a chilly February night. The noise came from inside Venkat's room. Ryan and I were in the corridor of our wing, returning from one of our visits to the canteen.

"Why are they talking so loudly?" Ryan said.

"I don't know. Normally muggu Venkat's room is pretty quiet."

Ryan put his ear on Venkat's door.

"What are you doing?" I said.

"Shh… I think they're having an argument."

"What do we have to do with it? Let's go," I said.

"Shh…come here," Ryan said.

At some level, even I was curious about the argument. *Was it a big one? What was it about?* I put my ear on the door, and every word could be heard loud and clear.

"Alok, this is too much. I mean, I have to study for ten hours a day to keep my GPA. The least I can expect is to count on my group partners," Venkat was saying.

"My dad has become unconscious. We are worried he may have had a stroke! Two calls have come from home…" Alok said.

"Listen, your mom always overplays your dad's illness. He will recover, how will your making a trip help?"

"I am the only man in the house Venkat. I want to go. Can't you take care of it this time?" "Actually, no. I have to study class notes for other subjects. I don't think you realize this, I mean how would you being a five-point something," Venkat said.

"Realize what?" Alok said.

"That I have to maintain *my* rank. The second guy in the department is only 0.03 behind me you know. Now should I finish this group assignment or read my notes?" Venkat said, or rather shouted.

"Bloody mugger," Ryan whispered in my ear. I signalled Ryan to keep quiet.

"Venkat you study all the time. Can't you just..." Alok said.

"I am a nine-pointer, *do you understand?* I have to maintain *my position!*" Venkat said, speaking more to remind himself than to tell Alok.

"But am I not your friend? You know I have to take care of my dad," Alok said, this time pleading more than protesting. "Enough!" Venkat said, "this assignment is worth ten percent. Alok, you can't go."

"Venkat please," Alok said, and voice started to sound like his mother's, which meant he was going to cry soon.

"This is too much, I am going in," Ryan said, kicking the door open. I would have tried to stop him, but Ryan acted in a nanosecond.

Alok was standing next to Venkat, who sat on the study chair. They turned toward us in surprise.

"What the..." Venkat said, "Ryan, what are you doing here?"

It was a valid question. What was a five-pointer doing in a nine-pointer's room? Venkat looked at Ryan as if a person searching for a bar had reached a temple.

"What's the problem?" Ryan said, completely ignoring Venkat.

I stood there silently, checking out Venkat's room. Apart from a bed and a few clothes, there were just books, books and more books.

"Ryan, it has got nothing to do with you," Alok said. I could tell he was shocked to see Ryan, yet somewhere deep down, like he felt his saviour was there.

The pathetic 'I-will-cry-any-moment' expression had vanished.

"I said, what's the problem?" Ryan said.

"I'll tell you what the problem is," Venkat said. "We have a Thermo assignment due tomorrow, and Alok and I are in the same group. It is ten percent. Yet, he wants to go home…"

"I am not off on some tour, Dad is really sick," Alok said.

"Do you want me to go?" Ryan asked.

I was left puzzled. One year of silence, and now this sudden offer of help.

Did Ryan really want to get back with Alok or was he just proving what a prick Venkat was?

"Huh? You? Where…home?" Alok said.

"Yes, I know where you live and I have taken your dad to the hospital before. I have a scooter too and will get there faster. Or, if you need to go, then I can help you finish the assignment, except I don't want to work with this mugger bastard friend of yours," said Ryan, stressing on the word 'friend'.

This was too much. Ryan was acting like a Mother Teresa for Alok. The person Alok had insulted and left, was today a cure-all fairy from heaven. I looked at Venkat, who looked like a younger version of any of the anally retentive profs in the institute. He had put enough oil in his hair to cook an entire Kumaon dinner, his forehead sported an ash-mark from his devout prayers. Yet, at that moment, it was Ryan who looked like an angel.

"Really?" Alok said.

"So I go then," Ryan said and stood up. Alok nodded and Ryan left the room.

We remained silent for a minute. Ryan had solved a problem that could save a sick man's life and offer a nine-point mugger a future. All with a scooter ride to Alok's home.

"Well, that settles it then. I'll leave you to do the thermal assignment," I said and stood up to leave the room.

"Wait," Alok said.

"What?" I said.

Alok walked out of the room with me. Wasting no time, Venkat took out the thermodynamics book, giving Alok a glance which meant 'come back soon'.

"Thanks," Alok said.

"Thank Ryan," I said.

"Yes, I will. Is he still mad at me?"

"Obviously not, or why would he have gone to your house?"

"But you know Ryan, he could do things for you and yet be mad at you."

"Yes, he can sulk. But what difference does it make. Just thank him later." I was getting irritated with Alok. I didn't think he had the right to say he knew Ryan anymore, certainly not as much as me. "Hari?" Alok said. "You think I can come back?" "Come back where?" I was bewildered. "You know, the three of us again." "Why? Venkat isn't working out for you?" "I didn't know what I was doing man. I want to move back." I couldn't believe my ears. The difference one year with an obnoxious nine-pointer can make! "You sure?"

"Yes, I am sure." Alok's voice was small.

And then, like sentimental fools, we hugged each other. I think Alok was dying for a cry and he shed a few tears that he always has spare. I was kind of mellow too, I'd never thought the three of us could be together again. I knew Ryan would do some drama, but finally he would agree. If he could spend hours taking care of Alok's half-dad, he certainly felt something for him. "Good. Welcome back then," I said.

"Yes. Right after this damn thermal assignment though," Alok said and we laughed together for the first time in over a year.

9

The Mice Theory

PREDICTABLY, RYAN POUTED OVER PRODIGAL ALOK'S return but not for too long as it was kind of pointless. After Alok had shed yet more tears, we all bear-hugged and just like that we were back to being a group once again. Venkat's hissed curses we ignored happily because he had his books, but we had each other.

Ryan threw a party to mark the historical event. He did the arrangements himself and that included cleaning up his room — a Herculean task in itself given he had not disturbed the layers of dust with as much as a sneeze for several months.

"Why is he calling it the Mice Party though?" puzzled Alok.

"Don't know. He has this new theory that he is going to launch," I shrugged.

Ryan had banned us from venturing near his room before the party. I heard him shout "Fatso, buzz off" at least six times at Alok. The guest list consisted of me, Alok, Sukhwinder, Anurag and Vaibhav, who lived in the last room on our floor and always had vodka in his room. To Ryan that meant he was good friend-material. However, I only later figured out the real criteria for the guest list; all the guests were in the five-point something range of scores, were underdogs and lived in the same wing. We all anxiously waited for ten o'clock for Mr Ryan to open his damn door.

"Come in, guys," Ryan called out after we had waited outside his room for like an hour, on the verge of going bananas.

We entered and it was dark, for Ryan had replaced the normal bulbs in the room with red ones so that a crimson hue spread over the study table, which now doubled as a bar. Ryan had laid out vodka and rum bottles, juice from the roadside vendor, coke from the canteen, lemons, ice, sugar and finally, joints for the guests. When ready-made joints are served, you know the host is someone who gives attention to detail.

That was not all. Nude women adorned the walls, posters extracted from US porn magazines, which made their way to Kumaon through ex-seniors in innocuous US university admission brochures via mail. Blondes, brunettes, red-heads, thin, voluptuous and petite, posed on Ryan's wall, uniformly wanton.

Alok stared at the posters, his mouth open as if a UFO had landed in his kitchen-sink. "These women are completely naked," he managed to gurgle eventually.

Thanks for the insight, Alok. His quality time with Venkat had made him miss out on a lot.

We all sat down on the floor in Ryan's room, where he had placed cushions for each guest. The first drinks, the customary 'cheers', the challenge to execute 'bottoms up' followed and Pink Floyd sang to us.

We finished the first drink soon and Ryan topped us up promptly, and then again. I knew the alcohol had reached my head when I reached out for the ready-to-smoke joints; I always ache for a smoke when three drinks buzz inside me.

Surd had his own way of being drunk, by becoming overtly affectionate, kind of spilling over on to others' drunken space. He sat next to Alok, putting his arm around his shoulder, occasionally squeezing, rubbing.

"Great party man. Alok, are you feeling happy-happy?" Surdy asked solicitously.

Alok nodded, delicately removed Surdy's arm and moved forward to speak. "So Ryan, what is the big theory that you are going to launch during this party?"

Ryan was sitting across us with Anurag and Vaibhav. "Let's have a good time first," he said.

"I am feeling very good man. Tell us," Surdy said and replaced his arm around Alok's shoulder.

"Yes, yes, tell us," Anurag and Vaibhav spoke in unison.

"Guys, my theory is called the Mice Theory. But before I tell you that, I need you all to answer one question."

"What question?" Anurag said.

"I want you to tell me exactly what you want from life."

"Yeah whatever," I said, "Just tell us your damn theory." I was familiar with Ryan's showman tactics. Besides, my brain had too much alcohol to answer deep questions.

"C'mon guys, work with me on this," Ryan said, "you will appreciate this much more if you think about your own life first. Just one question – what do you want in life? Think about it for two minutes."

We fell silent. Ryan took a commercial break from his theory and refilled everyone's drink. I was on drink number four and I had never felt more clueless about life. I watched everyone else think.

"Okay, enough time," Ryan said, "Surdy, what do you want?"

Surdy held Alok tighter and dragged him closer. Then he planted a kiss on Alok's mouth and whispered intimately to him, "Should I tell him?"

Alok determinedly extracted himself from the affectionate and inebriated grip again and nodded.

"I just want to reach the US. With my GPA, it's impossible, but just somehow, someplace, somewhere I don't know, I just want to be in the US of A," Surdy babbled.

Anurag muttered something about inventing a new computer language, and Vaibhav wanted to start his own business.

I could tell Ryan was not too interested in the others' life ambitions, yet he politely nodded to all of them. He wanted to hear from Alok and me.

Ryan nodded at Alok.

"Well, you know it," Alok said.

"Tell me again."

"I want to get a job in Delhi, so I can look after my parents and take care of our money problems."

"Really?" Ryan said, implying he did not find the response so convincing.

"Of course," Alok said robustly.

"Really?" Surdy said again, though more out of affection than anything else.

"You, Hari?" Ryan said.

"I don't know." I really did not know what I wanted in life. I had thought about the question. I did not want to have a five-point GPA, and I did not want to be fat and unattractive. I also did not want to get tongue-tied in the damn vivas every semester. I mean, I definitely knew what I did not want — as I had it all in that department. But knowing what I really wanted was difficult.

"Of course you know. Come on, be a sport," Ryan urged.

Sport, that is Ryan's word. Ryan is always a sport. And Ryan is always thin and attractive. And Ryan is always confident and carefree. I hated Ryan. Yet at that point I realized what I really wanted — I wanted to be Ryan.

"Nothing much," I said, as I tried to think of an answer. I surely could not tell everyone I wanted to be Ryan; after all, Ryan would never want to be someone else.

"Still, say something man. So we can hear the theory," Alok said.

"I want to be able to kiss my girlfriend, and kiss her any time I want. And even do more, like go all the way with her."

I still don't know why I said what I said. I mean, it was sort of true. Yeah, I did want to kiss Neha and everything, but I had wanted to say something different.

"Who is your girlfriend?" Surdy turned to me with interest.

"None of your business," Ryan said briskly.

"Anyway, tell us the theory now, sir," Alok said. Two drinks down, he did not mind Surdy's overtures that much anymore, settling down into the masculine embrace with a resigned look behind his glasses.

"Gentlemen," Ryan said, sitting on the bed. He was now above us all physically, showering our uptilted heads with his gospel knowledge. "Thank you for coming tonight. As I am sure you have figured out, you are the lowest GPA holders in our wing. We are, gentlemen, the underdogs. Cheers to the underdogs."

Though Ryan was shamelessly working us up, we felt special at being the failures in the IIT grading system, and held up our hands high to a big 'cheers'.

"And this IIT system is nothing but a mice race. It is not a rat race, mind you, as rats sound somewhat shrewd and clever. So it is not about that. It is about mindlessly running a race for four years, in every class, every assignment and every test. It is a race where profs judge you every ten steps, with a GPA stamped on you every semester. Profs who have no idea what science and learning are about. Yes, that is what I think of the profs. I mean, what have IITs given to this country? Name one invention in the last three decades."

Silence ran through the party crowd as Ryan's speech became serious. I hoped Ryan was really drunk, for there was no other excuse for such patronizing crap at a party.

"Anyway," Ryan continued, "screw the profs. Coming back, this system is an unfair race. If you are a mouse who thinks or pauses to make friends with other runners, or stops to figure out what you want to do in life, or drag baggage from the past," Ryan said, looking at Alok, "then you will be pushed behind. As we have been pushed behind by morons like Venkat."

Surdy blew a flying kiss. I guess that meant he approved.

"But we can change all that," Ryan said.

"How?" Anurag said. At least someone was listening to this trash.

"By living on our own terms. By being rats, not mice, work together and beat the system. I will not give up my friends for this system. In fact, my friendships will beat the system."

"How?" Anurag said again.

"That is for me and my close friends. You only get the theory, I did not say you get the practicals."

"We are not your friends?" Surdy asked, his tone dipping emotionally.

"Of course you are. But I can only do this with my close friends."

No one else protested. If nothing else, Ryan's theory formed core entertainment at the party. One vodka bottle, ten joints and three cassettes of Floyd later, the speech was just part of the evening. At one a.m. the others left. Alok and I helped Ryan clear the mess.

"That was a good party," Alok said.

"I know, Fatso. You missed out on all this with the bastard Venkat," Ryan said, and staggered to his feet.

"So, what is with the implementation of the theory? How does that work?" I spoke idly.

"C2D," Ryan said.

"What the hell is that?" It sounded like a code in those damn sci-fi movies.

"Cooperate," Ryan said and fell on his bed, only half-intentionally.

"Cooperate?"

"Yes, Cooperate to dominate, C2D..." Ryan said and closed his eyes. All that work for the party and the vodka had taken their toll. He had passed out.

"Come, fellow mouse, let's go to our room," Alok said.

The party was over.

I was in the machining lab with Ryan when I remembered my date with Neha the next day. This time, madam had asked for a gift. She made this whole big deal about how I actually never give her anything, and how other girls got gifts from their friends. I mean, it was asinine logic if you ask me, as there were things she could be giving *me*, and without much capital investment. To have the nerve to ask for a gift on top of this deprivation is something only a woman can do, as they are made differently after all. Anyway, I'd promised her I would not come without a gift and then had totally forgotten about it.

"Tomorrow morning?" Ryan said "How will you get a gift by then?"

"I don't know, I just forgot. Man, will she sulk! I'll just buy some chocolates, bloody expensive they are though."

"Yeah, but chocolates? That is not original at all. No wonder she doesn't give you any," Ryan said.

"Well whatever. You have any bright ideas?" I was irritated at his conclusions, which were probably right.

"Think man, think."

We thought for several minutes and threw out most ideas; clothes too expensive, perfumes too frivolous, books impersonal and so on. I had neither time nor taste to improvise.

"Make something for her." Ryan snapped his fingers.

"What?"

"Like, make an object right here, in the lab. A handmade original, from an engineer, how neat is that?"

It seemed like an interesting idea, even though completely impractical. And what if she was expecting me to spend some money.

"Make what?"

"I don't know. Think of some simple device she could use."

I tried to think of Neha's life. She had this big purse full of things. "How about a little box to keep her lipsticks? They kind of keep rolling out of her purse when she takes things out."

"Now you are thinking customer needs. Ok, lipstick box. How many lipsticks max?"

"Three...four."

"And size of a lipstick?"

"No idea. Say three inches by one inch by one inch."

"Cool. So, say we stack them two by two...and then we design with sheet metal of thickness..."

I saw Ryan transform from the irreverent IIT underdog he purported to be into this passionate scientist over my stupid lipstick box. For the first time ever, he pored over an engineering drawing like he really wanted to make one. He thought of other clever things, a snap-up lid, a little mirror, and her name etched on top.

After the designing, he broke up the task into various parts; cutting, bending, buffing – all concepts we found boring as hell in class were now suddenly interesting. We forgot about the actual assignment for the day, as we gave a damn about our grades anyway.

Three hours later, I etched out the last few letters of 'Neha Cherian' on her made-in-IIT lipstick box.

"This is pretty neat," I said, impressed at the snap-open mechanism, "she will love this. Thanks, Ryan."

"Any time man," he raised his thumb. Yes, I really wanted to be like Ryan, who I loved most of the time. At least I hated him less than myself.

I presented Neha's gift to her at our ice-cream parlour.

"What? What did you say this is?" She twisted the metallic cigarette box-sized case round and round in her hands.

"It is a lipstick holder," I said.

"Really? Never heard of them."

I asked her for her lipsticks. She had five, which meant our design was below capacity. Anyway, I took four — red, copper, brown and pink (why girls put coloured wax on their bodies continues to be a mystery to me) and placed them inside. Snug fit, snap cover — the design worked perfectly. One surface had a mirror, so the user could apply the coloured wax accurately and not paint their nostrils in the bargain.

"Why lipstick case?"

"I don't know. I like your lips I guess," I said.

"Very funny. And you made this?" she said.

"Yes, with Ryan. See, it is personalized." I turned the box to its lower surface. 'Neha Cherian', the most beautiful name in the world was written in the most beautiful letters.

"Wow," Neha said softly, and then fondled the lipstick holder from the IIT Delhi machining lab like it was a newborn baby. "Wow," she said again.

"What?" I said. (Okay, so I was fishing for a little more appreciation here than the monosyllabic 'wow'.)

"No one has done anything like this for me," Neha said.

And it was at this moment that by pure chance I came out with the right line. I don't know how it came to me, but it just did. "Well, no one has meant more to me in life."

Maybe it was not completely true. But it wasn't all lies either (and in any case, it is about saying the right thing to girls, who gives a damn if it is true or not. I am Hari, not Harishchandra).

"Really?" Neha asked.

"Yes."

"Thanks, Hari. See I am going to use it right now," she said.

I watched Neha's face as she applied her lipstick with the same concentration as Alok had when doing quanti problems. Girls are beautiful, let's face it, and life is quite, quite worthless without them.

"What time you got to go home?" I said.

"Say by nine," Neha said. "I told them I'm meeting girlfriends for dinner."

"Wow, pretty liberal of them," I said sarcastically.

"They know I was feeling down. Thinking of Samir again."

"Hey, you want me to take you to a secret place?" I said.

"Where?"

"The insti roof."

"What? Are you crazy. Right on top of the insti, as if there could be a worse place for going public!"

"There is no one there. Ryan and I have gone dozens of times. And the view from the bell tower is beautiful."

I could see Neha was excited about the roof. It took me a few minutes of persuasion, convincing her that no one would find out, as we could follow her standard 'five minutes apart' policy to walk up there.

"I'll go. But not today. It's close to nine. How about next time, and I'll cry for Samir the whole day so they let me go out until eleven."

I didn't really dig her idea of using her brother as a weapon to stay out late but her parents were certified weirdos and probably deserved such tactics.

"Next time meet me on the roof directly, at eight-thirty."

"Sure," she said, "you said it is safe, right?"

"Yes, trust me," I winked.

10

Cooperate to Dominate

"HERE, ONE COPY FOR EACH OF YOU." RYAN HANDED OUT papers to us with the title: THE C2D PLAN.

I had forgotten about the C2D theory, but obviously Ryan hadn't. He had in fact been working on the official document. We were sitting at Sasi's and Alok was busy with his second plate of paranthas, when Ryan dished out his plan for the rest of our IIT stay.

"Whassit?" Alok's greasy fingertips left marks on the sheet, obviously needing a tissue more than an IIT plan. There was something about Alok with his food that was too intimate to be watched.

I read out the contents.

Cooperate to Dominate. The IIT system is unfair because:

1. It suppresses talent and individual spirit.
2. It extracts the best years of one's life from the country's brightest minds.

3. It judges you with a draconian GPA system that destroys relationships.
4. The profs don't care for the students.
5. IITs have hardly contributed to the country.

"You have the time to do all this?" was Alok's response, which was stupid because Ryan had all the time in the world.

I read on: So, the only way to take on the unfair system is through unfair means – which is Cooperate to Dominate or C2D. And this is the plan that Ryan, Hari and Alok agree to for the rest of their stay at the insti. The key tenets are:

1. *All assignments to be shared – one person will do each assignment by turn. The others will simply copy it. Saves time, saves duplication of effort.*
2. *We will divide up the course responsibilities. For instance, if there are six courses in the semester, we will take care of only two each. One must attend all classes that one is responsible for, but can skip all others. (note: Ryan gets all Prof Veera courses) In each class you attend for your course – take copious notes. The rest will merely copy them.*
3. *We share lab experiment observations.*
4. *Our friendship is above GPAs. With all the new spare time, we live our lives to the fullest.*
5. *We combine our hostel rooms into one living unit – one common bedroom, one study room and one fun party room.*
6. *We split the cost of vodka regardless of how many drinks each person has had.*

Ryan looked at us as if he was expecting us to break into applause. We kept silent, hoping he would explain where he was going with this.

"So, what do you guys think?" he asked.

"What is this? Some kind of teenage club thing?"

"If you agree, sign it. Sign it with your blood."

"Yeah right," I said, "How old are we, like twelve?"

"I am serious man," Ryan said and then before we could say anything, he flicked out a razor blade from his pocket. In one nick, his thumb sprouted a dot of red.

"Ryan, are you crazy?" Alok squeaked, almost losing his breakfast at this gross act.

"No. Just want to drive the point home. You decide what you want to do," Ryan said, signing the document with a toothpick dipped in his blood.

"Can we discuss this first?" I said.

"What is there to discuss? I am not forcing anyone."

"Like this whole sharing assignments and observations. Isn't that cheating?" Alok said.

I agreed with Alok, though I was more concerned about the vodka costs, given that Ryan out-drank us every single time.

"It is not cheating, it is cooperation. They have divided us with their GPAs, we are just pulling together to fight back."

"I don't see it that way," I insisted.

"Are you signing or not?" Ryan put his hands on his hips.

I thought about the C2D one last time. "Well. I can sign it, though I am not cutting myself or anything."

"It just takes a second," Ryan said and flicked the blade on my forefinger and blood spouted out of me before I could form my denial.

"Fuck you."

Ryan laughed and said, "Sorry man, look at your face. C'mon man, get into the spirit. Just sign it."

I looked at Ryan in disgust and signed the sheet.

Alok sat there, petrified like a chicken in a butcher shop. The old Alok would have vociferously stood up to Ryan, but the new, improved version, just back with us, did not want to fight again. "I'll make the cut myself," he said finally.

And soon he did get some blood from his little finger and we signed the C2D document like primitive tribesmen. I have to say, the whole blood thing made this feel important. I was not sure of what I had done, but somehow it sounded exciting. We converted our three single rooms into one apartment the same day. Ryan's room became the party room, Alok's was the study room with three tables and my room had the three beds.

"So you friends moved in together," Neha said.

We were en route to the insti roof as per plan. She met me at eight p.m., her parents blissfully ignorant about her real whereabouts, picturing her by a cake at a non-existent friend's birthday party.

"Yes, sort of. We combined our rooms to one living unit," I said, panting as we climbed the back stairs to the building.

"Sounds exciting," she said, blowing the fringe out of her eye.

It was already dark when we reached the roof. As always, there was no one there.

"Wow, look at all the stars," Neha said.

"Yes," I said, proud as if I had finger-painted the sky myself. "And it's all ours. Check out the campus view. See — that's where you live," I pointed.

We couldn't see much, apart from the lights in the living room.

"Wow. We are so near to them, yet so far," Neha said dreamily, flopping on the concrete floor. "So?"

"So what?" I said.

"Where is the vodka? Don't you guys drink here?"

"Yes. But you don't drink, do you?"

"Says who? I'll have one if you have some."

"We do hide a bottle under the bell. Let me look," I said, surprised at Neha's request. She was a nice girl, I thought. Nice girls do not drink. But I kind of could do with a drink myself, so I came back with the bottle.

"Nice," she said, as she lay back against the dish antenna, "look at the stars above, just so beautiful. I wish I were a bird."

When people want to be birds, they are normally getting drunk. But she was getting trippy just from the idea of drinking on the insti roof.

"Oh, I could lie here forever. Give me another drink," she said.

"Don't have too much," I had to caution.

"I won't. My dad will kill me if he smells it."

"Of course you'll smell of it."

"Not much, check this out."

She opened her purse. Ten items later, she took out a pack of cardamom pods.

"See, one of these and I go home minty fresh."

"Really? Then have one now, be minty for me."

"What? Do I have bad breath?" she sat up straighter.

"I did not say that."

She held my arm and pulled me toward her. "Look me in the eye and tell me if I have bad breath."

"I don't know. I have never been that close to your mouth," I said honestly, even as the millimeters between our mouths lessened.

"Go to hell," she laughed and pushed me away.

"See, you are chicken. Just so chicken," I said.

"No, I am not. Look at me, a professor's daughter, getting drunk on the insti roof with a five point something loafer."

If she had not been laughing, I would have resented that, but I decided to milk the opportunity anyway.

"Loafer? So I am a loafer," I said.

"Yes, but..."

"But what?"

"But I love my loafer," she said and pulled me toward her again. Again, our mouths were millimeters away. She tilted her head sideways. Was she going to kiss me? Or rather, was she-plus-two-glasses-of-vodka going to kiss me?

"We don't need no ejju-kay-shion..." a hoarse singing voice startled us from our embrace. Someone had just come to the insti roof.

"What the..." Neha said, "I thought you said no one was here."

"I don't know. Shh...quiet," I said as we tried to hide behind the antenna.

I finally recognized Ryan's voice through all that bad singing and saw him heading for our vodka hiding place.

"It's Ryan!" I said in a voice mixed with relief and irritation at losing my moment.

"Ryan," I shouted.

"Hari," he shouted back, walking over. "Bastard, you are here and I was looking all over for you. Is there someone with you?"

"Ryan, I want you to meet..."

"It's a girl!" Ryan exclaimed as if he had spotted me with a dead rabbit. Neha continued to cower behind me, attempting anonymity.

"It's Neha," I said. "Neha, meet Ryan. Ryan, be nice and say hello to Neha."

Ryan's voice mellowed down instantly. What is it with men; they become another person in female company. So predictable!

"Hi Neha," Ryan said, trying to avoid staring too much at someone he had heard so much about.

"Hi," Neha said, still unsure if Ryan could be trusted.

"I was just looking for Hari to do an assignment," Ryan said.

"Drop it Ryan. We're having a drink," I said.

"Really?" Ryan said as if he expected Neha to be winged and haloed or something. "But I thought Neha was not like that."

"Like what?" she asked immediately.

"Uh, nothing," Ryan said and sat down on the warm concrete.

"So what have you heard about me?" Neha said.

"Lots," Ryan said and started telling her sacred details about all our past dates. They kept talking for like ten hours or something and I just kept getting more drunk. Ryan has a computer memory or something, and he told her about the times even I had forgotten about.

"He told you about the family planning documentary?" Neha tittered.

"Of course, he tells me everything," he said with considerable pride.

I wondered if Neha and I would have kissed and managed more if bloody Ryan had not dragged himself up here. I considered pushing him off the insti roof, but thought it would kind of spoil the mood anyway.

"So why did you say I wasn't that type of girl?" Neha said.

"You know, the whole vodka thing. You are supposed to be well...forget it," Ryan said.

"What? Tell me," Neha said with a firmness only good-looking women possess.

"You are like this good girl. Like why else won't you let him do anything? Dating for a year, still no kiss even. Just this goody-goody prof's daughter."

"He told you that?" Neha squeaked.

"Of course. You think you are dating a guy or someone asexual? You don't think he has needs?"

"Shut up, Ryan." This from me.

"C'mon man. Show some guts sometimes. This is for your own good."

"Needs?" Neha repeated, dazed.

"Yes, every man has needs. And pretty girls like you are either not aware of them or deny them for power games."

"Power?" Neha repeated.

I wanted to tell Ryan I had just been getting somewhere nicely, thank you, when he whistled by.

"Yes, power. What else?" Ryan said, calming down finally.

"I crave power? Now that is a joke. You guys just don't understand women do you?" Neha said, with a vodka-infused confidence that could take on even Ryan.

"Huh?" Ryan said, proving that we really did not understand women.

Neha had to go home soon after that, so we left the topic there. I wanted to scream at Ryan later, but he rolled two joints for me and gave me a scooter ride back to Kumaon, so I left it. Besides, Neha really did not seem mad or anything.

I had a hunch he might have helped my case!

11

The Gift

I AM A HORRIBLE PERSON ON THE INSIDE AND THIS I demonstrated while fitting in Alok for the morning classes, citing his practice of waking early during those Venkat days, laying on thickly the unreliability of Ryan and me for any sunrise job.

C2D was great, I found out, as I was responsible for only two courses in a semester. For the rest, Alok and Ryan gave me all the assignments (which I copied) and their notes (which I photocopied). I returned the favour in my courses. We now needed to spend only an hour or two a day in studies, leaving us with plenty of time for movies, scooter drives, restaurants, chess, scrabble, indoor cricket, sleep, squash (yes, Ryan was trying again) and of course, booze and grass. The first minors that semester were a breeze. We didn't like ace the class or anything, but our expectations were low – just maintaining our five-point GPAS. It is amazing how happy one can be with low expectations of one's self.

I was in the design class one day, a course for which I was responsible. Ryan chose to attend the class with me. I think he believes he is like this great designer or something. Prof Vohra was teaching us.

"Class, note down this problem that I want you to do in the next fifteen minutes. Design a car jack to lift the chassis in case of flat tires etc. Do a simple sketch."

Prof Vohra was a portly man in his fifties, who had an unusually kind face for a Prof. Of course, nothing in his nature supported this. With six term papers a semester and a lethal red pen that crossed out one design submission after another, kind was hardly how you'd describe Prof Vohra.

It was my course, therefore my hand that had to sketch the car jack with Ryan merely having to copy it. Prof Vohra had taught us enough for us to execute at least a basic screw-type design. I had just begun to draw when Ryan said, "What? You are going to make the same damn thing like the rest?"

"Yes sir, I am not Thomas Edison," I said, "and this is my course so just shut up and copy it."

"I have another idea," Ryan said.

I wanted to tell Ryan to screw his other idea and copy my screw-jack. But I never say anything to Ryan, and he never listens to anyone anyway.

So Ryan drew this 'modified screw-jack', in which one did not manually have to open and raise the jack. A flat tire did not mean the engine had failed, he said, hence one could attach a motor on the traditional jack and hook it up to the car battery. If one switched on the car ignition, the motor could derive power.

"What are you doing?" I said, worried about Ryan's sketches of the car battery, obviously irrelevant to the current task.

"You wait and see, the prof will love it," Ryan said.

I stuck to my traditional screw-jack like the rest of the class. The course was called Design, not Original Design after all.

Prof Vohra walked along the class rows, looking at the familiar designs that all his students drew year after year – the simple screw-jack. His stroll ended at our desk.

"What is this?" Prof Vohra said, twisting his head around to make sense of Ryan's unfamiliar drawing.

"Sir, this is a modified screw-jack," Ryan said, "It can be attached to the car's battery...."

"Is this an electrical engineering class?"

"No sir but the end need is the same..."

"Is this an internal combustion engines class?"

"Sir but..."

"If you don't want to be in my class or follow my course, you may leave."

Prof Vohra's face no longer looked kind. If only Ryan had kept quiet, he would have moved on.

"Sir, this is a new design," Ryan said, as if it was not painfully obvious.

"Really? And who told you to do that?"

Ryan did not answer, just lifted his assignment sheet. Then in one stroke, he ripped it apart in two pieces.

"There, it is useless now," Ryan said.

Prof Vohra's face contorted and turned red, "Don't act smart in my class."

"Sorry sir," I said, though it was not for me to say it.

But it broke the tension. The prof and Ryan looked at me via the corners of their respective eyes. Prof Vohra exhaled and moved on; Ryan sat down.

"That wasn't very smart. You know he can flunk you," I said to Ryan after class.

"I don't care. I can't wait to get out of this stupid place man," he said, kicking the scooter stand as if it was Prof Vohra's face.

It wasn't Ryan's course anyway and he did not attend any further classes in design. He directly copied answers of my assignments mindlessly, and never as much as looked at the question-sheet. Yes, our greatest designer gave up.

The three of us were in our common study room one day, copying Alok's thermal science assignment.

"So, Prof Vohra is mad at you now," Alok said.

Ryan kept silent.

"Of course he would be. You should have seen his face," I contributed.

Alok laughed, shaking his head.

"He can flunk me for all I care," Ryan stated.

"That is not the point," Alok began.

"Fatso, you won't get the point, so give up. By the way, Prof Veera called me to talk about my lubricant assignment."

"Really?" Alok and I said in unison, wondering if Prof Veera had caught us cheating.

"Nothing to worry guys. I gave him a separate paper. It wasn't a class assignment."

"You have time to do separate papers?" I said.

"I have time to do what I want. I had thoughts on doing some experiments with various substance mixtures to check lubricant efficiency in a scooter engine."

"Where?" I said.

"Well, ideally in the fluid mechanics lab. But then we need a scooter engine, and a small budget to buy materials. Until then, I tried a few tests on my scooter."

"Wow. you're screwing your scooter up. How will we travel?" I said.

"It is for science. I might be on to something. Anyway, I combined different types of oils to check mileage. I think I can beat normal lubes by ten percent."

I have to say, I was impressed with Ryan. Against all odds, this man was working to reduce our petrol bill. I thought of all the extra *paranthas* we could buy with a ten percent lower fuel cost.

"So, what did Prof Veera call you for?" Alok said.

"He said he'd help me get the institute's permission to use the lab and get some research grant."

"Wow! You will be a scholar man," Alok said.

"Yeah whatever," Ryan shrugged, "It is not that easy. One has to submit a proposal to Prof Cherian, detailing budgets, benefits, timing and all that crap, then a committee decides. It takes months."

"But if you do get it..." Alok blinked rapidly, "so neat man."

"I have to work hard on the proposal over the next few weeks. Don't worry, I'll do my courses, but no partying or movies," Ryan said.

Now, if Alok had said the same thing, Ryan would have blown a fuse. But this was Ryan, and we never said anything to him. Besides, I was kind of glad he was into something sensible.

"Sure, we'll tell you what you missed," I said and winked at Alok.

"Yeah, though that makes you the mugger now," Alok said.

"I am not a mugger. You are the mugger, Venkat-boy," Ryan retorted.

I have to say, it was never my thing to visit Alok's house. Just the thought assailed me with medicine smells, crumbling concrete and cooking smells, topped by a middle-aged woman wailing at the drop of a hat. Yet, there I was one Saturday with Alok, if only because Ryan was busy with his do-not-disturb-me lube research proposal. It was depressing to see Ryan work so hard and he did like three night-outs one week in the computer centre and the library. On top of that, he spent his days in the fluid mechanics lab mixing lubes and then testing them on the scooter. I told him about this movie at Priya in which there were as many as six topless scenes and he only looked blankly at me. I tried luring him with new cocktail recipes, but Ryan stuck to six straight cups of coffee a night. Objectives, scoping, budgeting, applications, past research – each section in his proposal was like a million pages. He submitted drafts to Prof Veera, who almost always wanted Ryan to do more.

So when Alok asked me to his house for lunch I found myself agreeing if only for the food. I had learnt to ride now and Ryan's scooter was free that day (though Ryan did give us the task of noting down the kilometres back and forth).

Delhi roads are a nightmare and I couldn't dream of driving as fast as Ryan. Alok and I couldn't go beyond fifty, and Alok kept talking as I navigated the cows and the cops to the suburbs.

"You think Ryan will get the project?" Alok said, sitting pillion.

"I think so. His proposal alone is eighty pages, which I think is a project in itself. And I mean, it is original work."

"Yes, but you know he has to put a cover sheet on the proposal."

"So?"

"The cover sheet carries the student's name and GPA. You think they'll fund a five-point something?"

"Why not? They'll read the proposal and decide."

"They are profs," Alok said, "and you know how they think."

"Prof Veera is with him."

"Yeah, let's see."

We reached Alok's house in an hour. I kind of stopped breathing to skip the medicine smells. Of course, couldn't do without oxygen forever but luckily Alok's mom laid out the food soon.

"Alok, see I have made paneer for you and your friend," his mother said.

For a poor family, Alok's family ate quite well. I mean, there was rice, rotis, daal, gobi-aloo, mango chutney, *raita* and of course, *matar-paneer*. I guess that explained the corpulence running in the family.

"Eat *beta*, eat. Don't be shy," Alok's mother egged me on.

The food was delicious but the conversation tasteless. Alok's mother recounted her last week, which was full of problems. The funny thing was almost all her problems had one solution – more money. On Monday, the five-time-repaired geyser had broken down and there was no money for a new one. On Wednesday, the TV antenna took a toss and a new one was too expensive. The family had to live with grainy reception until they could save some money. On Friday, Alok's father fell off the bed, which required a doctor to come home, another hundred bucks. There were other stories too – the ration shop had started charging double for sugar, and the maid had ditched twice that week.

"Ma, can you stop boring my friend," Alok said.

"No, it's fine," I said, reaching for more daal. Actually, the life Alok's mother led at home intrigued me. Somehow, her clutching her sari to wipe her tears had been the only image I had been stuck with for the past year but now I realized she had a life too. The challenges she faced were not quite lube research proposals, but pricey tomatoes nonetheless.

"And you know the sofa springs are coming out..." she was saying when Alok interrupted her.

"Mom, can you please keep quiet. I have come home after a month and that is all you have to tell me."

She looked surprised. "Who else will I tell my problems to? I have only one son."

"Enough mom," Alok said, his face turning red like an expensive tomato.

"I will keep quiet," Alok's mom agreed and started mumbling to herself as she ate her food, "earn for them, then work like a servant for them and then they don't even want to listen to you. Physics teacher Mrs Sharma tells me, these days sons forget their parents."

Clang, Alok threw his plate on the floor. Bits of lunch splattered all across the living room and he got up and left the room.

What was I supposed to do? Follow my friend, who had brought me here? Or sit and watch Alok's mother wipe her tears with her sari? I decided to do none of the above, focusing on the *matar-paneer*. The food was good, that is what I came here for, I kept telling myself, looking intently at the plate.

Needless to say, it wasn't a happy visit home. Alok kind of cooled down, came back to the living room, and sat on the sofa. Alok's mother cried her stock of tears, and went in to get *kheer*.

"Alok, what are you doing man?"

"You stay out of this Hari. You won't understand."

Yeah right, I should stay out of this, I thought. But he was the one who had got me into this.

"She has made *kheer* and everything. What is your problem?"

"They are my problem. You won't understand, shut up and wait for the *kheer*."

We did wait for the *kheer*, which was perfect. I was sure that Alok's family could solve half their problems if they stuck to a more frugal diet but good food seemed vital to them, even at the cost of TV reception. It was their situation, so I stayed out of it until we were on our way back.

"I know what you are thinking," Alok said.

"What?"

"That how can I be so heartless."

The only thing I had thought about Alok's heart was that it would be under tremendous strain with such a fat-intensive diet.

"Nah, just haven't seen you like that," I said as I turned on the Munirka crossing, narrowly avoiding a peanut seller.

"That is all they talk to me about; problems, problems and more problems," Alok said, "and what can I bloody do about them?"

"Hmmm. That is true," I said, wondering if Alok was now telling me a problem I couldn't do anything about.

Vivas — the most hated, dreaded moments of my student life. I avoided them like I did cows on the road with their tails twitched up. But like the cattle in Delhi traffic, sometimes you just couldn't avoid running into them. And this one Wednesday was the design viva. It was my course under the C2D, and I was supposed to take the lead on all questions. I tried to convince Ryan and Alok to help me, but the bastards didn't care and had gone to sleep at ten the previous night, leaving me to mug through the night and prepare for all expected questions. It wasn't much use, for in my case it wasn't about knowing the answers.

"Hari, what makes C40 steel better than C20 steel for making rigid structures?"

More carbon in C40, hence harder steel, I thought. Also, probably cheaper in terms of costs. C20 was soft and could buckle. I knew the answer... if only Prof Vohra would stop looking me in the eye.

"Sir, C40 steel is..." I said as I looked back at Ryan and Alok to evoke some pity.

"Look at me Hari," Prof Vohra said, "I am asking *you*."

I didn't want to look at him, and I really wanted to get the answer out. But all I got out was fat drops of sweat, on my face, arms and hands.

Four tries and three different questions later, Prof Vohra gave up. Ryan shook his head and smiled, as if he'd known all along that this would happen. Alok kept quiet, as he mentally calculated how many marks we had lost.

"Sorry guys," I said at dinner, "I let you down again. I hate vivas man."

The mess workers tossed rotis that you could make jeans out of; I tore one hard, hoping to relieve my tension.

"What happens to you?" Alok said.

"I don't know. Whenever someone asks me a question in a stressful situation, I can't say anything."

"Since when?" Alok said.

"Since high school," I said.

"Something happened?" Ryan said.

"No...I mean yeah, nothing," I said.

"What?" Alok said.

"Forget it. Pass the rice, I can't digest these rotis. They are like chewing gum," I said.

Neha's birthday was on December 1 and as usual I was clueless about what to get her.

"You have to make it special," Ryan said. We were skipping class and having lunch in the canteen.

"Special how? I have no cash. I can't even afford toothpaste right now," I said.

"You are not brushing your teeth?" Alok said, looking up.

"No man I'm using Ryan's," I said. "Anyway, come to the point Fatso, what should I do?"

"Think," Ryan said, knocking his head like he was solving a nuclear physics problem. He is a patronizing bastard, I tell you.

"I can't think of anything," I said. "No more 'make-your-own-gifts', did that with the lipstick box already, so it won't have the same effect. And I am so broke, I can't give her something expensive."

"How about something useful but cheap, like handkerchiefs?" Alok said.

"Shut up Alok," Ryan said.

I was glad he said it for me. Alok had as much of an idea of romantic gifts as his mother had about cabarets.

"Ryan, what should I do?" I was panicking.

"Well, it doesn't have to be expensive, as long as it's a surprise. Who doesn't like surprises?"

"Like what?" I said.

"Like being the first one to wish her," Ryan said.

Ryan's plan was quite original (and cheap); to break into her room, right through her window on the eve of her birthday. At midnight, I would be the first one to wish her and the surprise would sweep her off her feet (and hence eliminate the need for a real gift). It was a crazy idea, for we weren't just breaking into my girlfriend's house, but a prof's house, that too a head of the department no less. But Ryan made it seem easier than copying a thermodynamics assignment, and I agreed.

So, at eleven-thirty p.m. on a cold December night, Ryan, Alok and I quietly slipped out of Kumaon. Ryan drove us to the faculty housing complex and parked his scooter fifty meters from Neha's house. The entire lane was silent in contrast with Kumaon where the assignments and mugging had only just begun for the night. The profs slept blissfully, while their minions worked away through the night.

"Ryan, you sure we can handle this?" I asked one last time as we neared the lawns of Prof Cherian's house.

"Shhh... of course, we can, but if only you keep quiet," Ryan said as he lifted the latch off Cherian's gate.

Silence, apart from a gentle creaking of the gate as we entered the den of the beauty and the beast.

I looked up at Neha's window, imagining her sleeping peacefully, her beautiful face glowing in the dark. My heart quickened.

"Alok, come on you go first. On the pipe now," Ryan whispered.

"This is impossible," Alok said.

"I'll give you a push," Ryan said.

As he climbed up the flimsy steel pipe, he looked like a gorilla hanging onto a bamboo stick. There was serious risk of the pipe breaking, given his mass and the strength of galvanized steel (see, our engineering knowledge did amount to something), so we decided to wait until he reached the roof.

After Alok it was my turn, followed by Ryan, who shimmied up the pipe in seconds. Ten minutes to midnight, we were on Prof Cherian's roof.

It was pitch dark. Ryan finally switched on a flashlight and we tried to navigate through the water tanks and clothes left to dry on the roof.

"Where is her room?" Ryan whispered.

I pointed mutely and we moved toward the ledge.

"Here are the flowers," Ryan said as he pulled out a bunch of sunflowers from under his shirt.

"Where did you get these?" I said.

"Just now, from Cherian's garden."

"Are you crazy?" I said.

"Nice touch," Ryan said, "now get ready."

We knocked on Neha's window using some pebbles from the roof. Nothing happened at the first pebble, nothing on the second and third.

"It's not working, she probably sleeps too deeply," Alok said.

"Keep trying," Ryan said.

We kept throwing little pebbles like morons. Probably a million pebbles later, we had a reaction. The room light switched on, and the window became bright.

Climbing up a pipe was hard enough, but the next step was the real killer. I was supposed to dangle myself over the ledge, with Alok and Ryan holding my hands for emergency support. But first Neha had to open the window.

"Quick, say her name before she screams in fear," Ryan said.

"Neha, it's me," I said, not whispering for the first time in half an hour.

"Hari," Neha said as she opened her window, "What are you doing here?"

"I can explain. Let me come in first," I said, and sprung myself over.

"Are you crazy?" she said and rubbed her eyes even as my legs dangled in front of her face.

"Careful Ryan," I said.

"Who else is there?" Neha said, by now completely awake and completely in shock.

"No one... I mean only Ryan and Alok," I said as I swung myself inside the window.

"Careful," she said as I landed on some cushions on a rug, pretty and delicate as only in a girl's room.

I gave a thumbs-up signal to my friends and banged shut the window.

"Hari, what exactly do you think you are doing?" Neha said, "What if Dad wakes up?" She adjusted her hair as I noticed her nightclothes. She wore a sleeveless, simple cotton nightie with little blue triangles all over. As always, she looked beautiful.

"Happy birthday, Neha," I said, and took the flowers out from under my shirt.

The flowers were crushed and already wilted, but there is something about flowers and women. Somehow, seeing these reproductive tools of plant-life works wonders. It chills them out. Neha's anger vanished, and I could tell the idea had worked.

"Sunflowers," Neha said, "Where did you get these?"

"From your garden actually."

"What?" Neha said and threw a stem at me, "you loafer. Such a cheapo you are."

I took a cushion in response and threw it back at her. I was just getting excited about the impending flower and pillow fight when she nipped it in the bud.

"Don't mess with these cushions, I hand-painted the covers."

Hand-painting cushion covers, how can girls waste their time on such useless pursuits? I mean, Ryan and I didn't even have cushion covers, let alone painted ones.

"What are you thinking?" Neha said as she came close and held my hand.

"Nothing. And I'm sorry I startled you like that."

"It's okay, I like it," Neha said, "I guess it is kind of special. Come sit."

She made me to sit on her bed. I sat down as close to her as possible, my eyes drifting down to her chest. Girls don't wear bras at night I guess, which quite obviously suits them better. At the same time, I thought of the possibility of Prof Cherian walking in through the door.

"What are you thinking? Look into my eyes," Neha said.

"Huh…nothing. Happy birthday," I said.

"Aren't you going to kiss me?"

My eyes went wide as UFO saucers.

She drew back. "Wait a minute. You want to, right?"

"Yes, of course."

"So now?" she said.

"Now what?" I said.

"Are you going to kiss me or what?"

Maybe it was the flowers, or just the whole excitement of breaking in, or maybe even that she had finally grown up. I moved forward, and even though I had seen a million kisses in movies, I can't tell you how hard it is to deliver a good one the first time.

"Oops...not so hard," she said, "gentle, baby kisses first."

She led the path from there, and frankly, I was too excited and scared to do better. But I had my first kiss, right there in Prof Cherian's house.

"Shh...Daddy's got up for water," she said, pushing me away.

"Now what?"

"Nothing, he won't come up. But you should go now."

"I want to stay."

"Just go now," she said as she pushed me off the bed, in contrast to her loving looks moments ago.

It was pointless to insist. Besides, a part of me wanted to get the hell out of there before the gig was up.

"So, how was it?" Ryan said as I was pulled back on the roof.

"Nice. Very nice," I said with a big grin splitting my face which said it all.

Getting down was as much an art as climbing up, but the real problem was as we reached the lawns. Someone had switched on the living room light.

"How did the light go on?" Alok said.

"Don't know. I think Cherian woke up for water," I said.

"Let's crawl out," Ryan said as we bent under the window to be out of sight.

A bucket fell noisily as Alok crawled through the grass, loud enough to make all our whispers pointless.

"Who is it?" a male voice came from inside as we heard footsteps.

"Fuck, it's Cherian. Run, get the hell out of here," Ryan said.

We stopped with the slithery crawl and ran for our lives. If Cherian had seen us, he would have kicked our butts out of the college right then.

We were just outside the gates when the door opened and Cherian came out in what looked like his wife's nightgown.

"Who is it?" he shouted, adjusting his spectacles.

"Your father," Ryan yelled as we ran away from the house.

I don't know if Cherian chased us or was too scared to do so but the three of us did not stop running until we reached Ryan's scooter.

"Are you stupid or what? Why did you say that?" I reproved as we rode off.

"Yeah, right. I should have said, sir, it's only your son-in-law with some friends. He would've brought the drinks out then."

12

Neha Speaks

*S*AMIR BHAIYYA,

I don't know how and when you will read this, this letter that I've got to write anyway. I am always composing replies to that last mail of yours, the one you penned only to me though I am not happy about the exclusivity. But then I have told you that before.

Anyway, let me tell you about this boy I met. You could call Hari my boyfriend, though I don't. He is a student, can you believe it? Remember how we hated every IIT student who lived on campus? We met in this totally strange manner, there was something about him that drew me from the very beginning.

Not very good looking or anything, nor super smart but there he was, this silly bumbler. As you can guess, Dad and Mom have no clue, something that I've learnt to live with since you left but you can well imagine what will happen if Dad finds out. Remember how he called cops to arrest a man who whistled at me at the campus bus stop? And the time he changed the home phone number because a male classmate called for notes? He wants to bring up his daughter right. I am his mission in life. He doesn't want to make the same mistake twice. Did you have to do that to me, Bhaiyya?

I just want to tell you, don't worry about me for I know girls should be good. Sometimes I feel this guy is only interested in getting physical. Other girls who have boyfriends tell me all boys are the same, want the same thing. But can I tell you something? Even I want the same. No, no I haven't done anything yet. But then, every now and then I get curious, start imagining what Hari would do if I let him. Is thinking that a bad thing?

Oh no, here I go, throwing questions at you again. Let me tell you more about Hari. He has two friends - Ryan and Alok. They are nuts. Now don't think I have started liking IIT students or anything — just that these guys are different. For one, they can barely remain students with their five-point something GPAs.

I know what you are thinking, they are the kind of students Dad would hate, and you are thinking she is hobnobbing with them for precisely that reason. You are wrong, Bhaiyya. You know on my last birthday, they broke into our house, these loafers I am talking about. Hari came into my room and gave me flowers plucked from our garden! I hope Dad never finds out about him the wrong way. And I hope I can keep meeting him forever. Though there is so much more I don't yet know about Hari.

My plan is the day Hari gets a job, I will introduce him to Dad. I mean, Dad will still flip his lid, but at least there would be something going for Hari. Right now, he is a little bit of a loser if you ask me. Sorry, if I am being mean. But in some ways, he is. For one thing, he is besotted with Ryan. "Ryan this, Ryan that," bugs me no end sometimes. I don't think this Ryan guy is all that cool. Wears branded clothes, but that is only because his parents are loaded. I personally think behind all this guy's aggression there is a vacuum.

See, that is the thing with these IIT guys and their college, they all are too wrapped up in the bricks and walls to know who they really are and what they really want. I want to tell them — before you get all gung-ho about working for the future, work out your past and present but that will just sound so grandma-ish and I am, well, so young.

Well, that is all I shall write for now. I promise to write again, and I promise to be good. But do not tell Dad and Mom what I've been babbling about. See, I kept your last promise and have not told anyone about your letter to me how much ever that broke me, so keep mine. Yes, I know Mom would not have been able to take it. She hardly speaks these days anyway. Why did you leave us Bhaiyya? It isn't fair, you know that, right?

Missing you,
Neha

13

One More Year Later

WE WERE DRINKING ON THE INSTI ROOF. THIRD YEAR
students now, alcohol no longer a novelty. This meant we could
drink less and not throw up every time to certify having a good
time. We were drowning our sorrows today for two reasons.
Firstly, after a year of working the files, the mechanical
engineering department had coolly rejected Ryan's lube project
proposal. Secondly, I had messed up yet another viva. When
it came to screwing vivas, I am the man you want!

"Screw the lube project. I have wasted too much time on
it. But look at you, Hari. It is so bloody typical of you. Why
do you get so tongue-tied?" Ryan said, in whose veins
confidence corpuscles flowed larger than red.

"I wish I knew." I squinted, frustrated.

"You know the answer to the viva questions. You know the
answers, right?" That was Alok.

I nodded my head. It was pointless. Three years of practice in vivas did not leave me any less petrified.

"Ryan, you know I hate vivas. But c'mon man. You must feel like crap," I said.

"What crap? I only did ten night outs on the proposal, the revised proposal and spent like a hundred hours in the lab. But in the end, Cherian shot it down. 'Too optimistic and fantastic,' he said. I could wring his bloody neck," Ryan announced.

"But you know your idea is good," Alok said flatly.

"Of course it is. Even Prof Veera thinks so. But Cherian doesn't, and he is the head. Anyway, screw it."

"Is it completely over?" I said.

"From my side. Prof Veera might try private sponsorship or something. Pretty much over though I should say," Ryan said.

Alok sat quietly, picking his nose and sipping his vodka. It was disgusting, but it didn't bother me anymore. It is amazing how habit immunizes you.

I looked fully at Alok. "At least you are happy."

"Happy?" Alok echoed, "good joke."

"Now what happened?" I said.

"Nothing. Nothing bloody happens in my life situation. That is why I am never happy. Sister needs to get married, that is the latest I guess."

Alok had a point. A miserable home, pointless grades and loser friends was hardly the route to happiness. At least he had the joy of picking dirt out of his nose in the company of his friends.

"How's Neha?" Alok said.

"She's fine. That is the only thing that keeps me in IIT," I said.

"Yeah right. Have you gotten any further though?" Ryan said.

"Like what? I have kissed her now you know," I said.

"Yes, but like ten years ago. And there is much more than that. You know that right? Or do you get tongue-tied in front of her as well."

Alok tittered.

"Screw you Ryan," I said, "Neha is not that type of girl."

"But you are *that* type of boy. So make her *that* way," he said.

"How?"

"I can't tell you everything."

Once it was dark we decided to return to Kumaon. Time did go on, and thank god for that. For that meant we only had so many fewer days left in this place.

"I'll be happy when college is over," I said.

"At least we have perfected the C2D," Alok said.

"Of course," Ryan said and smirked, "when was the last time each of us did his own assignment?"

"It still scares me sometimes though," I said.

"Why? The profs never read the crap they give us carefully. They'll never find out," Ryan dismissed, cocky as ever.

"I heard Cherian is anal though," Alok said.

We'd find out soon; it was finally time for Cherian to start teaching industrial engineering and management or Indem.

"Yes, the bastard will teach us finally. I am not attending any of his classes," Ryan said.

"You don't have to. It's Hari's course under C2D," Alok said and winked, "our guy wants to impress the dad."

"Well, at some point I do want Neha to tell her dad about me. Wouldn't be a good start if I skip all his classes," I said.

"I hate him," Ryan said simply.

No one skipped Cherian's first class. That is, no one apart from Ryan. I was curious to see in person the devil who tormented my girlfriend and my best friend. Others went to see the head of the mechanical engineering department of the best engineering college in the country. They said Cherian was a perfect 10 in his IIT student days. I didn't know much about the man, apart from the fact that his daughter was a perfect 10 to me.

I had reached five minutes early, and for the first time in three years, had taken a seat in the first row. I don't know why, but I really wanted to do well in his course. Perhaps an A in Indem might give a good first impression, leading the way for Neha to introduce me. It just sounded better — "Dad, meet Hari — the guy who topped your Indem course," rather than "Dad, meet Hari. The loser who scraped a C in your course."

Prof Cherian walked in precisely at nine, and brought with him a huge pile of books as if he had just robbed a library.

"Pay attention everyone. Let us start with the lecture," he began in a firm voice.

There is something about seeing your girlfriend's parent for the first time. I couldn't help but notice how Cherian was an extremely bad replica of Neha. Like her wax statue had puffed up first and then begun to melt haphazardly. He had the same jaw and round face like hers, however, his face was twice as big, with chunks of loose flesh hanging where Neha had these super-smooth, taut cheeks. Instead of Neha's long and beautiful hair, Cherian had a bald spot bigger than a Nirula's hamburger. If she dressed to act in a horror movie, Neha would look like her father.

"Time and motion studies are the essence of Indem. As engineers you should be able to reduce human actions to measurable tasks and stop talking there in the third row," Cherian said as he threw a piece of chalk at two students who had found a private joke too good to resist sharing it in class.

"Meet your father-in-law," Alok whispered.

"Looks like he can eat me alive," I said.

Cherian heard the whispers and stopped writing on the board. He turned around and banged a duster on the table. "No one talks for the next sixty minutes," he pronounced in a no-nonsense tone that would make Saddam Hussein shudder, "is that clear?"

Chalk dust formed a cloud as if Cherian had burst a grenade in the classroom. Behind this, one could barely see his contorted face. I wondered how Neha had spent an entire life living with him, wanting to rescue her that very instant. I thought of eloping with her, making the escape through the roof while Cherian slept. But where would I take her? The hostel was hardly handy, what with all of us sleeping in one room.

Cherian's first example of time and motion study was of a shirt factory. Let us say there were five workers, now they could either make individual shirts each, or one could divide the shirt making tasks. For instance, the first worker could cut the cloth, the second worker put in the first stitch, the third sews buttons and so on and so forth.

"This breakdown of tasks is called an assembly line. But you have to ensure that each task is of equal time to avoid bottlenecks."

Therefore, if cutting cloth took six minutes and the first stitch took three, two workers could do the first job. "This way, you can have a fast assembly line. Workers focus and get more skilled at their tasks. And what is more, you don't need extra equipment – like instead of five scissors, you need only one," Cherian said.

It all sounded very reasonable. After all, that is what engineers should do right? Tell workers how to work more efficiently, thinking up clever ways to save resources.

"He makes sense," I said.

"Just take notes. Anything can come in the quiz," Alok said.

The Fatso will remain a loser, I thought, except at nose, where his pickings were rich. I mean, I am no great thinker or anything, but sometimes one does listen in class. All this guy wanted to do was mug in class and puke in tests. I thought of discussing Indem with Ryan.

Sixty minutes later, Cherian put his chalk down. He modified the shirt example ten times, to show various time and resource allocation combinations. In typical IIT fashion, the simple example somehow converted into complex equations. The prof gave an assignment for the next class using these equations, which meant two hours at least in the library that night.

"Are you stupid. You found this Indem crap interesting," Ryan said as I told him about the class.

"Why? Think about it, instead of each person cutting and then sewing…"

"So, you want to reduce each tailor to a cloth cutter or button sewer. What are they, bloody robots?"

"No, just being smart. See if you apply the optimization equation…"

"Screw the equation. What do you want the worker to say at home? That I made ten shirts today? Or that I cut fifty pieces of cloth? Do you realize how mind-numbing each job willl become?"

"That is silly," I said, "it is about improved efficiency."

"But what if each worker wants to make his own shirt and wants to improve the design? It is just the same Cherian crap, treat humans like mindless machines."

"I think you should attend his class, Ryan. I can't explain it. He seemed to make sense."

"Of course, he makes sense to you. You want to nail his daughter that's why."

"Aw, shut up, just come to class all right. It is high time you give this system a chance."

"It's a screwed up system, so no more chances. Now, give me the assignment so I can cog it."

I met Neha outside the insti gate for a walk-date. A walk-date is where you go with your girlfriend for a long walk to get some fresh air and quality conversation, or at least you say so. The real great thing about walk-dates is that they are free. To me, nearly broke as it was my turn to fill Ryan's scooter tank last time, it was the obvious choice. Neha chose the route, a five-kilometer return trip from the campus via nearby villages.

"So, tell me. What did you think of my Dad?" Neha said as if she expected me to jump in excitement.

"Don't really know him, but pretty strict I think. How do you live with him?"

"You know he is really impressed by good students. I hope you are going to do well in his course."

"I am trying. But I have never got an A. And he gives like a dozen assignments a week. Plus there is a viva component that I hate."

"If you do get an A, I'll probably tell him that we are friends."

"Well, I am trying. Anyway, where are we walking to?"

"Just keep walking, I have a place in mind."

I kept silent, hoping she had thought of a secluded place. That is all one wants when one is dating, an empty place with nothing to do, no one around. Yet, you see dozens of fast-food places, cinemas, and ice-cream parlours, all targeting the dating crowd. Why don't they just make rows and rows of empty rooms instead?

Neha took me through a mud-path that led to Katwaria village. A few semi-naked kids looked at us curiously as if we were a different species. Two buffaloes loose from their sheds were also taking an evening walk, and one seemed to follow us.

"Are you sure you know where we are going?" I asked doubtfully.

"Of course, I am. See that temple at the end of this path, over there."

I squinted my eyes. There was a temple flag, around a kilometre away. After a while, the buffalo following us gave up on the idea, and the two of us were alone.

We reached the temple and sat down at the parapet of the neglected steps. A stray snoozing dog opened an eye to look at us. In front of the temple was a railway line. I guessed it was for the Delhi ring railway, the local city train that no one really used and ran only once every couple of hours.

"What is this temple doing in the middle of nowhere?" I

said, casually picking up her hand. The dog didn't care, and no one else was really around.

"I think only some villagers use it on special days. But I like it here," Neha said, leaning against me.

We kissed, I don't really know who started it. That is the cool thing about having a steady girlfriend. You don't have to struggle every time you want to kiss. But that was the farthest you could go with Neha. I put my hand on her shoulder for support. Then in a completely planned but seemingly unintentional manner I let it slip down toward her chest. Maybe this time her reflexes wouldn't be as strong.

"No!" Neha said the moment it got interesting. She pushed me away and sat up.

"You are so beautiful," I said, trying to be as mellow as possible.

"Shut up," she said and giggled, "your corny lines aren't going to get you anywhere. Have some shame, we are near a temple."

Yeah right, I thought. As if kissing next to a temple was okay but somehow the classic 'slide the hand carelessly down' was not. Neha, I tell you, is the queen of contradictions.

I tried to get close to her again, it was useless to argue.

"Just kisses. You know this is wrong," she warned.

We did our making out, or rather me-trying-to-make-out routine for half an hour, after which she had to go home or something. We stood up, threw the dog a last glance and started walking back.

"Do you know my brother died on those tracks?" she said.

I hadn't really heard much about how her brother died. Gory stories kind of just put me off but I guess guys have to listen to their girlfriends. "Really? No, I didn't know. How did it happen?"

"I still remember the date, May 11. Bhaiyya had gone for a jog. We got the call mid-morning. I mean, Dad got the call. He told us only in the evening and I ...wasn't even allowed to go see the body." Her voice began to quiver.

We were nearing the village, so I wasn't sure if I should let her cry on my shoulder. But she herself chose to, and I couldn't do much.

"Neha, it's okay," I said, conscious of two urchins staring at us. The only time they had probably seen a guy and a girl embrace was on screen.

She only moved away from me when the number of kids watching us had gone up to eight.

"Wow, now where did they come from?" She wiped her eyes. The eight kids, mostly naked, looked at us intently as if they were watching a film.

"See, she is a heroine," I said to the kids.

"Raveena Tandon," said a three-year old in the crowd.

Neha started to laugh, much to my relief, given her moods tended to be long.

We walked further, until we came close enough to campus where we adopted separate paths.

"Perhaps I can introduce you as his course topper to him some day." She winked, walking ahead.

I waited the prescribed five minutes and then headed for campus. Was I in love with her? I kicked a pebble out of my way; if only she wouldn't be so good all the time!

14

Vodka

ALOK RETURNED HYPER-HARRIED FROM HOME.

"How are your dad and mom?" I asked, alerted by his unusual silence at Sasi's, not even asking what the daily specials were.

"Miserable as usual. There was another big drama at home last weekend. There's yet another suitable match for my sister but we can't cough up the suitable money. Hence, either we say no or sign IOUs, meaning give it later when I pass out of the insti, get a job and then pay for it."

"That's tough," Ryan noted, who had just joined us after waking up from his royal siesta.

"But it is my duty man and I love them. I don't see it as trouble," Alok said dully.

"So what job are you going to take up?" I said.

"Whichever pays the most, I don't care," Alok said.

"That is crap. Don't you want to do something you really like?"

"I like money," Alok said as he finished his food. Until he had the money, paranthas would do.

We were mid-way through the semester now, and every now and then I would start thinking about my goal – to do well in Indem. By third year, every IITian knows his place. We were now five-pointers frozen in our place; we had modest expectations, and our grades never disappointed us. However, in Indem I wanted an A, something that had never been on my grade sheet. Alok warned me about my lofty ambition. "Cherian will chew you alive man. You hardly sleep these days. You know he gives only two or three As, right?"

"I do. But I have to give it my best. It is not just a stupid grade, but Neha at stake."

"How much have you scored so far in the assignments?"

"Thirty-three out of forty. Worked like a dog on all of them."

"Yes right. You need eighty total to get an A."

"I know, out of that the viva is ten, and the major is fifty."

"So unless you get almost a full score in the majors, you have to do decently in the vivas."

"I know. So this time, I have to pull it through," I said, abjectly nervous at the thought.

"Just relax man, a B won't be that bad."

"An A Alok, I want an A."

"Fine then. All the best," Alok said as Sasi delivered more paranthas.

"How is your girl?" Ryan said.

"Neha is fine. Just took me to the place where her brother met with the accident. Isn't that weird?" I said.

"Maybe because you are special. And the place holds special meaning for her," Alok shrugged.

"Fatso is right. She likes you man," Ryan said. "When did her brother die anyway?"

"Around three years ago. May 11 to be precise. He had gone jogging when they got a call mid-morning, hit by a ring railway train."

"Wow, that is incredible," Alok said, "and I thought no one used the ring railway."

"He wasn't using it Fatso. He just got hit by it," Ryan clarified.

"Yes, pretty gory." I rolled my eyes.

"Though who goes jogging on a bloody hot May morning?" Ryan wanted to know.

"Shut up man. The guy is dead, and you are making fun of him," I protested.

"No. That is not what I mean. I mean, hey Fatso, what time does the first ring railway train run?"

"I don't know," Alok said, busy eating his paranthas and somewhat pissed at the frequent reference to him as Fatso.

"I know, ten I think. Why?" I said.

"Well, think about it, ten in the morning in May. I think it is close to forty degrees and crap hot. Who goes jogging on a May morning?"

"Well, he did. Otherwise he wouldn't have died, right?" Alok said, obviously irritated. He never went jogging, so I guess he didn't know better.

"I know he died. But my point is..." Ryan said, "anyway, forget it."

"What? I want to know," I said.

"My point is, was it an accident at all."

I woke up with a headache on the day of Cherian's viva. There were a couple of weeks left until the majors, but today would seal my Indem fate. "Try to sleep, try to sleep," I had told myself about a million times the night before, all to no use.

"God, you look a mess," Ryan greeted in the toilet as we were shaving together.

"Couldn't sleep much. Hell, I know I am going to screw this one up," I said and slapped water on my face.

Ryan pressed the nozzle of his Gillette shaving gel and prepared his twin-blade sensor razor. His parents had sent him all these contraptions to look even better as if the guy needed to improve his looks. Why couldn't he get a few pimples now and again like say Alok?

"Listen Hari," Ryan said making clean strokes across his cheek, "you have busted your ass for this course already. You mess this up, and there is no hope for you man. You probably know the answers better than anyone else."

"Since when has knowing the answers been a problem? And this is Cherian, even normal guys get scared," I said.

"See, I am not even going for his viva. But if you are so scared, I have an idea."

"You aren't coming? Ryan, it is ten percent. And Cherian will go ape-shit if a student doesn't even come to the viva."

"I have vowed not to view that bastard's face as much as I can. And who cares about ten percent, I don't have to impress the dad."

"Up to you. I still think you should come. Anyway, what is your idea?"

"I don't know if it will work."

"Just tell me man. I am desperate," I said.

Ryan wiped his face with a towel. He opened a bottle of some fancy overpriced American aftershave and splashed it liberally on his cheeks.

"Vodka: the solution to all problems."

"What? Vodka? I am talking about a viva Ryan, I am not organizing a party."

"I know. But you know how vodka makes one less inhibited and makes you talk more? Who knows, a couple of swigs and it may work for you."

"You are crazy. The viva is at eleven in the morning. It is hardly the time to drink..."

"If you get a zero in his viva, you think Neha will ever introduce you to daddy?"

The image of a zero and a B or C in Indem flashed across my mind. "How much?"

"Just a couple of shots. Come, I have some in my closet."

I went to Ryan's room where amidst branded clothes he hid his stash of alcohol. Alongside the bottle were envelopes, all with US stamps.

Ryan poured vodka in a steel glass, making it a third-full.

"What are those envelopes?" I said.

"Nothing. Here, one shot...one, two, three," Ryan said.

I couldn't believe the envelopes were unimportant. I mean, there were like a hundred of them literally.

"Letters from your parents, aren't they?" I hazarded a guess.

"Yeah. Here have another one," Ryan said.

"You sure this won't be too much?" I said.

"No. In fact have a third one just to be sure. Here, I'll accompany you."

With that, Ryan joined me in my third shot. The vodka went down like a fireball, hitting my empty stomach, spearing my intestines.

"All right then, off I go to meet the daddy," I said cheerfully.

"All the best, Hari. And listen, just don't tell Alok about the envelopes."

"Tell what?" I said. I hardly knew anything about them and I wouldn't have if Ryan hadn't mentioned it.

"Nothing, just don't mention it. They write every week, and send a cheque once a month. I never reply, that is all."

"Why don't you reply?" I asked, basking in the spirit inside of me.

"'Cause I hate them. Actually, I don't care about them. I mean, neither do they about me. So why pretend?" Ryan said.

"Ryan, you know this whole big deal you make about not caring about your parents?" the vodka spoke for me.

"Yeah, what about that?"

"I don't think it is true. I mean, how can it be true?" I said, ignoring his hostile stance. I kind of meant it. With all the Gillette and aftershaves they sent, how could he not love them?

"It's true. You are a kid in life man, just go give your viva," Ryan said and lit up a cigarette. Smoke made the man more profound.

"I am going. But if it were true, why would you keep all the letters?" I asked, beating a retreat.

Cherian was already in class. My turn came in ten minutes and I sat next to Alok.

"Where is Ryan?" he whispered, flipping through his notes. Alok always revises until the last minute.

"He is skipping it," I said.

"What? He is crazy man," he shook his head.

"Says he doesn't care. Just as he doesn't for his parents," I said, obviously the second phrase came because of the vodka.

"Are you okay, Hari? You sound kind of garbled. And what is that smell...wait have you been drinking?"

"Shh...keep quiet. Just a little bit. Ryan said it helps relax."

"Ryan, Ryan, Ryan. Do you ever think for yourself?" Alok said.

"Hari," Prof Cherian called my name even before I could answer Alok. My moment was here. My first A was to be decided in the next five minutes.

"So, what is the Japanese system for manufacturing that lowers inventories?" Prof Cherian started as usual without any greetings or pleasantries. Just a straight firm voice like from a machine.

"Good morning, sir," I said.

"Good morning, Hari. Now answer my question." His eyes looked like big, bulging versions of Neha's eyes.

"Good morning, sir," I said again, to kick-start my brain.

"That is fine, Hari. Now answer please, if you don't mind."

"Sir, the Japanese inventory lowering system..." I began.

"Yes, that one. You know the answer or not?" Prof Cherian said, his voice getting louder.

"I sir....I sir..." I said.

"It is JIT or Just in Time. Cannot believe students today cannot answer such simple questions. Next one, what is the difference between assembly line and batch manufacturing?"

"Sir, very simple question sir...hic," I said.

"Why are you talking like that? And what is this smell? Are you drunk Mr Hari? Are you drunk in my class?"

"No sir, sir, I actually know answer, sir," I reiterated desperately.

"You are actually drunk. The guts of these students today!" Prof Cherian said and threw a piece of chalk right at me. It hit me on the chest and hurt a little. Even though I was drunk, I knew something was going wrong. I was actually speaking at this viva, but not making any sense.

"Sir," I said.

"Get out of my class now. Get out now." Prof Cherian's face turned red and he slammed his files on the desk.

I picked up my notebook to leave when Cherian came toward me. He took out a red pen and marked a circle on my sheet. Then he made another circle over it.

"Zero, that is what you deserve. I wish I could give you negative," he said, "and you better do well in your majors for I am not going to let you get away from this that easy."

I kept quiet. All those shots for a zero, which I could have earned myself anyway with or without vodka.

"Fuck!" Ryan slammed a fist against his palm when he heard the story back in Kumaon.

"What fuck? Who told you to suggest such a weird idea?" Alok said.

"I thought it would work but the shots were too big," Ryan said. He was playing with a basketball, bouncing it back and forth on the wall.

"Will you cut out that noise?" Alok said, "So what are you going to do now Hari?"

"Do what? I lose the A for sure. And Cherian thinks I'm a drunkard. Way to go for his daughter's boyfriend," I said, covering my face with my hands.

Thump, thump, thump. Ryan kept silent as the only noise he made was with the ball.

"Stop it," Alok said, grabbing the ball from Ryan, "say something solid now!"

"Alok!" someone shouted from outside. It was the security guard downstairs.

"Phone call for Alok," the guard shouted.

"Must be from home," Alok said, "Come Hari, no point discussing Indem now."

I came down with Alok if for nothing else but to be distracted from the Indem fiasco.

"Hello, Mummy. How are you? Yes, I know I have not come home for a long time," Alok said on the phone.

"What? Didi got engaged? Oh, you mean the boy's side have agreed," Alok said, his voice excited.

"Yes, I am really happy, how is Dad...I know...of course I'll pay for everything once I get a job Mom...yes, you are taking a loan for gifts..."

I could hear only half the conversation, but could pretty much figure out what was going on. Alok's parents had finally managed to palm off their daughter to someone. As he explained later, the groom's family wanted a Maruti car in dowry, but had agreed to defer it until Alok passed out and started working. That's when the marriage would take place but at least they had a deal.

"Congratulations, your sister is getting married. Is your family excited? Or like sad or something since she'll go away?" I said to Alok after the call.

"They are relieved more than anything I think. I just hope I get a job that pays for this damn affair. Apart from the car, there will be a function as well."

"Why don't you guys marry her off later? What is the big hurry?"

"The older she gets, the more dowry people will demand. Waiting will mean more expense later. I'm happy the deal is cut."

It sounded like credit card debt. If you don't get rid of it now, it will cost you a lot more later. The relief was understandable.

"What does the groom do?" I said.

"Oh. I don't know. I forgot to ask," Alok said.

Several weeks later, we were in the Kumaon mess eating dinner. It was Thursday I guess, for that is when Kumaon had 'continental' dinner. In reality, it was just an excuse for mess-workers to not give us real food. The menu sounded nice – noodles, French fries, toast and soup. It tasted awful. The cooks made the noodles in superglue or something – they stuck to each other as one composite mass in the huge serving pan. The French fries were cold and either extremely undercooked or burnt to taste like coal. The cream of mushroom soup could have been mistaken for muddy water, only it was warmer and saltier.

"This is bad man," Alok said as his noodles refused to vacate his fork, "I told you let's go out."

"I didn't know it would be so bad. And the semester is almost over. I am totally out of cash."

"That is right actually," Alok said, "better start studying for the majors. Less than ten days now."

"Yes, not that I care now. After Indem messed up, I don't really care beyond passing each course."

"Ryan, I think you should focus on Indem. Cherian didn't like you missing the viva. He smirks when he mentions your name in class attendance."

"I know," Ryan said, dropping his half-eaten French fry in disgust, "I got sixteen out of forty in quizzes and zero in viva. Need twenty-four out of fifty in majors to pass it."

"Not that easy," I pointed out the obvious.

"Worse case, I flunk. So what?" Ryan said and tried the soup. Without caring for etiquette, he spewed the contents out from his mouth back into the bowl.

"Cherian will make you do it again, it's a core course," Alok said. "Like drinking the soup you just spat out."

"Fuck," Ryan said. I wasn't sure if his comment was aimed at the food or the prospect of repeating Cherian's course.

"Man, if only I had an A, I could finally get Neha..." I said.

"I think we can still do something," Ryan said.

"What? Drink enough to forget Neha?" I mocked.

"No. If you completely crack the majors, you can still make it, right?"

"I have thirty-three on forty, need eighty for an A. Major is fifty points. How am I going to get forty-seven on fifty?"

"No way man. Ryan, don't trouble the guy more. It is over."

"It is not over, my friends, it never is. If I tell you that you can get a perfect score in majors, will you believe me?"

"Don't be crazy. I'd have to spend twenty hours a day on Indem and will probably not make it. Cherian's major test will be full of surprise questions. I am screwed…" I lamented.

"What if you knew the questions?" Ryan said.

"What if, what if? Ryan, are you dreaming?" Alok said.

"No I am not dreaming, Fatso. I am trying to help my friend. I think we can get the major paper."

"How?" I was arrested.

"By sneaking it out of Cherian's office," Ryan said.

Alok and I fell silent for a full minute, took us around that much time to digest the preposterousness of the idea, along with the unpalatable food.

"You mean steal it? Steal a bloody major paper from an IIT prof? Is that what you said?" Alok said.

"Don't make it sound so dramatic. It is not such a big…"

"Are you nuts? Tell me, are you nuts?" Alok said and walked out of the mess. I went out as well, preoccupied with my coming encounter with Neha, especially with how I could dismiss my past encounter with daddy dearest.

15

Operation Pendulum

THE NEXT DAY AT KUMAON LAWNS RYAN WAS HIS LORDLY best. "Guys, just listen to me."

"No way, you can't do this. Please, stop this nonsense," Alok said.

"He has a point," I conceded, not fully sure of what it was though.

"Can you guys just listen to me for a minute? You don't have to do anything," Ryan said, sounding almost reasonable.

"Sure," I said.

"We have lived in this place for three years, right? And what have we got?" Ryan said.

"Oh, don't start about the system being crappy, Ryan. Just come to the point," Alok said.

"I will, I will," he said, realizing that he didn't exactly have a patient audience in hand. He took out a sheet from his pocket — two A4 sized sheets stuck together — and laid it out on the grass. Employing two pebbles as paperweight, he began with a flourish, "This, gentlemen is a map of the insti building. All profs get the major papers ready and printed a week prior to tests but our Cherian's a paragon, so his must be ready even earlier. Here, Cherian's office is on the sixth floor. The roof is on the ninth floor…"

Ryan's face was intense like Alok's while writing his exam paper. This was not a casual conversation; he had pondered over this for a while.

"I told you the whole idea was crap. How can you force these details on us as if we've said yes," Alok said.

But that is how Ryan is, he decides, and then he proposes, and then he does whatever he wants to anyway.

"Ryan, what is all this man?" I said.

"Just listen to me. Hari, I could get you the A grade you want here. Imagine, your girl will finally not be ashamed to acknowledge you. And you too Fatso, an A won't look so bad on your grade sheet when you apply for jobs either."

"But it is so warped, so…so wrong," Alok protested, looking at me for support against Ryan's latest madness. But I was already thinking of walking hand in hand with Neha in the insti gardens when the moon was out. Could I really get an A?

"It is wrong only if you get caught right?"

It was kind of hard to argue with Ryan's logic, especially if you were dreaming about your beautiful girlfriend at that time. Yes, it is a crime only if someone catches you. Otherwise, it is just a neat plan.

"But…" Alok tried again.

"Anyway, let me finish," Ryan said, without letting Alok finish now that I looked half way there.

"The roof is on the ninth floor. So, if I suspend myself with ropes and then sail down to Cherian's window, I can get to his room. You guys can help me, just like we got Hari into Neha's room."

"Are you crazy? Neha's room was easy, no ropes or anything. And the insti building is nine floors high," I said.

"I am not scared. I have done rock climbing in school," Ryan said.

"What if the window is not open?" Alok said.

I could see Ryan liked Alok's question. Not only because Ryan had thought about it before, but because it meant Alok was buying into this. But wait a minute, was I on board with this just because it was Ryan? An A would be nice though.

"Yes, what about the window?" I said.

"The insti windows have latches that are weaker than rubber bands. They are the same windows as in Kumaon hostel. One bang on the back and it opens."

"Still, you will suspend yourself from the roof?" I said.

"I said I wasn't scared."

"What if someone sees us?" I said.

That is the thing about Ryan. He is brilliant, but also fearless. This machismo might lead to an over-confidence that could kill the plan.

"No one will see us," Ryan said.

"Yeah right. Just three guys hanging on to the insti roof as usual. Institute security wouldn't care, eh?" Alok smirked.

"Fatso, it will be super dark," Ryan said.

"But we could make a noise, or the movement could be seen by the security jeeps on the roads. Remember, we are not on the roof, but hanging by the sides. We just might be seen."

"C'mon guys..." Ryan said, looking bored.

"Too risky. Forget it," Alok said, tearing blades of grass. I had to nod, too. Besides, just the thought of Ryan bungee-jumping upward made me sweat.

"Well, you got any better ideas?" Ryan said, irritated.

"What were you planning to do next anyway?" My curiosity got the better of me.

"Okay, here are the next steps," Ryan pointed to the side of the paper. "One, switch on light on the opposite right wall. Two, scan the room for a sealed brown bag. Three, open the seal with a knife, and take out one copy of major paper. Four, using a candle and fresh seal, fasten the bag back. Five, get the hell out of there."

"Sounds simple enough after that," Alok said, "but I guess we can't get in. Let's go now, I'm hungry."

"There could be a way," I said.

"What?"

"Through the door. His main regular office door," I said.

"How? Break the lock? Of course, you know that is impossible, with the noise and everything. And he'll know the next day," Ryan said.

"No lock breaking. Just get in elegantly with the key," I said.

"Key? Where the hell will you get the key?" Alok said.

"From Neha's car keys. Her dad's office keys are in the bunch," I said.

Everyone fell silent for five seconds. It was the silence of admiration for sheer brilliance.

"Wow. I guess you just have to steal the keys then," Alok said.

"Why not just sneak them out for half an hour and make a duplicate?" Ryan said.

"I guess. Not the easiest thing to do, but can be done," I said, and smiled smugly at my own genius. Cherian's office was an open door.

"Hari, you are a killer man. That is awesome," Ryan said.

He finalized the revised plan again. It seemed simple enough now, and we had invested too much time in it to walk away from it.

"So we go up at night, just as we go to the roof for the vodka. But we stop at the sixth floor and raid Cherian's office," Ryan said.

"Not raid, just turn the key and slide in," I said, impersonating a mock key with my fingers.

"Yes, up yours Cherian," Ryan poked air with his middle finger. We all laughed and shook hands.

"Let us give this operation a name. Something sexy, something unsuspicious and simple."

"Something that will swing our miserable fortunes in this place," I said.

"Yes, this swinging operation can be called Operation Pendulum," Ryan said.

And on that bright lawn with our sun-lit eyes, we blithely cheered in unison, "Operation Pendulum!"

16

The Longest Day of My Life I

THEY SAY NO ONE DAY CAN BE TOO SIGNIFICANT IN YOUR life, but I tell you the day of Operation Pendulum was the most memorable and longest of all my IIT days. Each moment, each event is vivid and fresh in my mind as if it happened yesterday. It was the day that changed our lives, or at least changed us.

There was no formal date set for Operation Pendulum. It was kind of like, we'd do it the day I got the key thing done. The majors were less than a week away, so we were sure Cherian would have the papers by now. And of course, we'd need some time to figure out the answers to those questions. So the sooner the better.

April 11, the day of Operation Pendulum, a day that started with my date with Neha. I should have seen the signs the moment Neha told me she'd sprained her ankle.

"What?" I said over the phone, "I am dying to meet you. Don't cancel today. The majors will begin after that."

"But Hari, I can't even walk ten steps. Please, can't we do it some other time?"

"Can I just see you for half an hour. How about I come home?"

I knew Neha's mom would not be at home that day. It was the eleventh, the day she went to that temple by the tracks and sobbed for her son. That is why Neha had agreed to the date in the first place.

"Home? Are you mad? What if someone sees you?"

"Third year is ending, can you stop being so scared?"

"But..."

"And what if I get an A, you'll introduce me then anyway right?"

"Okay, but only for half an hour. And come exactly at 11.30, so I'll leave the doors open," she said.

"Great. I'll see you then," I said, keeping the phone down with a sigh of relief. I just had to see her that day, or rather see her car.

"Everything okay?" Ryan quizzed as I left Kumaon.

"Of course. See you in two hours," I said.

"Shh, quiet, just come in quickly," Neha said, whispering quite unnecessarily.

"No one is here," I said.

"You're crazy. So, why the big urge to see me today?" Neha said, leading me to her room.

"Well, you know third year is ending and majors and everything," I said, my eyes roving around the room to spot any key-racks.

"So?" Neha said.

"So I thought meeting you would be good luck for the exams," I said sitting down on the bed by her side.

"Wow, how romantic!" she said, "and I thought my loafer was pining for me and dying for me and whatever..."

"Oh, I was," I said and leaned forward to hug her. It was true. I was always pining for her. She looked beautiful. Even with her sore ankle, all pink and wrapped in a crepe bandage, she managed to look beautiful.

"Ouch, careful," she said, pushing me back on the bed, "I know what you pine for."

"What?"

"My body, not me," she said, nose up in air.

What is the difference? I thought. You just cannot understand girls sometimes.

"That is not true," I said, just guessing that it would be the right response.

"Come here," she called me and kissed me.

"When does Mom get back?"

"In two hours. You know, Samir Bhaiyya's date."

"I know, it's the eleventh. You know Neha, I wanted to ask you about that."

"What about it?"

"I was talking about it to Ryan..."

"You talked about Samir to Ryan?"

"No, just discussing how he well, died. You know the jogging and everything."

"So?"

"So Ryan made a point. A good point."

"What was that?"

"That who goes jogging on a hot May morning?"

She fell silent, released me from her hug and sat away.

"Neha?" I prompted.

"Hari," she said and sobbed, "Hari, I didn't want to tell you this, but I have to."

"What?"

"Wait," she said and went to open her cupboard. A bright mélange of clothes appeared, quite unlike an average Kumaon guy's closet. Neha took out a folded piece of paper. "Read this," she said.

I opened the page and my eyebrows jumped up in shock, it was signed Samir.

Dear Neha,

I love you my little sister, as much as the day I first held you in my arms when you were born. I was so proud that day, and will remain so forever.

Neha, can you keep a secret? By the time you get this, I may not be in this world. But you must understand that no one in the world must know of this letter.

I have tried three times to get into IIT, and each time I have disappointed Dad. He cannot get over the fact that his son cannot handle physics, chemistry and maths. I cannot do it Neha, no matter how hard I try, no matter how many years I study or how many books I read. I cannot get into IIT. And I cannot bear to see Dad's eyes.

He has seen thousands of IIT students in his life, and cannot see why his own son cannot make it. Well Neha, he sees the students who make it, but he doesn't see the hundreds of thousands who don't make it. He has not spoken to me for two months. He doesn't even talk to mom properly because of me. What can I do? Keep trying until I die? Or simply die?

If anyone finds out that I took my own life, Mom would probably not be able to survive. But I had to tell someone — and who else but you. I love you Neha. And you tell them I went jogging.

Yours in eternity,
Samir

"What the heck is this," I said, feeling creepy. It is not every day that you hold a suicide note in your hand.

"It's true. I should have never told you. But I'm so close to you and you start all this investigation thing and…" She burst into tears.

"Listen, now calm down," I said, speaking more to myself than to her. She stopped crying after five minutes and I gave her a glass of water.

"You want to know what happened in my viva?" Maybe it would make her laugh. "Ryan made me have vodka shots," I said.

Neha lifted her head up and squeaked, "That was you? Dad mentioned it. That was you?" She started hitting me with a pillow. She was laughing again. She looked beautiful, and I could have sat there admiring her beauty forever but I was on a mission today, to get the keys for Operation Pendulum.

"Stop, that hurts," I said, moving toward her on the bed.

"Don't come near me, you drunk loafer. You know Dad brooded for two hours that day." She was laughing so hard, she had to press her stomach with a hand.

I curled up next to her and held her. She turned her face towards me, almost in reflex. We kissed, and then we kissed again. Then she held my hand and did something that she had never done before; she put it on her breast.

Wow, my head went into a tizzy. What happened to this girl? Had she lost her mind? I certainly lost mine and forgot about Operation Pendulum.

My hand slid under her T-shirt and then clumsily under The Bra. Life would be so much better without hooks.

"Easy Tiger easy," she said. I liked it that she called me Tiger.

She sat up to remove her T-shirt. And then the rest. I sat there transfixed, trying hard not to let my tongue hang loose and pant like a dog.

"Well Tiger, are you going to remove anything or not?" she said.

"I..I…" I said as she pulled me close.

Half an hour later, we lay on the bed, spent but completely content. I looked up at the old ceiling fan in Neha's room, going around in awkward circles and felt dizzy with happiness.

"So?" Neha said.

"So what," I said, regaining my equilibrium.

"Say something."

I was bloody beyond happy. If I did not have that key to steal, I would have stayed put forever.

"That was quite…amazing," I said in an understatement.

"Thanks. I liked it too. I guess I am a bad girl now," she said.

"No, you are not," I said, scared she might regret this and never do it again.

"Yeah, right. Here I am, lying naked with a man who was drunk in his viva, while my Dad is less than a kilometer away in his office," she said and laughed, "It's so liberating."

"Really?"

"Yes, so liberating, yet so sad," she said.

"Relax, Neha," I said, fearing an inexplicable round of tears. "Do you want to go out?"

"No. Why, don't you like it here?"

"I do. Just wanted a cigarette," I said.

"Oh yes, I have heard cigarettes are great after sex. Please get me one too," she said.

"You don't smoke!"

"I don't sleep with guys either. Hurry, get me a fag please."

I saw the opportunity, and jumped at it. "Can I take your car?"

"Why? You didn't get Ryan's scooter?"

"No, he wanted it for squash. Can I?"

"Okay, the keys are on top of the fridge. Be quick though," she said as she got up and picked up my shirt.

"Hey, that's my shirt you're wearing," I pointed out.

"I know. I like it, it is so loose and perfect for a little nap," she said and pretended to fall asleep.

"Neha. Don't be ridiculous, how am I supposed to go out?"

"Wear my top," she said lazily.

"It's pink, and all tight. Are you nuts?"

"Just take one of Dad's shirts in the closet downstairs."

"Neha, don't be silly…"

"Get lost and get the fags Hari, you have tired me out," she said and threw a pillow at me.

Thinking if I could take Prof Cherian's car and daughter, I could totally take his shirt, I took out a white shirt from his closet, plain apart from the DC monogrammed on the sleeve.

I picked up the bunch of keys from the fridge. Six of them, one surely for Cherian's office.

"Yes!" I said to myself as I left the house.

I drove out on the empty road, as the mid-day sun had forced most people indoors, drove to Jia Sarai and went straight to the duplicate key shop.

"Which one?" the shopkeeper said.

"All six," I said.

As the shopkeeper carved the new keys, I bought a pack of cigarettes. This was simpler than I thought. I lit one and drifted into thoughts of hugging Neha again. This had to be the most wonderful day of my life.

The keys were ready soon. I put the new bunch in my pocket and drove back into campus through the insti gates.

Just as I turned toward faculty housing, I saw a bicycle ahead of me. I am mad, I am stupid, a freaking jerk I thought as I honked – and turning around to look at me was Cherian.

17

The Longest Day of My Life II

THERE ARE TIMES IN YOUR LIFE WHEN YOU ARE SO SCARED you scream, and there are times you are so beyond scared you just freeze. I mean you kind of get fossilized in an icebox and never come back to life ever again. When Cherian got off his bicycle and walked toward me, or rather his car, I went into deep freeze.

He came and stood next to me. I should have probably got out, but I was crap scared to move an inch. I heard my heart, which was louder than Cherian's words. "This is my car," he said.

True, I thought, ten out of ten. I can control this, I said to myself and tried to breathe. "Yes, sir," I said.

"Who are you? And what are you doing in my car?" he asked next.

"Sir, just driving back...sir," I said, probably looking as stupid as I sounded.

Cherian parked his bicycle on the side of the road and abandoning my role as a wax model, I got out of the car. Oh, where were the dinosaurs when you needed them?

"Were you driving to my home?" Cherian said, opening the front door. Yes, he was going to drive now. Could I go home?

"Yes, sir."

Suddenly his mighty brow furrowed. "I know you. You are a student, right? What is your name?"

"Hari, Sir," I said, glad he had asked the only thing I was sure about.

"You are the one who was playing tricks in my viva?"

I nodded, guilty as charged.

"Get in," Cherian said.

I quietly opened the other front door and sat next to him. He started the car.

"Who gave you the keys?"

I jumped at the last word. My hand caressed my trouser pocket from the outside. Yes, the set of duplicate keys was still there. I had to think of something now. Any reason why I could be driving his car apart from buying post-coitus cigarettes for his daughter.

"Neha, sir," I said after a deliberate pause.

"You know Neha?" the professor's eyebrows shot up.

"Sir, I met her on the road. The car had a flat tire."

"So?" Cherian said.

"Sir, I was passing by and offered to push the car to the mechanic. She had to go back and I offered to bring the car home."

Silence from Cherian. Had he fallen for it? I guessed he had, for he started the car and started driving it slowly.

"Why did you offer that?"

"Just wanted to help," I shrugged modestly like I go about scouting for good deeds all day.

"And you don't have classes to attend?"

"A free period, sir."

"Silly girl," Cherian spoke aloud to himself, "Gives the car to any stupid stranger. I have to talk to her about this."

I kept silent; a new thought had crossed my mind; if Neha would be dressed. The last thing I wanted right now was a surprise hug from her when she opened the door. If only I could get ten seconds before she spoke to Cherian. Or if only I could disappear.

Cherian parked the car at his house.

"Sir, can I go now?"

"No, come in. This stupid girl should at least thank you. Not that I'd ever let boys like you come near my house."

"Right, sir." I totally understood him.

Cherian pressed the doorbell. Neha opened the door wearing just a bed sheet.

"Have you..." Then she saw her father. "Dad," Neha said, blinking her eyes and adjusting her bed sheet to cover the maximum. Surely, this was one hell of a kick compared to cigarettes.

"Your keys, ma'am," I spoke quickly, "Don't worry, I got the puncture completely fixed and brought your car back."

"Huh?" she looked at me.

"Neha, are you out of your mind? Why aren't you dressed?" Cherian said, controlling the volume of his voice only because I was there.

Neha blinked again before disappearing into her bedroom, presumably to change.

"This daughter of mine is mad. Sit down," Cherian said.

"Sir, we pushed the car for twenty minutes. She must be tired," I said. Well, sex was like pushing a car sometimes, only a lot more pleasant.

Neha came back wearing a very daddy's-good-girl salwar-kameez and holding a tray with two glasses of water.

As Cherian drank his glass, I repeated, "I was just telling your dad how your car got a flat tire and I helped you take it to the mechanic and then brought it back. I met Sir on the way here you see."

"Oh?" Neha said, striving for an intelligent facial expression.

"How can you dump the car on a stranger?" Cherian asked her.

"Sorry Dad," Neha said and collapsed on the sofa.

"Sir, can I go now?" I said.

Cherian gave half a nod and I was out of the house. I walked as fast as I could without running.

"Hari," Cherian shouted when I was at the gate.

I froze and turned. "Yes, sir."

"You are not that smart, you know," he said.

I'd always known of Cherian's disdain for students with low grades. I didn't know he'd be so direct about it.

"Sir, I know sir. I will study harder."

"That is not what I meant."

"Sir?"

"I was a student once too you know. And the best one, a straight 10 all four years."

"I know Sir."

"And if you think you can mess with my daughter and get away with it, you are wrong."

I stood silent.

"You drink in my viva, and now I find you fooling with my daughter, in my car and wearing my shirt," Cherian said and tugged at my collar. "You watch it Hari, you watch it. This is IIT, not some bloody regional college. First the viva, and then my daughter. My daughter!"

"Sir, it is not what you think."

"Don't tell me what to think. I knew my daughter was distracted these days. God, and because of scum like you! You stay away from my home and my daughter. Just away, understand?"

"Yes, Sir," I said, wishing Cherian would let go of my collar. I was beginning to go limp. I mean being caught by him on top of losing my virginity was hardly conducive to strengthening me.

"Good. I don't want people talking, so I won't bring this up again. But you stay away from her and focus on your courses. For, Hari, one slip in the insti and I will ruin you. I will bloody ruin you," Cherian said, his face an unpleasant red.

"Sir, I will stay away. Just let me go," I pleaded.

He released my collar, his fingers still trembling. I ran out of his gate and toward Kumaon. It was the fastest jog of life. I stopped only once, when I passed Cherian's bicycle. I don't know what struck me. I turned to make sure no one was around, and then released the air from both the tires. Damn, that monster deserved some revenge. And that just might make the bastard believe there are flat tires in this world.

"No way man," I said, panting as I reached Ryan's room.

"No way what? Did you get the keys?" Ryan said.

I tried to catch my breath.

"What happened?" Alok asked as he came to Ryan's room.

"Hell. Hell happened." I regained my pulse and related the whole story.

Ryan started laughing. Even though he is bold and everything, that is not what I expected from him. Cherian was there, holding my bloody collar and threatening to ruin me.

"Fuck Ryan, this is not funny," I said.

"Oh really," he said, laughing even harder, "then what is it? Cherian's shirt, Neha in a bedsheet. The prof must have gone psycho," Ryan paused to laugh some more. "I wish I was there."

"Shut up. This is added tension man," Alok said.

"What tension? You got the keys right?" Ryan said.

I nodded as I took out the bunch.

"So we're still doing this?" I said.

"Why not? How does Cherian know about this?" Ryan said and dangled the keys in front of him like a tempting bunch of ripe grapes.

"I don't know. I'm scared Ryan. I really am."

"Just relax dude. You are in shock, sex and horror on the same day," Ryan said, laughing again.

"Hari is right. We should re-evaluate Operation Pendulum."

"Nonsense," Ryan said and became serious again, "if at all, it makes the case stronger. Hari's only hope is if he cracks the majors. He can then still make Cherian feel that he is not such a loser after all."

"Thanks Ryan," I said.

"Oh come on Hari. You had a few hitches today, but still managed fine. Let Cherian think what he wants."

"Wonder what he will do to Neha," I said.

"You can't do anything about that, can you? And not today at least. Let's get the major paper and then worry about other stuff."

"You should talk to Neha after a few days only. Don't worry, Cherian will try and bury it. He wouldn't want the world to know. And he doesn't look like the dad who can talk to his daughter about this sort of stuff," Alok said and put his arm on my shoulder.

"We are friends man. Just have to wait for the evening now. Remember co-operate to dominate," Ryan said and hi-fived both of us.

Two hours later, at exactly five p.m. Alok got a call from home. We were sitting in Ryan's room and playing cards.

"Alok! Urgent phone call!" the guard below shouted at the top of his voice. Alok threw back his set of three cards.

"What is it?" I said.

"I don't know. Maybe my sister's engagement date got fixed," he yelled as he ran down the stairs.

"Let's go down. If that is true, we can get Fatso to treat us," Ryan said as we followed Alok down to the booth.

"Yes Mom, yes, I am fine. What happened, you don't sound so good," Alok said.

Ryan and I looked at each other and shrugged our shoulders.

"Really? What? I mean how could they?" Alok said as his own face dropped. Ryan and I backed away from the booth. No treat this time.

"What happened to Dad? Mom, speak louder this line is not clear. What happened? Not eating anything? For how long?" Alok said as the line got disconnected. The phone had gone dead.

He sat down on the floor of the telephone booth. The flimsy wooden box shook with the weight. "Can you believe this?"

"What? The phone has been giving trouble all week," Ryan said.

"The boy's side cancelled the proposal," Alok said.

"Why?" I said.

"They wanted a portion of the dowry right now. To lock in the boy. Mom said she will apply for a loan but it will take a few months. Meanwhile, they get another deal and it is all over. Bloody idiots," Alok said.

"That sounds sick. Why would you want to marry your sister off to such a family anyway?" I said.

"I don't know. All boys-side families are the same. And Dad is upset and has not eaten anything since I don't know when. There is mayhem at home, and the bloody phone is dead."

"It is probably good the phone is dead. What could you have done? Get up now, let's go up and talk," Ryan said, giving Alok a hand.

We went upstairs and stayed quiet for a while. Ryan finally broke the silence.

"Six o clock," he said like a don to fellow-gangsters, "four hours more. We leave Kumaon at ten for the operation."

I nodded my head, barely listening to him. I was wondering what Neha was doing right now.

"Ryan," Alok said, "I am really not comfortable right now..."

"About what?" Ryan said.

"I am getting nervous about this operation. First Hari runs into Cherian. Then Didi's proposal flops. And Dad might just fall sick again if he doesn't eat properly. I mean, we don't have to do this, do we?"

"Hey wait a minute now," Ryan said as he stood up, "what has your sister's proposal got to do with this? And your dad will be fine."

Alok remained silent with an unconvinced expression.

Ryan look at me and then back to Alok a couple of times. He paced around the room and started speaking again, "But tell me, is this the time to discuss all this? I thought we had made the decision. Look, we even have the keys."

He jingled the bunch in his hand.

"But Ryan, we don't need the risk now," Alok said.

"There is no risk. Just four hours, and we will have the paper. End of story."

"Hari, what do you think?" Alok said.

"Wait a minute," Ryan said, his voice louder. "Are you going to make him take sides again? Hari, does this Fatso want to do what he did after the first sem?"

"Relax Ryan," I said, interrupting my re-playing of the last moments with Neha, "why are you shouting?"

"Then tell Fatso to make up his mind," Ryan said and sat down. He lit up a cigarette and took a hurried puff.

"Of course I don't want to split, guys," Alok said.

"Or does he want to stay here and make us do the work? So he can get the paper for free?" Ryan said.

"See, that is what he thinks. He doesn't trust me," Alok said.

"Relax guys, I said, "I think all of us are getting tense here. We have four hours until the insti gets empty. We have the keys. We want the paper. If we do it, we do it together, right?"

"Right!" Ryan said.

We looked at Alok.

"Right" Alok said in a volume one-tenth that of Ryan.

"And we have thought through the risks right?" I said, looking at Ryan "Of course," he responded.

"Then let us just go for it. And Alok, your didi will find another match. If not now, maybe when you get a job and can pay for the wedding. What is the big hurry? Right?" I said looking at Alok.

"Right," Alok said, his voice sounding more confident and relaxed.

"Friends?" I said, looking at both of them.

"Of course," Ryan and Alok said in unison. "I'm in," Alok said.

"Good. Let's stay quiet for the next few hours," I said, wanting to dream about Neha.

We kept quiet for the next three hours. Alok said something about being worried about his dad. But we told him to relax, as his mom had handled such situations before. We did not go down to the mess to eat dinner. Somehow, we felt the crowds in the mess would read our minds.

"Ten o' clock," Ryan said and we jumped up as the clock struck the hour.

18

The Longest Day of
My Life III

WE WANTED TO LEAVE NO TRAIL OF OUR PRESENCE. FOR the first time in years, we walked to the insti instead of using Ryan's scooter. We walked quietly past the hostels, with books in hand as if going to the library for some midnight reading.

"So why did your parents start looking for your sister so early, how old is she?" I whispered, nervous as hell.

"Just twenty-three. I think they should look for a boy only when I start working. It would be much easier for me to get a loan," Alok said.

I agreed.

"If I get a job that is. Not much out there for a miserable five-pointer," he said.

"Well, maybe this A will lift you up a bit," I said.

"Shh," Ryan said as we reached the insti building.

We were being overcautious, as we scanned every corner for insti security guards. They never hung around the lobby at this time, and we'd sneaked up the stairs dozens of times for our vodka sessions. But we still split up and looked around all sides of the building — there was no one.

Cherian's office was on the sixth floor. There was minimal lighting on the stairs, and we counted aloud as we finished each flight of stairs.

"...and six. That is it guys. We get out, and Cherian's office is seventh door on the right," Ryan said.

We stepped on to the sixth floor. There was only one small bulb lighting the entire corridor.

"D C Cherian, Head of the Department. Bloody pig," Ryan said as he read the nameplate outside Cherian's office. Alok crouched behind me as Ryan examined the lock.

"Keys," Ryan extended his left hand.

I took out my bunch of keys and they jingled as if on stereo.

"Keep it quiet," Alok said.

"Stop being so scared, Fatso. No one knows we're here." He was freaking me out. "Ryan, find the right key man," I said.

"I'm trying. There are like a million of them in this bunch. Wait this one, no this one, no this... ah I think this is it."

"It is?" Alok looked dazed.

Ryan opened the bolt in one stroke, kicking the door open. There it was, the lair of the head of the department of IIT Delhi Mechanical Engineering was ours. Ryan searched the wall and flicked the light open.

"What are you doing?" Alok asked.

"How else will we search, Fatso? Just relax, no one can see us. Take your time and search. And I want to search for something else too."

"What?"

"My lube project proposal. Cherian bloody stuck it in his office and it got nowhere. Prof Veera told me there is a copy here somewhere with his comments."

"Whatever Ryan. Can we search for the paper first?"

"Where do we start?" Alok said as he scanned the piles of paper kept on Cherian's shelves. This could take all night.

"Look for brown bags with a red wax seal. They always open the seal at the time of the papers," Ryan said.

We divided the shelves to save time, and started a quick scan. I ran through journals, administrative documents, course outlines and timetables. Nothing for twenty minutes.

"Anything?" I asked.

Ryan and Alok shook their heads.

Ten minutes later, Ryan stepped back and sat on Cherian's chair.

"What?" I said.

"I have checked my shelves. There is nothing in mine. Got my lube project though. He just says 'no commercial viability or academic value'. What a prick."

"Well, I can't find anything either. Do you want to help?" I said.

"Red seal and brown bag. Indem Majors - Confidential. Is this what you are looking for gentlemen?" Alok said and waved the bag in front of us.

We jumped up.

"Fatso, this is it man!" Ryan said.

"Yes," I said as we hi-fived each other.

"I cannot believe it," Alok said.

"That is because you don't trust me. Though we still have stuff to do. So, wait while I deal with this seal," Ryan said as he emptied his pockets. A blade, candle, lighter and some wax to re-seal the bag.

"Man, you come prepared," Alok said, not able to resist a smile of relief.

"Well, what do you expect? Give me a few minutes now." Ryan held the blade between his thumb and the forefinger and got to work. He slowly sliced the seal open as neatly as possible.

"Where did you learn all this?" I was impressed.

"I am training to be an engineer. This is not that hard to figure out. Now keep quiet," Ryan said.

"How long?" Alok said as sat down on the chair opposite to Cherian's. "Ten minutes. Quiet now else I'll rip off some of the paper," Ryan said. Two minutes passed. I looked at Alok, who sat with his hands in his face. I could tell he was thinking about home again.

"I hope Dad feels better soon. He can really fall sick if he doesn't eat properly. I wish I could do something."

Given Alok's family's love for food, I was pretty sure either of them would fall sick if deprived of it.

"Don't worry, it is nobody's fault. The guy's side seems too greedy if you ask me," I consoled.

"They are all the same. I just want to check on Dad. If only the bloody phone in Kumaon was working," Alok said.

"Yes!" Ryan said as he opened the seal with minimal damage. There were a hundred crisp sheets inside. The fresh copies of the major paper!

"Wow, it's the paper. Let me see it," I said.

"No. I know you guys. You'll just start discussing it right now. I am keeping this with me until we wrap up and get out of here," Ryan said.

"What else needs to be done," Alok said.

"I have to put a fresh seal. Why do you think I brought the candle?" Ryan said.

"Anyway, I think he'll take another million hours to finish," Alok said.

"Hurry up, Ryan," I said.

"Shut up," he said as he heated a fresh blob of wax on the candle. He looked like a craftsman intently at work.

"Hey Hari, Cherian's office has a phone," Alok said.

"Yes, it's right there," I said, pointing to the bookshelves where the instrument was kept.

"Maybe I can just make a quick call from here," Alok said.

"Really? Don't you want to wait and call from outside?"

"It'll get really late. Besides, I just need to check how Dad is. What else do we have to do now?"

"Okay," I shrugged.

Alok stood up and went near the phone.

"I think you have to dial nine to get an outside line," I said.

"Now what the heck are you guys doing? Can't you just sit still," Ryan scolded as he spooned molten wax from the fresh seal.

"Just calling home for a minute. It is too much to wait for you to finish," Alok said.

"Can't you call from outside," Ryan said, "or you are too cheap to spend a buck."

"I just need a minute. You just pay attention to the seal," Alok said as he dialled the number.

He got through pretty soon, and it was clear that his mother had been waiting for Alok to call back. Alok hardly spoke, as his mother vented about her miserable life and the hapless fate of his didi.

Ryan continued dabbing some fresh wax on the underside of the old seal. I tried to pass my time flipping through Ryan's lube proposal. This is when the wires got ahead of us.

I did not know this then, but this is how the insti phone system works. Each prof has a phone in the room that is part of the IIT network. One uses it mainly to dial internal campus numbers. To dial outside, the network connects to a few external lines. When nine is pressed, the internal phone requests an external line, and the campus telecom exchange switches the lines. A control switchboard in the telecom exchange does this automatically. The switchboard lights up a small red bulb for every engaged line. Every time one requests an external line, the light turns green. This control room is in the institute security office on the ground floor of the insti building. One night operator and a guard sit there at night, mostly gossiping and snoozing through their shift. So, a little red bulb lit up on one of the sixth floor phones, and then that red bulb turned green. What was Prof Cherian doing in his room this time of the night? the guard wondered. The operator had the option to listen in to the conversation if he wanted, and he did. This wasn't Prof Cherian. It was a mother reciting the sad tale of her daughter to someone called Alok. The security guard opened his walkie talkie, and requested patrolling guards to check on Cherian's room. The patrolling guard was joined by another guard as he walked up to the sixth floor.

Unfortunately, like I said, we did not know all this then.

"There are some comments given on some of the pages though," I said.

"All crap. Cherian just didn't want to give this project a shot. I have demonstrated results of efficiency improvements. How could he close this because of no viability? That bastard, ouch!" A drop of wax fell on his fingers.

"Don't worry. You concentrate on the seal. And hurry up, Alok," I said.

The two guards came and stood outside our door. They must have been standing there for two minutes before they opened the door. A lit candle, melted wax, someone on the prof's chair, a few strewn papers. The guards did not need to be too educated to figure it out.

Alok dropped the phone from his hand as he froze. His poor mother must have felt the phone go dead again. Actually, we all went dead. I froze in my chair too, and I don't know how, but Ryan figured out what to say first.

"Oh, guard sahib. Hello, come in let me explain," he said, trying to be as calm as possible.

"Who are you?"

"Guard sahib," Ryan said as he stood up, almost ready to dash out if needed. Alok and I came up behind him as well, waiting for any sudden instructions.

"Don't come near us," the guard said, "we are calling the prof now."

"Oh no guard sahib, listen to us," Ryan said as he went near the door. It was clear we had to make a dash now.

The guard picked up our intentions or something, or maybe he was just scared and stupid. He backed off, and shut us inside the office. We heard him bolt the door and tell his fellow guard to call the prof and the chief security officer. Ryan tried calling the guard again, but it was to no avail. There we were, three of us locked in Cherian's office on the sixth floor at midnight.

We didn't say a word, we just looked at each other's faces. We could do nothing but wait and wait and wait. The longest day of my life wouldn't get over...

19

The Longest Day of My Life IV

I KIND OF WENT INSIDE MYSELF IN THAT SHORT SPAN OF time before Cherian's office door opened again and sealed our fate, just sat quietly and ignored what Ryan and Alok said, that is if they did say anything. Future scenes erupted in my mind. By tomorrow morning, all profs, all students at Kumaon and other hostels would know about us. Caught stealing the major paper from Prof Cherian's office, no less! Probably the insti director would also come on this special occasion. Cherian would get us all shot if he could, but either way he would definitely not go easy on us. What did they call it? Disciplinary Committee or Disco, for deciding the fate of the students who broke discipline. Suddenly, my five-point GPA seemed wonderful to me. If only I could pass out of this place with a simple job and this could all be over. But even keeping that GPA and passing out was not going to be easy now. *Will Cherian soften if we grovelled? Should we just deny that we had come here to cheat? Should we just admit everything and apologize? Can we just rewind a few minutes and stop Alok from making that call? Could I just re-live this one day?*

These stupid questions darted about like rabbits inside my head. I took a deep breath; we just had to live through these moments.

"Someone's come," Ryan said and we stood up. The bolt was opened and around ten people swarmed in. I recognized the two security guards and the chief security officer by their uniforms. The other guy with them was the telephone exchange operator, I knew since he wore an insti uniform. These morons with dull jobs were the heroes of the day.

And then it was a couple of profs from the Mechanical Engineering department. Even Prof Veera was there. And of course, there was the man whose office we had temporarily occupied – Cherian. He stood there shocked, wondering how his office was broken into so cleanly. It was the Who's Who of IIT, most of them in their pajamas. People get more pissed off if they are disturbed in their pajamas.

The guard told everyone to come inside the room, keeping an eye on us as if we'd try to make a dash again.

"You?" Cherian said, looking straight at me. He must have been wondering: his daughter in the morning and his office in the evening. I'd be pissed if someone screwed all over my life in one day.

"What are you doing here?" Prof Veera said, probably aware of what we had been up to. The guard had told everyone what he had seen a million times; the candle, the seal and the major papers. Maybe Prof Veera was just giving us a chance to verbalize a good lie to get out of this.

We said nothing, hoping silence would evaporate us.

"Cheating, sir, stealing major paper. My boys caught them," the security chief said, proud as if they had broken a CIA ring.

"You were stealing the paper from my office? How did you get in?" Cherian asked me directly.

"You know him?" one of the profs asked Cherian.

"Not really. I have just seen him in class, a very poor student. He was even drunk in my viva, you know Dean Shastri. Yes, that is the only time I remember him from, Hari Kumar, isn't it?"

I guess Cherian did not want to mention our morning tryst to the rest of the profs.

"And the others? What are your names?" the Dean said.

"Alok Gupta, sir. Kumaon hostel, Mechanical Engineering," Alok said.

"Ryan Oberoi, same," Ryan said.

"And you think you are too smart?" the Dean said.

"No sir. That is why we wanted the paper, sir," Ryan said.

Slap! The Dean slapped Ryan right across the face. I don't blame him, Ryan could have chosen a better time to make a wisecrack.

Slap! Slap! Before I realized what was happening, the Dean deposited a slap on Alok and me as well.

God, I tell you, it was humiliating. Profs, security guards and Cherian all staring at us while our faces turned red on the left. But we kept quiet. I secretly hoped they would all slap us and get it out of their system. Heck, they could trash us senseless as long as that was the only punishment. Please don't do a Disco and screw with our career.

"You are criminals. You realize? You are criminals. Call the police," Cherian said, his whole being trembling, as if he was the one being slapped around.

He was walking to the phone when Prof Veera spoke, "Cherian sir, one minute before you call the police sir, this will become a big deal."

"It is a big deal," Cherian screamed out loud. Just slap us, Cherian, I thought. I know he wanted to, especially me.

"Dean Shastri, you explain to him. Police will mean the case will hit the papers. I mean, do you really want IIT in the news for all the wrong reasons," Prof Veera reasoned.

"Hmmm," Dean Shastri said, rubbing his hands.

"Sir, we have mechanisms in the insti to deal with this, right? The police will not arrive without reporters," Prof Veera said.

"Veera might be right. I don't want the IIT name in mud because of these miscreants."

Even in this situation, I felt the word 'miscreant' was quite cute and funny. I almost smiled.

"Sir, I don't want to spoil the IIT name either. But I want these boys to suffer. Who do they think they are?" Cherian said as he stopped cuddling the phone.

"I agree, this is quite outrageous. We cannot decide their fate so easily. We have a mechanism, not that we use it often. Take them to Disco."

It was time for us to shiver as we heard the last word. Maybe our silence was not so golden after all. Do something oh clever

Ryan, I wanted to say but he stood silent. Only Alok did something. In his usual manner, he began to cry.

"Sir, please sir. We are so sorry, sir..." he said.

"No more discussion. Bloody standard of these students falling every year. We'll talk in an urgent Disco — tomorrow!" declared the Dean.

"Dean sir, you can test intelligence in entrance exams, but how to test for integrity?" the security chief said. He probably got less credit for his achievement that night.

A crowd gathered around the Kumaon hostel notice board the next morning. On a small piece of paper, the size of a bank cheque, the short notice was enough to start long conversations.

"This is to inform that there will be a Disciplinary Committee meeting starting at 10:00 pm tonight in the Mechanical Engineering Department Conference Room. The agenda of the meeting is to decide the course of action for alleged disciplinary breaches by Hari Kumar (Kumaon), Alok Gupta (Kumaon) and Ryan Oberoi (Kumaon) on April 11."

The three of us were too ashamed to come to the notice board. We cut through the crowd as quickly as possible, even though we heard some questions.

"What happened?" said Anurag, "skipping too many classes or what?"

"That doesn't lead to a Disco. Must be something else."

"I think this is big. They are holding the Disco in one day," another Kumaonite said.

"Yes, at night too. Something to do with the Mechanical Engineering department."

We let the smart inmates of Kumaon figure out what was going on. We simply looked down and headed out of campus. Courtesy Neha, I knew a few places where no one would find us. The ice-cream parlour seemed perfect. Alok reached straight for the counter and came back with three strawberry cones.

"Ryan, you got cash? I don't have any," Alok said, passing us our treats.

"Fatso, you can't resist food even at this time," I said.

"It is ice-cream man. Just trying to distract myself, you know I didn't sleep for two seconds last night."

"Me neither," I said.

"What do you think they'll do?" Alok said.

"Maybe an F in Indem," Ryan hazarded a guess.

"An F! I have never got an F. And we'll have to repeat the course," Alok said.

"I know. But it is not the end of the world," Ryan said.

"Are you guys dreaming? They will hold a night-time Disco with all these profs and all to give just us a measly F?" I said.

Ryan and Alok looked at me as if I just stolen the cherry off their ice-cream.

"Sir, come to reality. The Disco meets rarely. And when they do, they have no mercy."

"So what can they do?" Alok said.

"They could expel you from college. Or more commonly, suspend you for a year or a semester."

"Expel?" Alok said, shivering as if the ice-cream had given him a cold.

"They won't expel. That has never happened. Even to people who have been caught stuffing coke bottles you know where," Ryan said.

"They could suspend you for a semester or a year. That is enough to fuck your future. You try getting a job after that," I said.

"For a whole semester? What will we do then?" Alok said. Looked like our man was just waking up.

I kept silent. Ryan finished his strawberry cone and tossed the tissue straight into the bin.

"Say something guys. What will happen then?"

"Figure it out Fatso. Your grade sheet will have no grades for a semester or two. It may actually have 'suspended' stamped all over it. Makes for a great conversation starter in a job interview, eh?" Ryan said.

"I think no one will give you a job, the bloody US types take this cheating stuff pretty seriously. No admission to MBA colleges either – they will ask the same in an interview."

"In other words, our lives are screwed," I said, noticing I had not touched my ice-cream. The cone was a gooey mess, I passed it to Ryan to chuck into the bin.

"And you guys are calm about it? How can you be so calm about it? What will my parents think? What will happen to Didi?" Alok said, putting his elbows on the table and pulling at his hair. Then he tucked his face in his arms, to hide his tears.

"Who the hell says I am calm about it?" Ryan said and stood up, his voice loud enough to stir the sleepy cashier at the counter.

"Be quiet and sit down. There might be people from the insti here," I said.

"Fuck the people. And fuck the insti. And fuck this Fatso who feels only he loses sleep at night and cares about his future! Wake up Mr Alok, this is not the time to cry and pull hair. We have a bloody Disco in ten hours, and maybe we should think about how we are going to answer the bloody profs."

"Oh yes," Alok stood up this time. I guess it is easier to shout when you are standing up. "Oh yes, Mr Ryan," Alok said, "so it is you with all the brains to think strategy at this moment. I say, fuck you and your strategy. What happened to Operation Pendulum?"

It was pointless for me to try and keep them quiet. They needed this I guess.

"Operation Pendulum? You are telling me that was bad strategy? Which bloody baby had to call Mom?" Ryan said.

"Oh yes. And which IITian in history breaks into a prof's office? 'Nothing can happen'. My bloody ass nothing can happen."

They argued for five minutes after which I broke into tears. They were coming on their own, even though I didn't think this Disco would get the better of me. Man, I was crying like Alok. It was embarrassing as hell, but at least they noticed me.

"What is wrong with you now?" Ryan said.

"Nothing. Just stop shouting both of you. This won't help. We need each other now."

"He is right. Sit down, Fatso," Ryan said.

All of us sat in the ice-cream parlour for the next five hours. Over two banana toffee cones, one mint chocolate chip and three raspberry delights we figured out the best arguments to save our lives. There was little hope, but we had to do what we could. Our strategy was hardly creative – it was to be honest, stay calm and beg for mercy. We only reached Kumaon at six p.m., where I had at least six phone messages from Prof Veera. He wanted to see us before the Disco, and we agreed to meet him at nine.

"You got duplicate what made?" Prof Veera asked again, more in shock at the story we had told him.

"Keys sir. For six rupees at Jia Sarai," I said.

Prof Veera sat back in his chair and burst into laughter.

"This is incredible. I have never heard this in IIT. So Ryan, you thought you could just go into the head of department's office and steal the paper and end up with an A."

"Yes sir," Ryan said in a suitably humble voice.

"And you Hari went and sneaked out the keys from Neha, who you say is your girlfriend, so that you could steal from her dad's office."

"That is correct, sir," I said.

"And you Alok, just went along with this crazy plan of theirs."

"They are my friends, sir," Alok said.

I have to say this statement touched me. For a moment, I forgot the hell around me and felt good that Alok found that reason enough.

"You guys are idiots. You know, just big idiots, that is what you are," Prof Veera said. He seemed pretty harsh, but we liked him. Besides, he was right.

"Sir, we almost made it. Alok made this phone call…" Ryan said.

"Almost made it?" Prof Veera interrupted, "is that what it is all about? You think I am calling you an idiot because you got caught?" The tone of Prof Veera's voice had become firmer. This was the closest he got to being real mad.

"You, Ryan Oberoi, I thought was one of the most brilliant students we had ever had. Your lube project was the best work I have seen come out of a student. I don't care about your grades at all. But you were stupid enough to risk your future for a stupid letter on your grade sheet."

Ryan hung his head.

"And the three of you are best friends. But none of you was able to stop each other from this madness. You know Cherian would have thrown you into jail."

"Sir, we'll say we are sorry sir. Maybe they will be kind," Alok said.

"Kind? This is the Disco, not Mother Teresa's home. You saw Cherian's face," Prof Veera said.

The three of us became silent. We could hear the clock ticking in Prof Veera's office. It was nine-thirty.

"So what is your plea to the Disco? Guilty or not guilty?" Prof Veera said.

"Guilty. They caught us red-handed sir," I said.

"Hmm. I think the first thing you have to do is get the expulsion stuff out of the way," Prof Veera said.

"You mean there is a chance?" Alok said.

"Not too high, unless Cherian is hell-bent on it. What are you going to say about the keys?" Prof Veera said.

"I don't want to bring Neha into this. I thought we'd just say we collected lots of keys and tried them until one worked," I said.

"Why not tell them the truth? You have told me everything," Prof Veera said.

"I don't want Neha to know," I said.

"Listen boys, I am trying to help you here. I think you are in a big mess but if you can twist this a bit, you may save yourself some trouble."

"Like how?"

"One, we should try and present some alternatives of punishment. I will be there, so I can suggest an F in the course, a public apology and hundred hours of community service."

"What is community service?" Ryan said.

"Just helping around in the campus – painting cycle parks or planting trees - that kind of stuff," Prof Veera said.

"I hate that stuff," Ryan said.

"Shut up Ryan. That is fine. Please continue sir," I said.

"Two, I want you to twist the story a bit. I hate lying, but you won't have much of a chance otherwise. So, instead of saying you tried different keys, say that Neha gave the keys to you," Prof Veera said.

"What?" all three of us said in unison.

"Listen, if you say that you know Neha, and somehow she was upset with her father and gave you the keys to get even, it will get personal. The Disco committee will think you didn't actually break in. I don't know, they may see right through it, but I think you should take a chance."

"What will Neha think when she finds out?" I said, "No way we can do this."

"An upset girlfriend is better than a tainted degree and no jobs after college," Prof Veera said.

"Prof Veera is right Hari," Ryan said, "you bring Cherian's family into this and he may withdraw. Last thing he wants is everyone to know that you are his daughter's boyfriend."

"But this will let the whole world know," I said.

"You don't have to tell the whole story. Just say Neha is a recent friend of yours. I am sure Cherian will not dispute that," Alok said.

"Alok, even you think this is the way?" I said.

"Yes, we have to save our ass right? C'mon, it is just a last-ditch survival strategy. Last-ditch survival," Alok said.

I hated myself for agreeing to that story. What would Neha think when she heard what I said? That she helped me by giving the keys? She'd probably hate me forever. The clock struck ten, and it was time to go to the departmental committee room.

Romance was secondary to survival right now.

20

The Longest Day of My Life V

THE IIT DISCO IS ABOUT AS FAR AWAY FROM DANCING AS it can get. Here the lighting is dull, the room dead silent and almost everyone elderly. Around ten profs sat around a semi-circular table, while the accused students were bang in the centre. Profs fire questions at students from all directions, the location placing us at minimum distance to each one of them. It is essentially a more efficient design of a courtroom, I guess, Indem-inspired.

Dean Shastri asked us to take our places. Dean Shastri, Director Verma and Prof Cherian formed the co-chairpersons. Prof Veera was one of the other seven profs who mattered little in the scheme of things. A lot of them yawned, probably used to being in bed at this time. Of course, for their students, dumped with another set of assignments, the night would have just begun.

"May the disciplinary committee begin, fellow co-chairs," Dean Shastri said in what I felt was a complete waste of courtesy.

"You may begin," the Director and Prof Cherian said. I guess this formality gave them an extra sense of power.

What if I was speechless today, I thought and sweat broke out all over me. All the profs opened the special Disco file, which contained a description of last night's shenanigans.

Ryan noticed my nervousness. It is amazing how people who know you well can sense everything. "Hari," he whispered.

I looked at him.

"I know what you are worried about. Remember, this is not a viva. If you don't open your trap here, you will be in deeper crap than a bloody zero. You understand, don't you?"

"Uh, yes," I said.

"And I want you to know that even though I hate to admit it, you are a bloody stud," Ryan said.

"Why?"

"Because, in front of you lies a man who controls your future right now. Yet, whatever he may do, he can't take away one fact."

"What?"

"That you went and slept with his only daughter in broad daylight. That my friend is a true stud," Ryan said.

"You think so?" I perked up.

"I do. I salute you man. I am proud to have a friend like you," Ryan said.

I beamed.

"No talking amongst the students," Dean Shastri said and looked up from his file.

"Sorry sir," I said. Ryan and I pointed thumbs at each other. Damn it, I could answer these old bozos any time.

"Mr Hari Kumar, the files here state that you were found in Prof Cherian's office last night with two friends. Is that right?" Dean Shastri said.

"Yes sir," I said.

"Ryan Oberoi, we learn that security found you with a candle, wax seal and the packet of major papers in hand. Is that right?"

"Yes, sir," Ryan agreed.

"Alok Gupta, we learn that it was you who was making a call from Prof Cherian's phone last night."

Alok nodded.

"Do you boys realize the gravity of this incident?" the director said.

"Yes sir, we got carried away sir," I said. Man, I was surprised I was taking the initiative to answer these questions.

Other questions were part-rhetoric, part-moral in nature. I can't even remember all of them now, it was about integrity and strength of character and all that stuff. We just apologized, probably a million times. Ultimately they asked the question we were waiting for.

"How did you get into my office?" Prof Cherian said.

"We had the keys, sir," Ryan said.

"How did you get the keys?" He looked baffled.

"Sir, we sir..." I said and turned silent. No, I couldn't do this.

"Hari's friend Neha gave it to us," Ryan supplied.

"Who is Neha?" Dean Shastri asked.

"Neha Cherian is Prof Cherian's daughter. I know her as a friend for the past three months," I said.

The room fell silent as Dean Shastri and Director Verma's mouths went slack. They turned toward Prof Cherian, as if he was next in the firing line. But that was not Disco protocol.

"What? You sure of what you are talking about?" Dean Shastri said.

"I am. She was upset with her father and wanted to get even. She offered the keys and we got carried away," I said.

There were not too many questions after that. But somehow, every prof wanted to talk to their neighbour. Even the seven sleepy profs woke up; this was more interesting than a simple caught-red-handed case.

Cherian whispered something in Dean Shastri's and Director Verma's ears. Dean Shastri nodded and made an announcement.

"We are done with investigating the students. I think we now need to deliberate in the committee to come up with the important decision. This may take some time, even a couple of hours. But once we finish, we will have a final decision. No appeals, no pleas. The students may leave now."

Dean Shastri signaled us to leave the room. We left the Disco room and came out to the campus lawns.

"How do you think that went?" Alok said.

I shrugged my shoulders. The thought of Neha kicked me in the stomach.

"Who knows? Let's wait near here," Ryan said, sitting down on the wet midnight grass.

"It could take hours," I said.

"What else do we have to do? But let's not wait near here. Let's go to the insti roof," Alok said.

I liked the idea of the insti roof. It was the one place where we felt secure now, as even Kumaon was difficult to be in right now, with a million eyes on us.

"How will we find out they are done?" Ryan said.

"We'll keep looking down. The corridor light is on. When they come out, we should be able to see something."

"Fine, let's go up," Ryan said.

We sat on the roof of the institute building, each of us five feet apart at the ends of an imaginary triangle. The moon shone too audaciously for what is, after all, just reflected light. It was different on the roof that day. I hated myself for dragging Neha into this. In fact, I hated myself for being a cheat. And for everything else – agreeing to duplicate the keys, being a part of Operation Pendulum and bringing my life to this. *How did I get here? I was a topper in my school all my life. That is how I got into IIT, right? But then why am I now a low-performer, five-point something cheat sitting on the insti roof at midnight, unsure of my future?*

It is funny how your mind comes up with questions. Damn it, it is up to the mind to come out with the answers, so why can't it just keep its doubts to itself? I realized I was not making sense. Two sleepless nights in a row didn't help. But the questions would not stop.

I looked at my friends. *Friends? What the hell is that anyway? Who is this Alok? And what the fuck do I care that his father is half-dead and his sister can't be married without cash?* Then I turned to look at Ryan. Yes, the stylish, smart and confident Ryan. The man who was so sure of himself, he could take on the world. He wanted his revenge on Cherian. *Now what exactly is the point of that?* Doesn't seem like all his ideas are quite so smart after all. *Why do I listen to him and not Alok? And why is everybody so quiet now?*

I bent my head to check the time on Ryan's Swiss watch. It was three in the morning.

"Tea?" Ryan said, rubbing his hands.

"No, I'm already wide awake, thank you," I said.

"Yeah. I am fine too," Alok said.

Tea. That is the best Ryan can come up with right now. A shot of caffeine as compensation for throwing away everything that mattered to us.

"It's cold here," Ryan said.

I nodded my head. Yes Ryan, it is miserably cold, infect, almost like a December night in Delhi, I wanted to say. But you know what, I don't feel it. There are more important miserable things happening right now. Like we could be thrown out of IIT in a few hours, and may never find a respectable education or job again. I chose another response. "Yes, must be five degrees," I said.

Half an hour passed. Ryan stood up and walked to the precipice of the roof. Nine stories high, this is the highest point in the institute. Yet, there is no parapet, as the roof is officially out of bounds. One step more and Ryan could enjoy his last few seconds of free-fall weightlessness. He stands on the edge and bends forward to look down. He extends one leg out.

"What are you doing?" Alok said.

Yes, what exactly are you doing Ryan, I thought. Haven't we lived on the edge long enough? Isn't our life screwed up enough already? Can't we wait for the Disco results in silence without engaging in attention-seeking behaviour, please?

"Come back, Ryan," I called out.

He turned around. "It is really high here." Slowly, he retreated and came back to where he'd been sitting.

Yes, it is high. Yes, it is cold. Any other insightful statements, sir, I wondered.

If there is one thing men completely lack, it is the ability to communicate during tough moments. Alok and I have no words at all, while the best Ryan can come up with is comments on our thermodynamic and spatial state. So different from Neha who always has something appropriately verbal for any occasion. But there won't be any more Neha after this, especially after Alok's so called "last-ditch survival" strategy in the Disco interview. No more Neha — my stomach churns as the fact finally registers. So here I am, sitting with my two best friends, one will get me thrown out of the college that I worked two years to get into and endured for another three years. The other has ended whatever semblance of a love life I ever had.

"You think the Disco might be lenient?" Alok said.

"It is the disciplinary committee, not a joke. You know the Disco never spares," I said.

Disco, what a name, I find it funny even at this hour, even when I am in the middle of it.

Ryan looked up at both of us. "This was all a bad idea," he said.

Thank you, Ryan. It is cold, it is very high and yes, Operation Pendulum was a bad idea. Just keep these obvious statements coming.

We heard a noise downstairs at four-thirty. A few scooters started, as tired profs wanted to rush back home. That was our cue; the results were out.

"C'mon guys, we need to race down," I said.

"Yes, let's go. Prof Veera should be there," Ryan said.

"I am going to stay here. Just come back and tell me," Alok said.

"Just come down, Fatso," Ryan said.

"No, I can't face the profs when they tell me," he said.

"Whatever then. Let us go, Hari," Ryan said.

We ran down the stairs. Most of the profs had left. Dean Shastri, Cherian and Veera remained.

"Prof Veera sir," Ryan said as he approached him from behind.

"Ryan," Prof Veera said, "just a second."

Prof Veera spoke to Cherian and Dean Shastri for a few more minutes. Soon all of them wished each other good night. Cherian went to his car, the one that had allowed all this to happen.

"Sir?" I said.

"Ryan and Hari, you have not been expelled," Prof Veera said.

"Really? So what was the decision?" I said.

"We talked for hours. There was divided opinion, but ultimately the Disco decided that the three of you are suspended for one semester."

"Sir?" I said.

"I tried guys. But the Disco doesn't go easy. You lose a semester, which means you have only one last semester to do fourth year courses. Also, you get an F in Indem, and you have to repeat it again. Not to mention the final year project. As of now, insti rules do not allow to take that much course-load," Prof Veera said.

"So we have to do courses next year. And we can't sit for job interviews either," I said.

"I am afraid so. I tried talking to Prof Cherian about allowing some project credit in the suspended semester. I asked if you guys could work with me. But he just said no. Suspension means full suspension."

"It's over. Our grade sheets are ruined. We can't get a job. And we have to wait an extra year to get a useless degree," I said.

Ryan kept silent.

"I am sorry it turned out this way guys," Prof Veera said, patting our shoulders. He walked past us to his scooter. A few seconds and some exhaust smoke later, he was gone.

We climbed up to the insti roof, where Alok waited with his hands folded. Maybe he was praying. Or maybe he was just cold.

"Kicked out for one sem. F in Indem. Need to stay until next year to complete course," Ryan said, summing it up for Alok.

"What?" Alok said, coming out of his trance.

"Prof Veera tried, saved an expulsion. But it is still pretty screwy. I don't know what we'll do," I said.

We sat down again. It was five a.m., just one hour before daybreak.

Alok stood up without saying anything. I wished he would, as his face seemed tense as hell. He walked to the edge of the roof where Ryan had stood just an hour back.

"You were right Ryan. It is pretty high here," Alok said.

"You okay Alok?" Ryan said.

"Yes. You think only you can stand on the edge of the roof?" Alok asked.

"No. Just come back and let us go down. I have had enough," Ryan said.

Alok continued to look down as he replied, "For once Ryan, I agree with you. I've had enough too. I think I'll just go down."

There was something messed up in the tone of Alok's voice. I turned around to look at him. He stood straight, then one jump up and then straight down. In half a second, he was out of sight. Gravity had done its job.

21

The Longest Day of My Life VI

I HAD NEVER BEEN INSIDE AN AMBULANCE BEFORE. IT WAS kind of creepy inside. Like a hospital was suddenly asked to pack up and move. Instruments, catheters, drips and a medicine box surrounded two beds. There was hardly any space for me and Ryan to stand even as Alok got to sprawl out. I guess with thirteen fractures you kind of deserve a bed. The sheets were originally white, which was hard to tell now as Alok's blood covered every square inch of them. Alok lay there unrecognizable, his eyeballs rolled up and his tongue collapsed outside his mouth like an old man without dentures. Four front teeth gone, the doctor later told us.

His limbs were motionless, just like his father's right side, the right knee bent in a way that would make you think Alok was boneless. He was still, and if I had to bet my money, I'd have said he was dead.

"If Alok makes it through this, I will write a book about our crazy days. I really will," I swore. It is the kind of absurd promise you make to yourself when you are seriously messed up in the head and you haven't slept for fifty hours straight...

The ambulance took us to AIIMS, the biggest hospital in Delhi. The blood and two sleepless nights had made me numb. I don't know who called the ambulance, or who made the choice of hospital. Maybe it was the security guard. Everyone around me seemed to be acting urgently.

More medical professionals at the AIIMS emergency ward. This was a government hospital, so lots of people but little service. Ryan screamed at a few of them, shaking them into action.

"Nine stories?" one of the stretcher-bearers asked, probably wondering if it was even worth it to carry this heavy weight to the intensive care unit.

The doctor told us to leave the ICU and wait outside. Damn, I was tired of waiting. I sat outside on a wooden stool. Relatives of patients fighting for life inside sat around me; mothers, daughters, sons and fathers. I tried fighting sleep, but it wouldn't work.

Ryan woke me up at noon. My entire left side had cramped.

"He is going to make it! Doctor said it is pretty bad, but he is going to make it!"

"What? How? I mean really?"

"Yes, he fell on his bottom, right into the fountain by the insti building. Can you believe that? Doctor said his fat bottom and the six inches of water cushioned the impact."

Thank god Alok was a fatso. And thank god they made that useless fountain by the insti building. Eleven fractures in the legs and two in the arms isn't so bad. Given how much Fatso eats, he could probably build his bones back in a day.

"I thought he'd die, I really thought he would," I said and hugged Ryan. And then I started crying. I don't know why I did an Alok then. It was embarrassing but kind of okay in a hospital.

"Is he awake?"

"Not much. But mostly because he hadn't slept for two days. Let us go pinch his butt," Ryan said.

We went inside the ICU and saw Alok asleep.

"Patient needs time to rest," the nurse said and signalled us to keep quiet. We left the ICU and took a bus back to Kumaon.

On our way back in the bus, Ryan turned to me. "You know Hari, I owe Fatso a lot."

"Really?" I said.

"If it weren't for him, I would have never studied to even reach a five-pointer," Ryan said.

I guess he was right. It was only he who brought us to our books. And now as he lay there, we didn't have any books to study from.

"You think he will be okay?" Ryan said.

"He will Ryan. He will," I said and hugged Ryan. For the first time, he felt more heavy than strong. He hugged me back tighter.

"I am sorry Hari," Ryan said and his voice sounded like he was fighting back tears, "I am sorry."

"It's okay, we can get through this," I said.

All of us needed time to rest. And we had time — four months of it — to take all the rest in the world.

22

Ryan Speaks

I BLEW IT. DAMN, FATSO WAS IN THE ICU BATTLING TO *breathe. That really was disaster, eh? This whole Operation Pendulum was a mistake — in hindsight of course. It could all have been different you know. If Fatso had just not tried to save a buck and make that phone call, or better yet, if he hadn't come at all. If nothing else, at least he should have known better than to jump. What is it with Alok, or for that matter, even with Hari? When will they grow up?*

Now you will say, I really don't want to accept that it was my fault. Ryan will blame anyone — his parents, his friends, his college, even god — anyone but himself. He is that boy with the grudge!

I don't blame you. You are reading Hari's version. How can he be the bad guy, right? After all, Hari is just a bumbling IITian who can't get his grades or life in order. He is just kind-hearted and confused – hopelessly in love, physically unappealing, wants to keep his friends together, fumbles in   vivas – whatever, whatever, whatever. Can't help but feel sorry for that guy right?

Did it ever occur to you that at one level Mr Sorryboy has a layer to him that he doesn't want to unpeel and will not bring up in his, yes that is the key word – HIS, book? Like he will never really bring up his parents. Or if you think he will reveal the big bad story about why his vivas get screwed up – sorry, no luck there. Or why does he always make fun of Alok's family – I mean it is funny but it isn't what you could call sensitive.

No, he won't go into all that. Maybe I can touch on it at least (too much and he'll edit it right out). But before that, I want to come back to Alok. Man – you don't jump nine stories because some old bozos do a Disco on you. Or if you can't pay for the car that will buy your sis a loser for the rest of her life. Why is he so stupid? If he was so mad, he should have pushed me instead.

You know what, despite what you might think, I like Alok. Yes, we fight, we argue and sometimes I hate his mugger-whiner guts. But at the end of the day, the guy lives a selfless life. He doesn't really want to get that high average in the quiz. Damn, he doesn't even want to be an IITian (but then, who would). It is something he does for his folks back home, day after day after day. Just as he has been serving his dad since he was twelve, locked in that room full of books, medicines and misery. That is why he never grew up. That is why he thinks its okay to – ugh – cry at twenty.

And that is why he never had fun. But does that mean he doesn't want to? Why do you think he stuck with us? Or why did he come back? Because at one level, he knew that he wasn't

Venkat. He was just a boy who wanted to be an artist — and couldn't become one. And he was a boy who never had real friends in his life — but he wanted them. And when I saved him from that hideous ragging, it wasn't something that happened to him every day. So he stuck with me, and fought with me, and cursed me and hated me — while all he was doing was fighting, cursing and hating himself. I shook his convictions — one didn't have to care for parents at all costs, one didn't have to accept the system, one didn't have to sacrifice fun. I pushed him, he resisted and liked it at the same time. And I pushed some more, and more, until I went too far. God, please let him live.

But Hari? Him I want to ask a few questions. Like what's with your parents Hari? Is there going to be no chapter covering that? What about your Dad — the colonel in the army? What is the rule in the house — no TV, no music, no laughing loud? It is all for discipline, right?

And your mother — she turns silent for days, right? Oh, wait a minute, I am not supposed to talk about that. What about the belt your father hangs in the closet. Do you still dream of that sometimes, Hari? He told you not to answer back. If you answer your superiors back, you will be punished. Severely. Is it viva-time? Does it still hurt, Hari?

Okay, I think I am pushing it. Hari is okay, he just has some issues he doesn't want to talk about. And just because one writes a book doesn't mean one has to bare all. After all, this is a book about IIT — the place where one makes a future. What is the point of digging up the past?

So let me come back to IIT. Hari (with more vodka inside him than he can handle) once told me his view on friendship.

He said, "Ryan, you are stupid to want to sacrifice so much for your friends. In some ways, it is the same madness that Alok has for his family. Both of you have lost touch with what you really want."

Profound eh? So, I asked him if he was in touch with what he wanted. And he nodded.

"What do you want?" I asked.

"To be you."

"What?" I hadn't heard right!

"I want Neha," he said and passed out, the horny bastard.

So what's the deal here — he may not live for others, but he wants to be like others? Confused, I tell you.

23

Kaju-burfi

TWO MONTHS INTO OUR SUSPENDED SEMESTER, ALOK finally returned to Kumaon. The casts were still on, and doctors said that even when they came off, he would be left with a slight limp in his left leg. Small price to pay for one's life I guess, though it meant Alok would never forget that night for the rest of his life.

We visited him daily in the hospital, as we had nothing else to do anyway. We never discussed going home for the semester. Somehow, we knew we had to stay in Kumaon and be near each other. No one really talked to us much. If they did, they only wanted to know the inside story — what we did, what was the Disco like, why did Alok jump etc. It suited us to stick to our rooms and limit our outside trips to the hospital.

Alok swore us into keeping his high jump a secret from his family. His bones healed gradually and after a month he could at least hop-and-walk to the toilet and not embarrass himself with company there. Though docs had warned us not to mention the fall, Ryan couldn't resist asking once, "Stupid or what?"

But Alok kept silent. A couple of times, Prof Veera visited at the hospital. He kept our spirits high, saying how he would try to get us to take extra course-work in the last semester to complete our credits. He even unsuccessfully tried talking to Cherian on a mercy plea.

Prof Veera even came to Kumaon, to welcome Alok back. "So Tiger, you are back in your den," he greeted.

Alok was sitting on my bed, his torso propped up on pillows. "Sir, you shouldn't have bothered to come."

"No big deal," Prof Veera dismissed and took out a box from his bag, "Here have some sweets. On Alok's return home and for something else."

Alok looked at the box and almost snatched it out of Prof Veera's hand. When it comes to food, Fatso forgets all formalities. The box contained *kaju-burfi*, his all-time favourite.

"You shouldn't have, sir," he said, the three pieces stuffed in his mouth muffling his voice.

"Just enjoy guys. Thirteen bones broken and home in two months, that is worth celebrating," Prof Veera said, stroking Alok's head.

We were happy at Alok's return too, and now at the box of *kaju-burfis*. If only Alok would leave the box alone for one second.

"Sir, what was the other reason for the sweets?" Ryan eventually enquired.

"Yes, of course. I have some good news for you guys finally," Prof Veera said.

"What? Cherian wants to do another Disco?" Ryan said.

"Easy Ryan," Prof Veera said, "I know it has not been cool for you guys. But this time I arranged it through the Dean."

"What?" Alok and I said in unison.

"You remember the lube project? Well, Prof Cherian never approved further research, but I went to the Dean and said we would like to revise and re-submit our proposal based on Prof Cherian's feedback."

"I am not working on any feedback from that bastard," Ryan declared.

"Will you relax, Ryan? Sir, why would we re-submit?" I said.

"That is where lies my idea. If they allowed us to re-submit, we will do some more experimentation in the lab to prove that our lube additives do have potential. In some ways, doing some of the research at the proposal stage," Prof Veera said.

"And?" Ryan squinted his eyes.

"And that means you guys can help do those experiments. I asked the Dean if he would allow you guys to work in the lab to revise the work we had done, since it will be a productive use of your time. And the good news is the Dean agreed. Of course, on a non-credit basis."

Ryan snatched the box away from Alok's hands, took two pieces of the sweets, and sat down to light a cigarette. "Will someone explain what will be the point of this? Working our butts off for no reason," he said.

"There maybe a benefit," Prof Veera said, pulling the cigarette out of Ryan's mouth and stubbing it on the floor, "for one, you could later explain the absence in your grade sheet. And I don't know, if they like the proposal this time, you may be allowed extra credit for this work in the next semester."

"Really?" Alok said, "You mean we will be able to graduate like normal students, in four years?"

"Wow! Sounds like you gave it a lot of thought Prof Veera," I said.

"Cherian will never allow it. I am not falling for this," Ryan said.

"Maybe he won't. But if the work is good and the Dean likes it, who knows? At least you have something to do in your spare time."

"We have plenty to do in our spare time," Ryan said.

"Ryan, will you talk properly to Prof Veera," I said. Somehow, the Disco had changed my attitude toward Ryan. It had become easier for me to tell him things he didn't want to hear. He didn't argue much either.

"It is okay Hari. Ryan is obviously mistrustful of everything about the insti. But guys, this is the only chance you got. And if you do more work on the lube proposal, who knows, we might get an industry sponsor this time?"

"Sir is right, Ryan. And we can't do this without you. It is your project."

"You guys really want to do this?" Ryan said.

"Yes," Alok and I said.

"On one condition then," Ryan said.

"What?" Prof Veera said.

"I get the rest of the *kaju-burfi*," Ryan said.

"Ten o' clock in my lab then, we start tomorrow," Prof Veera said even as we burst into laughter.

24

Will we Make It?

NEHA. THE NAME THAT DID NOT ALLOW ME TO SLEEP nights.

True, my engineering degree was in the dumps. True, we probably pointlessly slaved in Prof Veera's lab mixing one type of grease with another all day. True, I may get expletives in my grade sheet that would prevent me from getting a decent job. However, none of these bothered me enough to cause insomnia. In fact, the four months off were great to catch up on sleep. But the one person whose voice, smell, image, feelings crept up next to me at night and made sleep impossible was Neha.

I tried calling her on an eleventh. She hung up in two minutes, telling me she never expected me to be like this. I guess for someone she called a loafer, she had pretty high expectations.

I had called right back, trying to explain in vain how the whole idea was not mine, and it was stupid for me to fall for it.

"You used me Hari. Like all men, you used me," she said. *Like all men? How many men had she been with anyway, I thought. What has she been reading these days, some Femina-Cosmo crap?*

I was just trying to sneak out a major paper. Okay, it was pretty sick of me to duplicate the keys — but I did it only because it was convenient. Ryan would have found another way in any case. I tried telling her that, but she was like 'you men just don't get it, do you?' I thought she wasn't getting it either, but I still loved her like mad.

"And you told the Disco I gave you the keys? I Hari? You know Dad still believes that?"

Wow, I was kind of glad Cherian believed it. How would Neha understand? If they knew we had duplicated the keys, we would have resembled those real criminals. We probably were real criminals. But that was not the point. *Man, why is it so hard to explain stuff to girls. Can't she just get on with it? Should I say something dumb that she wants to hear?*

"Neha, I know I did all those things. But at one level, it wasn't me. It wasn't your Hari," I said. Obviously, I made no sense. But that is the thing with girls. Give them confusing crap and they fall for it.

"Then why Hari? Why?"

"I don't know. Can I just meet you once?" I said.

"No way. We are through."

She hung up after that and took her phone off the hook for the rest of the day. It meant I had to wait another month, or suffer another thirty sleepless nights.

Then the next eleventh came around, and I couldn't wait to make that call.

Woke up at ten the next morning. The eleventh finally, I told myself and left my room immediately. I had to make my call fast and think up really good lines this time. I was on my way downstairs when I noticed an elderly lady come up. Probably someone's parent, I thought even as I couldn't help thinking she looked familiar. Then it struck me – Alok's mom.

"Hello Aunty. It is me, Hari," I said.

"Oh hello Hari beta. Where have you all been? I had to come to the hostel because Alok hasn't been home for two months. Is he all right?" she asked, breathing heavily.

"Huh? Alok is fine Aunty. Must have been busy with the project," I said, thinking of a way to prevent her from meeting Alok.

"Uncle is downstairs in an auto. Call him quickly, we are all worried for him," she said.

"Yes Aunty sure," I said as I ran up. Alok was sitting on his bed, reading a magazine and eating chips.

Ryan sat next to him, a porno mag in hand, his cigarette filling Alok's room with smoke.

"Are you guys nuts? Smoking and porn early morning," I tut-tutted.

"What are you so worked up about? Why not do the best things when one is still fresh," Ryan said.

"Alok, your parents are here," I said.

"What?" Alok said as the chips in his hands fell.

"Yes, your mom is climbing the stairs. She sounds mad and worried you didn't call."

"You mean she is coming here?" Alok said, waving his hands to get rid of the cigarette smoke.

"Yes, and I think she is going to see your broken bones now."

"Fuck," Alok said.

"Just stay in bed. We'll cover your legs with sheets," Ryan said, stuffing the porno under Alok's mattress.

"Can't. His dad is downstairs waiting to see his only son," I said and dug into the chips. It was fun to see these two guys worked up now.

"Fuck. Fuck. Fuck," Alok said, trying to arrange his pillows.

"And I think you should keep the curses down," I said.

Alok's mom knocked about a minute later. It is amazing how much can get done in a minute. Ryan threw out the ashtrays, pornos and vodka bottles. He also arranged the course books and assignments on the study table. All dirty clothes stayed hidden in an overstuffed cupboard.

"Hello Mom. What a pleasant surprise," Alok said.

"Alok. I am not talking to you. You have completely forgotten us," Alok's mom said as she put boxes of sweets on the study table. I wondered if it was okay for us to strike at them now.

"I was busy," Alok said.

"Shut up. Two months have passed. You haven't called since that day you called about Dad and Didi's proposal. What happened? You don't want to talk about our problems?"

"No Mom. It is just this assignment for Prof Veera. It keeps us so busy," Alok said.

"My son works too hard," Alok's mom said looking at me and Ryan, "You guys should take a break now and then. After all, your jobs are just a semester away," she said.

Ryan and I smiled, continuing to stare at the boxes of food. *Please Aunty, offer them once.*

"Alok, you must come home next weekend. Look, even Dad had to come all the way in an auto," she said.

"You took an auto! It is seventy rupees," Alok said.

"So what to do with Dad? And after all, my son will be working soon," Alok's mom said, "and Hari, why don't you have some *laddoos* I made."

Ryan and I jumped on the boxes before she finished her sentence.

"Mom but still," Alok said.

"Keep quiet. Look Didi also sent this new pair of jeans for you. She saved her pocket money you know," she said, passing a brown bag.

"Thanks Mom. I'll keep it for a special occasion," Alok said.

"But at least try it now. Come get up," Alok's mom said.

"No Mom. I'll do it later," Alok said.

"What later? We can change size now if it doesn't fit. Don't be lazy get up," Alok's mom said, shaking Alok's leg. I am sure that hurt.

"No Mom," Alok said, clenching his teeth.

"Get up," Alok's mom insisted, pulling the bed sheet off him. She shouldn't have. For Alok still had the signs — plaster casts covered both thighs and legs. The feet still showed marks where doctors had done the stitches. It was something even we didn't fancy seeing.

"Oh my god," Alok's mom said as her face dropped along with her hands. "Mom please," Alok said, pushing her away and wishing she had never come.

Alok's mom felt nauseous and Ryan had to help support her back to a chair. I gave her a glass of water.

"What is going on? Will someone please tell me?" she said.

Ryan looked at me. It was time for us to leave the room.

"We'll go downstairs. We'll say hello to Uncle and say Alok is in the lab. Okay Aunty?"

She nodded, her eyes filling with tears. Could any male in her family stand up on his own legs?

"Easy Mom. It was a scooter accident that night..." Alok said as we shut the door behind them. I was sure she'd know he was lying. A scooter accident with Ryan and me perfectly fine was somewhat unbelievable. We saw her leave after half an hour, wiping her tears. We stood by the auto, trying to make conversation with Alok's dad. He was in a happy mood, probably enjoying his rare day out.

"Alok busy eh?" he said, pursing his lips.

"Yes. They have an important project," Alok's mom said, sitting in the auto.

"Bye Aunty," Ryan and I waved.

"Back to Rohini madam?" the auto driver said, starting the scooter.

"No. Take me to the Mechanical Engineering department."

"Aunty?" we chorused.

"There are things which a mother can sense, even though her son may not talk about it. I want to meet your Prof Veera before I go home," she said as the auto buzzed off.

"She'll find out. She'll find out about the Disco," I said, shaking Ryan's shoulder.

"Let her. She deserves it," Ryan said as he put his arm around me.

We went to Sasi's for breakfast after Alok's mom left.

"I have to make my call today," I said.

"Is she real mad at you?" Ryan said.

"She was a month ago. She's got to miss me right?" I said.

"I don't know. What is the whole deal about missing people and not doing anything about it anyway?" Ryan said, and took out a brown envelope from his jeans pocket.

Sasi served a plate of paranthas. Ryan left the letter on the table and started tearing up the hot paranthas.

"It is so different when you come and eat here without Alok. There is no frantic urgency about eating," Ryan said.

"Is that a letter from home?" I said.

"If you say so. Where are they now – LA or something," Ryan said.

"How often do your parents write?" I said.

"Used to be every week, then once in two weeks. Now they write once a month," Ryan said, smothering each chunk of parantha with yellow butter.

"Do you write back?" I said.

"No. Not unless it is a couriered letter. In that case the delivery guy asks me to write a few lines right there."

"So what is the deal here Ryan? I mean, they are just abroad trying to make a buck. What have you got against them?"

"I have nothing against them. I am just indifferent. I need another parantha."

"Shut up. How can that be? I mean, how come you save all their letters? I saw them, hundreds next to your vodka stash."

Ryan stopped chewing. "It is too complicated. I don't want to talk about it."

"You won't talk to *me*?"

"They are too strange. I kept telling them let us stay together after my boarding school. But the international business was really taking off then and they had to leave. I guess what I wanted was never in the picture. So, okay I get the dollar cheque, thank you. But spare me the we-miss-you shit. If you do, what the hell are you going to do about it?"

"Did you tell them about the Disco?" I said.

"Are you crazy?" Ryan said.

"You know, you could join their business after IIT. I mean, you know what our job scene will be. But you won't have to worry."

"No way in hell," Ryan said, and clenched his hands. "Never. I will open a parantha shop, become a coolie, wash cars but I am not going to go to them."

"They are your parents..."

He gave me a dirty look. "So thank you very much. I am going back to Alok. You have a good time with your girl."

"Ryan, could you give up your lube project right when it was about to become successful?" I said.

"What?"

"Answer me," I said.

"That is the only good thing I ever did in IIT. It is my passion, my sweat, and my belief. No, how could I give it up?"

"Maybe this pottery business is your parents' lube project," I said as I stood up too.

He picked up his letter again and walked away.

"Reply to it Ryan," I shouted across the road.

He put the letter back in his pocket.

"Neha, is that you?" I said, even though I was a hundred percent sure it was.

"Hari?" she said, her voice unable to hide the fact that she was expecting this call.

"Before you hang up, can I just say something?" I was suitably humble.

"I am not hanging up. What do you want to say?" she said.

"I miss you. And I love you. God, I was so close to you and then I blew it up. I wanted an A in your dad's course. I thought I could impress him. Somehow, in our twisted minds we planned this Operation Pendulum. And they did a Disco on us, ruined our lives. And now you also don't want to talk to me..." My voice dwindled to a whisper.

"Hari?"

"What?"

"I missed you too." She broke into tears.

I wished I could cry too. But her words made me too happy. I mentally hi-fived myself and tried to control my elation. Keep serious tone, keep serious tone, I told myself.

"Oh Neha, don't cry," I said, probably to make her cry a bit more. I can't tell you how good it feels when a girl cries because she missed you.

"I can't Hari. I can't forget you. Why did you do those things?" she said.

Okay, this is progress, I thought. From 'how could you' to 'why did you' is not bad. Twisted they may be, but I did have my reasons. And I didn't have to give them all now.

"I can explain more. Can we meet? Just for ten minutes," I said.

"Should we? I mean, Dad made me swear I'd never see you," she said.

Now how does one answer that? I tried to think of some rational premise on which swears to dad could be broken. Nothing came to mind.

"I miss you, Neha," I said. When in doubt, be sappy.

"I miss you too. Can you come to the ice-cream parlour at two," she said.

"Sure. But on one condition," I said.

"What?"

"Can we not have strawberry this time? I like chocolate more," I said.

"Shut up, Hari," she said, unable to hide a laugh. There, I had done it. Tears to titters in one call. Plus, a tiny date thrown in too. I did a mini jig at the public phone booth, which made the other customers in the shop think I had won a lottery.

"See you then," I said and hung up the phone. I heard the coin go in. What a wonderful way to spend a rupee.

Neha stayed at the ice-cream parlour for two hours, twelve times more than the ten minutes she had come for. By the end, I'd told her everything. She couldn't really remain upset for too long. I guess it could be because I bought strawberry as well as chocolate, but maybe it was because she was just happy to see me. We fixed the next date for a week later, and soon we were back in the 'fix the next date on the previous' cycle. It helped me pass all the idle time in the dropped semester. We worked eight hours a day in Prof Veera's lab, sometimes ten or twelve. Ryan worked longer, even up to sixteen. He ripped open his scooter for experimentation, making it a pain to move around in the insti. Alok used crutches for a month and then got by with a limp. Prof Veera liked the second proposal a lot, and he kept informing the Dean of the progress we were making. He never brought up the issue of a clean grade sheet or extra credits, but we knew there was little chance until we finished the proposal. We gave the final draft to Prof Veera one week before the semester ended. It was two hundred pages, and from Ryan, Alok and I this time.

"Wow. This is a fat proposal," Prof Veera said.

"It's literally the whole study. We have isolated the optimum mix already," Ryan said.

"I know. This is way beyond a proposal," Prof Veera said as he flipped through the pages, "I cannot believe the four months are over."

"Me neither. I guess it will be time to attend classes again," I said.

"And loads of them. Maximum credits this time, and I am not skipping any more," Alok said.

"Me neither, right Ryan?" I said.

"Yeah. I'll come along as well," Ryan said, "So Prof Veera, what do we do with this tome now?"

"Well," Prof Veera said, putting the proposal on his desk, "let me take a final read and unless there are big corrections,

I'll just submit it. Good job and take your week off before your loaded semester begins."

"And the credit and grade sheet, sir," Alok prompted.

"Later guys. It depends on the reception to the proposal. Don't be too optimistic, but we shall see," Prof Veera said.

We left his office, leaving our work of three months. It could get us nowhere, but we had given it our best shot. The final sem began on Jan 5, just a week from now. And six days later, on the eleventh, was my big date with Neha, when she would be free for the whole day. If she would let me come to her home again, I thought.

25

A Day of Letters

THE FIRST DAY OF OUR FINAL SEMESTER FELT AS SPECIAL as the first day of classes in the institute. We got up at six-thirty for the eight o' clock class. Ryan took a shower and then proceeded to carefully comb his hair for the next twenty minutes.

Even then we made it before class began. It was Prof Saxena's 'Refrigeration and Air-conditioning' or RAC class. He was a senior prof, and touted to be next in line for head of the department. That is, if Cherian moved on to something else, retired or just died. None of that was imminent as of now so Prof Saxena was content teaching final year students how to keep things cool. We were the first students to arrive, and he was already in the class.

"Welcome, welcome," Prof Saxena said, "now this is a surprise. Who would have thought fourth year students will reach early for class."

I guess he was right. In the final semester, people were more interested preparing for job interviews and MBA admissions. We hadn't even bothered to see which companies were recruiting this time, for we didn't know if we were getting a degree this year.

"Good morning, sir," Ryan said as we took front row seats. We were sitting in a classroom after four months. A blackboard never looked so great. I wondered when the class would begin.

"What are your names?" Prof Saxena asked.

"I have heard those names," he said after we told him. His forehead developed creases as he tried to remember.

"We had a Disco last semester, sir. You were part of the committee," Ryan said.

"Oh yes," Prof Saxena said, "Yes, the Cherian case. So, this must be your first class in months."

We nodded solemnly.

"That explains it. So, what is your situation? Will you be graduating on time?" Prof Saxena said. I couldn't say if there was real concern in his voice or if he was just passing time before class.

"We are five credits short, sir. Even though we have loaded up courses for this semester," Alok said.

"How many courses do you have?"

"Six," I said.

"Wow. Most final semester students do just two. And that too they hardly attend class. You will be in classes all day," Prof Saxena said.

"Yes sir. No choice." I shrugged.

"Have you talked to Cherian about credits?" Prof Saxena said.

"Prof Veera is trying for us," I said.

"Hmm. Anyway, the system is harsh. Look at you boys, could have got a job even with your low GPAs. Lots of software companies this time. But this Disco might spoil your entire degree," Prof Saxena said.

A few other students trickled in over the next few minutes. I think there were ten of us in class, while over thirty had signed up for the course. I remembered earlier eight a.m. classes, how we never attended them even in the second and third years. But right now, I couldn't wait to learn.

"Third law of thermodynamics," Prof Saxena said as he got up to turn to the blackboard.

Ryan, Alok and I took out our pens and jotted down every word the prof spoke for the next hour.

I met Neha a couple of weeks into the final semester. For the first time, I had to scramble to make it for a date. I had to finish five assignments on the weekend, not to mention revise notes for the coming minor tests. I couldn't afford to fail in any course, and somehow I had this big urge to learn a lot in my final days at IIT. But a date with Neha was a date with Neha, so stapling my sheets for the ergonomics assignment, I ran out to the ice-cream parlour.

"Twenty minutes late! Do you realize you are twenty minutes late?" Neha said.

"Sorry, this assignment..."

"I have to go back early today. Dad's elder brother and family are coming for dinner. Dad is going mad preparing for

them. And since when were you into assignments so much?"
She hadn't removed hands from hips.

"I don't know. Just don't want to take any chances. Can
I buy you an ice-cream?"

"No thanks. I have already had one waiting for you. And
with my relatives home tonight, there will be a big meal. And
I am trying to reduce," she said.

"Reduce what?" I asked.

"My weight," she said.

"Really? Why? You look great," I said.

"No way. You should see the girls in my college. Anyway,
what have you been up to?" she said.

"Classes, classes and more classes. Eight to six every day.
Then another three hours in the library. Then another two for
assignments and revisions. I am going mad. But what to do?
Never had this much course-load before."

"What about Ryan and Alok?" she said.

"They are equally overworked. And we'll still fall short of
credits," I said.

"What about your C2D, the whole cooperate to
dominate..."

"That was all crap. It doesn't work that way Neha. I know
it doesn't. I might be busy now, but at least I am learning
something. I am not just cogging assignments and beating the
system. That is not what it is about."

"Wow, my loafer has become all serious. What is it about
then?" Her voice went playful, always a good sign.

"It is about knowledge. And making the most of the system,
even if it has flaws. And it is about not listening to bloody Ryan
all the time," I said.

"You are getting all wise. I miss my loafer," she said.

I became quiet and looked into her eyes. Then, in one instant I got up and kissed her on the lips.

"Hari! Are you crazy? People know me here," she said.

"Just to let you know the loafer is still there," I said.

"Yeah right. Anyway, look what I got," she said and took out a piece of paper from her bag.

"It's your brother's letter," I said.

"Yes, his last. I want you to keep it," she said.

"Why?" I said. It was a weird gift, to say the least.

"I don't know. Dad doesn't trust me anymore. And he comes and searches my room now and then. I don't want him to find this."

"Really? Is he giving you a lot of trouble?" I said.

"Not much. I just don't speak to him much. I did hear him talk about you guys the other day though."

"What? Where?"

"I'll tell you. Will you keep my letter then?"

"You know I will. What did he say?"

"Dean Shastri came home the other day. They were talking about this proposal."

"The lube project," I said.

"Yes, something like that. Prof Veera had given each of them a copy. Dean Shastri was quite impressed with the findings."

"What did your dad say?" I said.

"I don't think you want to hear it," she said.

"No tell me," I fairly shouted. Why do girls take so long to come to the point?

"He said it was an okay-ish effort. But he told Dean Shastri not to trust these students. He said, 'who knows? They have cheated once, they could have cheated to make the findings. They just want their credits,' and that was it."

"Complete crap. That is complete crap. You know Neha, how much we worked our asses off on it."

"I know. But that is what he said. And Dean Shastri told him to think about it some more."

I put the letter on the table. I spread it out; Samir's last words. Someone so sick of his father's desire to get him into IIT that he preferred death. I wondered how much a train passing over you could hurt.

"Two large bricks of strawberry please," I heard a voice in the background.

"Hello Cherian sahib. What happened, big guests tonight?" the counter boy said.

"Yes, my brother is coming from Canada. He loves ice-cream," I heard Prof Cherian's voice.

I froze at my table, like all the flavors of ice-cream in the fridge. Neha froze too. We were sitting right opposite him, and couldn't run out of the parlour. We silently prayed he wouldn't see us. But this was Cherian. A reflection on the steel counter frame was enough.

"Neha!" He turned toward us. I think all the ice-cream in the parlour melted at that tone.

Neha didn't say anything. I didn't move. I recalled last seeing Cherian when he was head of the Disco. Will he ruin me again? I hadn't even ordered my ice-cream.

Cherian came and sat next to me. My heart raced as it attempted to leave my body and escape the parlour.

"You have guts. You bloody rascal, you do have guts," Cherian said as he stared at me.

Neha cleared her throat but he signaled her to keep quiet.

"Sir, I just…sir…just had to…sir just ran into her," I said, talking and thinking at the same time.

"Are you bluffing me again?" Cherian banged his fist on the table. It landed on the open letter and almost tore it.

"Dad, be careful," Neha said as she tried to push his angry fist away.

"What is this?" Cherian said.

Neha opened her palms and covered the letter.

"Nothing. It is nothing, Dad," she said.

"What is it, you rascal?" Cherian said looking at me, his fist still firmly on the letter, "love letters you write to trap my daughter. I told you to stay away from her. So one Disco wasn't enough?"

"It is Samir's letter," I said.

"Hari, shut up," Neha said, as a reflex.

I don't know why I said it. But I wasn't going to repeat it.

"What did he say?" Prof Cherian said.

Neha and I kept silent.

"Remove your hands, Neha," Cherian said and glared at her. She withdrew her hands, only to bring them to her face to wipe her tears. Cherian picked the letter up and read it silently.

He tried hard to retain his composure, but his eyes contracted and his fingers started to shiver. He read the letter again and again and then again. The two bricks of ice-cream he had bought were melting and creating a puddle on our table. but, the puddles in Cherian's mind were causing us more concern. He removed his glasses, his eyes then did the unthinkable. Yes, here he was, the head of our department, the tormentor of my life and his eyes had just become wet. Two fat tears squeezed out of the edges. And there I was, sitting with the Cherian family as they cried. I could have joined in, but I wasn't in the mood. Besides, ice-cream parlours are hardly the place for group cries.

"Dad, are you all right?" Neha said, wiping her tears.

Her father then cried uncontrollably. It was strange to see a grown-up man cry. I mean, you expect them to make you cry. I wished Ryan were here.

"Let's go home, Dad," Neha said as she got up.

Cherian surrendered himself to his daughter. I gave Neha the bag of ice-cream, mostly a syrupy mass now. Her father kept kissing the letter.

They left the parlour and I hadn't gotten a chance to fix my next date with Neha. But I felt damn lucky to survive meeting Cherian again. Neha drove the car with her dad still sobbing in the front seat.

"Sir, are you going to pay for that ice-cream?" the counter boy asked me.

"You mean Cherian was in tears. Like real crying-crying?" Ryan was disbelieving.

"Howling man, with hands on face and lots of tears right until he left. Damn it, I had to pay for two bricks of ice-cream."

"Totally worth it. I would pay for four for a repeat performance. Yes. Even he suffers. Yes!" Ryan performed a little jig.

"It isn't funny Ryan. He must have been in shock," Alok said.

"So? Not my problem. But I missed it. If only I was there," Ryan said.

"Can we do the assignments for tomorrow then? Do we have RAC?" I said.

"Yes, we do," Alok said, "So what is going on about the proposal?"

"I don't know. Neha told me Cherian wasn't so keen. Let us talk to Prof Veera some time next week."

"The companies have arrived you know. I saw the recruitment notice board. Many new ones in the software sector," Alok said.

"No point looking at them yet. If the credits don't work out, we'll have another year to think about it," I said as we opened fresh sheets to do our assignment.

I slept at four that night. Cherian's face after he'd read the letter swam before me. Sure, it was somewhat funny as Ryan said. But it was also sad. How could a strong man like Cherian get like that? *What are these tough people really made of?* And the way Neha took her father back, she must love him a lot. And Cherian must have loved his son a lot, even though he drove him mad enough to kill himself. Do all parents love their kids? What about Ryan? Did he love his parents? Did they love him?

And then I got up. At four a.m. I had the urge to write a letter. Maybe the havoc a letter had wreaked that morning influenced me. I left Kumaon and went to the computer centre. The twenty-four hour center had students working away on their resumes. The job interviews were coming, yes, but not for us.

Dear Dad and Mom,

This is Ryan. I am sorry for typing this. I just had to write tonight to tell you what has been going on in my life. And not all of it is good. But if I don't tell you, who else will I talk to...

I kept writing for like two hours. I don't think I made much sense at all times, but I did write about a lot of things. About our GPAs, our Disco, our tainted grade sheets, Prof Veera, and our stuck lube project. I also wrote about how they had never really loved me enough to keep me with them. I kind of knew I was doing wrong, posing as Ryan and typing away his life story, his deepest secrets. Simply said, Ryan would kill me if he found out. But I kept writing until daybreak. I thought I'd done a good job with the text, better than Ryan for sure. When I finally took the printout, it was ten pages long. It was easy to fake Ryan's signature, and his parents would hardly compare for identity. I had stolen the address from Ryan's room. It took thirty rupees of stamps to mail the damn thing.

"Where are you coming from," Ryan said as he noticed me come to my room at dawn.

"Nothing. Just went for a walk," I said.

Is lying bad?

26

Meeting Daddy

PROF SAXENA HAD TO INTERRUPT HIS CLASS THAT DAY. A peon had delivered a message to him, which he read and then turned to the class.

"Who are Hari, Ryan and Alok?" he asked, fully aware we sat in the front row.

We duly raised our hands.

"Go to Prof Cherian's room. He wants to see you right now."

I tried to be calm, but my heart was beating fast like it had a mind of its own. *Could it be the end of the lube project? Will Cherian hold another Disco? Will he hand me over to the police for buying Neha an ice-cream? Did he realize I paid for his bricks as well?* Irrelevant thoughts darted back and forth until we reached Cherian's office, where I noticed there was a new lock.

Inside, Prof Shastri and Prof Veera sat next to Prof Cherian. No one asked us to sit down.

"Sorry to bring you boys out of class. But just thought we'll talk to you while we were still together," Dean Shastri said.

Profs together is always trouble, I thought. We maintained a deep and meaningful silence.

"We have gone over your work with Prof Veera and your proposal, and we understand you worked on it in your suspended semester," Prof Shastri said.

We looked at Prof Veera.

"Yes sir, they worked for three months in my lab," Prof Veera said.

"Now Prof Veera has made an appeal that we show your absence in the seventh semester for research work instead of disciplinary reasons. Is that right?"

We had promised ourselves not to say a word in that room. It was a simple question, but we didn't want any more trouble.

"Answer Dean Shastri," Prof Veera bade us.

"Yes sir," Alok said.

I never made eye contact with Cherian, but his silence was unnerving. Why wasn't the kingpin in all this saying anything?

"Then I guess you will have a clean grade sheet, right?" Dean Shastri said.

Alok, Ryan and I nodded.

"Well, the final decision in these matters is with your head of department. And you well know your mistakes are quite unpardonable. But this time, Prof Cherian has agreed to show your seventh semester as a research semester."

"What?" the three of us said in unison. Sometimes, even good news can be a shock.

"Yes, Prof Cherian has agreed. Congratulations and good work," Prof Veera said.

I looked at Cherian for the first time. His face remained frozen, as if he was not part of this room. What is up with him? Has he tripped out on grass, I wondered. Whatever the reason, I wanted to get the hell out of that room before he changed his mind.

"Thank you sir. Thank you so much," Alok said.

"Thank you sir. Can we go sir?" I said.

"Sure. We were leaving as well," Dean Shastri said as he and Prof Veera stood up.

"By the way, how is this semester going?" Dean Shastri said.

"It is okay sir. We are still five credits short," I replied.

"Short for what?" Dean Shastri said.

"We don't have enough courses to finish the degree in four years. So we can't apply for any jobs or admissions," I said.

"Well, did you take a full course-load?" Dean Shastri said.

"Of course. We have packed classes," Ryan said.

"Well, again this is a departmental issue. That is why I tell these boys not to get into disciplinary trouble," Dean Shastri said and left the room.

Prof Veera patted my shoulder and left as well.

"Thank you sir," I said to Cherian. I don't know why I did it, kind of just felt like a good exit line.

"Hari, can you stay back for a minute," Prof Cherian spoke for the first time.

"Sure," I said as Alok and Ryan gave me curious glances before vacating the room.

"Sit down," Cherian said and pointing at a chair before him, he got up to lock the door.

Why did he ask me to stay back? Was he going to kill me?

"So five credits short, eh?" Cherian said. So he was listening to what people had said in his room.

"Yes sir," I said.

"You know if I sanction you all to work with Prof Veera this semester to follow through on this project, we could get you laboratory credits."

Now what was that supposed to mean – 'if I sanction'? Was Cherian just reminding me of how much he controlled my fate. Hell, I know that Sir. I am just excited to have a clean grade sheet for now. Maybe one day after several years I might get a job. Can I go now?

"What are you thinking?" Cherian said.

"Uh, nothing sir," I said, returning hastily from my thoughts.

"I said I could get you lab credits, that is if you are ready to work on this project this semester. I know you are already overloaded," Cherian said.

Had Cherian totally lost his mind? What was he saying? He was offering to rescue my degree. And if I was ready to do some lab work. Hell, I'd live in the lab for the next four months for five extra credits. I'd eat lubricants for lunch to get my degree on time.

"I think we can manage some extra lab work, sir," I said when my Adam's apple allowed me.

"Good. Let me speak to Prof Veera and see what he can get you guys to do. If all is fine, we'll add five credits to this sem."

"For all of us sir? I mean, Alok and Ryan too."

"Yes, of course," Prof Cherian said.

"Thank you sir," I said, wiping sweat off my forehead. This wasn't a real moment.

"Thank you, Hari," Cherian dismissed me.

"For what?" I said.

"Nothing. I think you should go back to Prof Saxena's class. And start preparing for those job interviews," Cherian said.

"Of course, sir," I said and stood up.

"And don't behave in the interviews like you did in my viva," Prof Cherian said and started laughing. I tried to sense if there was malicious intent in his laughter, but he sounded genuinely amused. I joined in the laughter.

"Right sir," I said and left his room grinning like an idiot.

We had promised to drink less since the Disco, but Cherian's news was huge and worth intoxication.

"Open the second bottle," Alok said, "today I am telling you Ryan, open the second bottle."

"Take it easy, Fatso. We still have assignments and lab work, not to mention those job interviews," I said.

"How? How did you do it Hari?" Ryan said, by now already high.

"I didn't do anything. I really thought he was going mad. But that is what he said." I shrugged.

"You are awesome man," Ryan said as he came forward and kissed my cheek. I hate it when he does that.

"Which is the next interview then Alok?" I asked, pushing Ryan away.

"Okay guys, here is the deal," Alok said, taking out a file full of brochures of companies, "we are five-pointers, remember? So a lot of these jobs won't even short-list us."

"I don't care man. Tell me any job that will," Ryan said.

"Software. That is the hot sector this year. They hire in droves and don't have GPA-based short-listing criteria," Alok said.

"I love software," Ryan vouched.

"When is the interview?" I said.

"Well, a good one is in three weeks. What do you say? All of us apply? Who knows, we can all be together," Alok said.

"We will be," I said and raised my glass.

"Cheers, to five credits," we all said in unison.

The alarm rang at six a.m. The big interview day had arrived. For the first time that semester, we skipped the first three classes. The last few weeks had been backbreaking with Prof Veera's lab work adding three hours to the already full fourteen hours a day workload.

But today was the software company's interview; the best chance for low-GPA students like us to get employment.

"Wake up, Fatso. We need to dress up for these interviews," I hollered.

"Will we get it?" Alok said.

"Not if you stay in bed," Ryan said, pulling his quilt away.

IITians really dress up for interviews. For the first time in four years, I wore a tie. It was a weird tie, with orange spots on black or the other way round, I forget. But it had worked for a senior last year and Kumaonites considered it lucky. Ryan had got a new Italian silk tie from his parents, bastard. For some reason, his gifts had increased the last few weeks. I wondered if they had received my letter.

Ryan's scooter was now engineless, so we had to take an auto to the institute. We couldn't walk and spoil the creases on our shirts and trousers, as Ryan pointed out.

"Technosoft Software interviews here," said a sign in the insti building. There were over fifty of us, all students from my batch dressed like we were attending our wedding.

"Apparently, half the batch has already got jobs. This is the best chance for the under-performers like us," Alok sighed.

I tried to think of the day when I had started relating so well to the word under-performer. Was it the first quiz we messed up? Was it our first GPA? Was it the Disco? I guess there were enough things we screwed up to earn our place in that club.

Amongst the three of us, Ryan had his interview first, followed by Alok and then me. Before the interview, we took an aptitude test. It had simple IQ type questions that any IITian could answer after a bottle of vodka in him.

"It is the interview. That is where they decide," Alok said.

We submitted our grade sheets. The seventh semester column was blank, with 'Research Absence', emblazoned across it. The rest of the semesters were pretty ordinary, lots of Cs and Ds.

"Best of luck, Ryan," Alok said as he hugged Ryan.

"Careful, don't spoil the crease," Ryan warned.

He came out after twenty minutes.

"How was it?" Alok said.

"Don't know. Not too great I guess. They only asked about my low grades, and why I wanted to do this and all that," Ryan said.

"So what did you say," I said.

"Just whatever. Let us just wait and see," he said.

Alok went for twenty minutes. It was my turn as soon as he came out.

A thirty-year-old man welcomed me into the interview room.

"Hi, I am Kamal Desai. You are Hari, right?" he said.

"Yes sir," I said.

"Sit down, sit down. And don't sir me, call me Kamal."

I sat down quietly. Kamal browsed through my files and then stopped at the grade sheet.

"Hmmm...5.48 overall, what happened?" He looked into my eyes.

It was right at this moment when I should have had my panic attack. But I didn't this time. I don't know why, but ever since I saw Ryan's plan fail, Alok jump and Cherian cry, the whole wide world didn't intimidate me anymore.

"I screwed up my first semester, sir...I mean Kamal. And it is really hard to come back in IIT if you miss the first time."

"That is very interesting. What happened in the first sem?" Kamal said

"Don't know. Felt like enjoying college life a bit. I guess IIT is not that type of college," I said.

"Yes, IITs are truly different. Tell me, do you like IIT?" Kamal said.

It was a loaded question. A question no one had asked me before. I had thought I'd be quick to say how I hated every living moment of it, but couldn't. I remembered my first day – the day Ryan saved me from Baku and his coke bottles. Four years, and soon it would be time to leave this place. Did I like it here?

"I don't know. There are things I'd rather forget. But I met my best friends here, and hopefully this place will get me a job," I said.

Kamal laughed. I could see him as one of the students ten years ago. I wondered what his GPA had been in his time. That is the thing about IIT, you see people and you wonder what their GPA was. You kind of need that to judge them. Sad.

Kamal asked me a few more questions about why I wanted to join the software sector. Hell, I'd kiss any sector that would give me a job. And this was my one chance.

"It was very interesting talking to you. That's all for now," Kamal said as he escorted me out of the room.

"Interesting talking to you" – I repeated the phrase three times in my head. *What was that supposed to mean? Just a polite way of saying I was weird and stood no chance? Or did my pathetic resume file really charm him?*

We waited another hour for the results. And that is when I realized that for once my luck might have turned for the better.

"Hari, you and I have made it! You got an offer in Bombay and I got Delhi," Alok said and tugged at my shirt.

I became numb and couldn't answer him for the next five minutes. A crowd of students almost crushed me in their rush to the notice board. I was lost in my thoughts. Just a few days ago, I was planning to spend an extra year to complete five credits and collect a tainted grade sheet. Now I had a way out. And I had a job.

"I didn't get it," Ryan said.

"What?"

That had to be a mistake. How could Alok and I get a job while Ryan not?

"What happened?" I said.

"I don't know. Fuck man, fuck-fuck-fuck," Ryan said as he walked away from us.

"Where is he going?" Alok said.

"I don't know," I said.

For a couple of moments I forgot my own job. *Ryan had not got a job? He was the creative, confident, smart one. He was what I always wanted to be. So he had almost the lowest grade in the insti, but this is Ryan, hello?*

"We got a job, Hari. Six grand a month," Alok said.

"Huh? Oh, yeah," I said, suspending my concern for Ryan for a while. "So, we're not just five-point somethings anymore, we are five point somebodies."

Alok spoke to his parents on the phone for two hours that night. I think he read out the whole offer letter to them. His mother noted down the entire package – basic salary, travel allowance and of course, the much needed medical benefits. Alok was thrilled.

I was still kind of numb. When good things happen to you, you kind of feel there is something odd. Like this could be a dream. That Kamal Desai of Technosoft will call me and say it was all a bad joke. And then again, the job was in Bombay.

"What is with you? You don't seem so excited," Alok said as he got out of the phone booth.

"I am. I am. But it is in Bombay. What about Neha?" I said.

"What about her? You'll still continue after IIT?" Alok asked naively, as if she had been part of my curriculum here.

"Why not?" I said, placing my fingers in the booth's grill.

Alok shrugged his shoulders. It was pointless talking to him. He would have rather discussed the dental benefits that the job gave us.

"Where is Ryan?" I said.

"I think he went to the lab. He said he wanted to talk to Prof Veera," I said.

"I hope he finds something. I think that is the other reason why I can't be so fully excited," I said.

"It's hard for him. He is only 5.01, and the last in class. It is difficult for him to get placed," Alok said.

"But he is so smart. I mean, the lube project is basically all his," I said.

"GPAs matter," Alok said and walked away.

Ryan did not get a job for another month. Our semester sped by really fast, especially since we were so busy trying to meet our deadlines. Ryan kept applying to companies, but he only got two more interviews. The last guy in the class always found it hardest to get a job. For that matter, if Kamal Desai was not into honesty appreciation that day, I might have been in Ryan's situation.

"You guys can't lose heart. Ryan, you must keep trying," Prof Veera exhorted as we stood in the lab.

Ryan's scooter engine was running at full blast. Today's mixture had an unusually bad smell, stinking up the whole lab. I kind of wished this was not the optimal mix for our final lubricant.

"I can't Prof Veera. It is not going to work," Ryan said, looking at the exhaust fumes coming out of the engine.

"Of course, it will. But I do feel you are made for better things than a run-of-the mill software job," Prof Veera said.

"What do you mean?" Ryan said.

"I mean you should work in research. What is in a software job? You are contract labour at cheap prices for foreigners. Ryan, you really think you will be happy there?"

"I would be," Alok said.

"I am asking Ryan. You guys are friends, but you all could want different things you know," Prof Veera said.

"Like what? What else can I do?" Ryan said.

"Would you like to work as my RA?" Prof Veera said. "Research Assistant. I can get you a two-year contract. Will not pay a lot, say two thousand a month. But you live on campus, and you can continue research on lubricants."

I saw Ryan's face. The Rs 2000-number was writ large on his face; a third of what our jobs would pay us. Would Ryan be able to accept that?

"It is an idea," he said eventually.

"It is a great idea. And if we find an investor who is willing to commercialize your product, who knows how successful you can be," Prof Veera said.

Ryan looked at me. Somehow, I felt he wanted me to make a decision for him. I thought about it less than I should have, but gave my answer.

"I think you will be happy doing this, Ryan. And I am sure you will find an investor for it one day," I said.

"I project the market for this product at atleast ten crore. You'll get a royalty of, I don't know, say ten percent. Of course, if we find someone who invests in the factory first," Prof Veera said.

"I'll do it," Ryan smiled, "I am your RA, sir."

"Yes!" I said and hi-fived him.

"I guess all of us are officially employed," Alok said, "can we party now?"

"Of course, you should. But go easy on the vodka," Prof Veera said but he was grinning.

27

Five Point Someone

IT WAS THE CONVOCATION DAY, OFFICIALLY OUR LAST DAY at IIT. We'd struggled unto the end, but had finally made it! We had passed all our final semester courses, finished our lab work and had all secured some sort of a job. It is the least any IITian can expect in four years, but to us it was nothing short of a miracle. I had hardly spoken to Neha in the past few weeks. I called once after I got the job, and she cried because (a) she was so happy for me and (b) because it was in Bombay. It is not easy to figure out how girls cry for two different reasons at the same time. But I didn't push her much. She also said it was best we didn't meet for a while, lest Cherian find out and flare up again. Frankly, that was fine with me (even though I made a big fuss) with all these damn courses. I had not seen Cherian after that day in his office when he was stoned enough to pardon me. But today, I would see him again. After all, the head of the department makes a speech to the passing-out batch. We were part of the passing-out batch and that was celebration in itself.

Alok, Ryan and I wore our graduation robes. As usual, Ryan looked the best. "I am not sitting in front. You can't fall asleep in front," I protested, as we reached the convocation hall.

"No, it is our last day. I want to see everything," Alok insisted.

"Then get your glasses fixed," Ryan said.

Alok insisted on sitting in the first row and we sat down facing the podium. We looked back at the guests' gallery.

"That is my mom and didi in the aisle. See Dad is there, too," Alok said as he waved at a wheelchair.

"Your parents are here too, right?" I said to Ryan.

"Yes, they flew in last night. I told them not to come, but they did. See, there they are in the third row," Ryan pointed out with quiet pride.

Yes, there they were, along with the parents of three hundred students. The huge convocation hall held them all, the whole insanely proud lot.

I saw Neha. She had come with her father, and sat primly with other faculty families. I waved to her and ten other profs waved back.

"Sit down Hari. It is about to begin." Alok pulled me down.

Prof Cherian took the stage, all the waving and murmurs ceased, and the convocation hall became silent as a tomb.

"Good morning. As head of the Mechanical Engineering department I welcome everyone to this convocation ceremony. Today we are proud to give a new batch of the brightest mechanical engineers to this country. I give this speech every year, and I have done so for ten years now," Prof Cherian said and paused to have a sip of mineral water.

"Ten years! This guy's really been around," Alok whispered.

"To torment class after class," Ryan supplied.

"Shh!" I said.

"And every year I make a similar speech, congratulating our best students and talking about how they should continue to achieve in the future. In fact, I make the speech by looking at what I said last year. However, this year I am going to do something different. In fact, I don't even have a written speech. I just want to tell you a story."

A murmur threaded through the crowd. No one expected Cherian to tell stories. Announce the toppers, wish everyone the best and close it. What was going on?

"Once upon a time there was a student in IIT. He was very bright, and this is true, his GPA was 10.00 after four years. He didn't have a lot of friends, as to keep such a high GPA, you only have so much time for friends."

The crowd dutifully chuckled.

"But he did have classmates. Classmates who this bright boy thought were less smart than him, classmates who were selfish and wanted to make the most money or go to the USA with minimum effort. And the classmates did exactly that. They went to work for multinationals and some went abroad. Some of them opened their own companies in the USA – mostly in computers and software. This was twenty years ago mind you, so computers were a very new thing."

Prof Cherian paused again for water.

"What is his point?" Alok said.

"I don't know. I told you not to sit in the front row. We can't even sleep now," Ryan said.

"But the bright boy stayed behind. Because he had principles. He did not want to use his education for selfish personal gain. He wanted to help the country. He wanted to do research and he stayed back at IIT. Of course, getting a research project approved in IIT is harder than inventing the telephone," Prof Cherian said as the faculty in the audience smiled.

"So our bright boy was disappointed. He still kept trying but apart from being a Professor, there isn't much one could achieve here. Ten years passed, when his friends from college visited home. One of them had a GPA of seven point something, and he had his own software company. The turnover had reached two hundred million dollars. Another friend was heading a toothpaste MNC, and came in a BMW. Of course, this didn't bother the principled bright boy. Or so he thought.

"As you guessed, that bright boy was me. And at that time I thought it didn't matter if others had achieved more personally. I was still the one with the better GPA, the smarter one, the brighter one. Somehow, on that day, I decided my son must get into IIT. I wanted him to carry on my family's strong intellectual tradition. Strong intellectual tradition – that is what I called it. But it was just my big ego. My son wanted to be a lawyer, hated maths. I hated him for hating maths. I pushed him just as I pushed students in my class. He failed to get in the first time and I made life hell for him. He failed a second time and I made his life an even bigger hell. Then he failed to get in the third time. And this time, he killed himself."

The crowd gasped. Students and even some of the faculty members started whispering.

"You all know that I have a daughter. But I also had a son, who died in a rail track accident five years ago. At that time, we thought it was an accident. But this..." Cherian said as he pulled out Samir's letter, "is my son's letter I got only a few weeks ago. He wrote this to my daughter on the day he died. He killed himself because he did not get into IIT. He killed himself because of me," Cherian said and paused for a long time. He removed his spectacles and wiped his eyes. The audience was silent enough to hear Cherian's mild sobs.

"He is crying," Ryan said.

"I told you. This is nothing compared to..." I stopped as Cherian began again.

"I am sorry everyone for bringing up this sad story on your special day. I told myself that if I admit to my mistake publicly, perhaps my son will forgive me. And I wanted to thank the one student in this class because of who I found out the truth. It is my daughter's boyfriend – Hari. And he is here sitting right in the front row."

"Wow!" Alok and Ryan said in unison. All eyes turned to me. I have never been so embarrassed in my life. This is not the limelight one wants. I wished he'd just move on from here, but he didn't.

"Let me tell you something about this boy Hari and his friends Alok and Ryan. They are the under-performers. That is what I used to call students with low GPAs. And they do have a low GPA – five point something is low, right?" Cherian asked in a jestful manner.

"My daughter found it easier to trust Hari with the letter. She defied me, lied to me and ignored me just to meet him. Somewhere down the line, this perfect ten-GPA Professor standing in front of you had gone wrong. Really wrong."

I sat back, listening to Cherian carefully. I kind of felt sad and for the first time felt he just may have a heart.

"And that is when I realized that GPAs make a good student, but not a good person. We judge people here by their GPA. If you are a nine, you are the best. If you are a five, you are useless. I used to despise the low GPAs so much that when Ryan submitted a research proposal on lubricants, I judged it without even reading it. But these boys have something really promising. I saw the proposal the second time. I can tell you, any investor who invests in this will earn a rainbow."

"Did you hear that Hari?" Ryan said.

I nodded.

"Anyway, this is my message to all you students as you find your future. One, believe in yourself, and don't let a GPA, performance review or promotion in a job define you. There is more to life than these things – your family, your friends, your internal desires and goals. And the grades you get in dealing with each of these areas will define you as a person.

"Two, don't judge others too quickly. I thought my son was useless because he didn't get into IIT. I tell you what, I was a useless father. It is great to get into IIT, but it is not the end of the world if you don't. All of you should be proud to have the IIT tag, but never ever judge anyone who is not from this institute – that alone can define the greatness of this institute."

The crowd responded with wild applause.

"And lastly, don't take yourself too seriously. We professors are to be blamed even more for this. Life is too short, enjoy yourself to the fullest. One of the best parts of campus life is the friends you make. And make sure you make them for life. Yes, I have heard the stories. Sometimes I wish I had had a friend, even if that meant a lower GPA. It must be good to have vodka on top of the institute roof at night.".

Cherian got a standing ovation.

The applause got louder, in fact it was right under my ears, on my shoulder.

"Wake up you lazy bozo," Ryan said, clapping my shoulder so hard my dream paused and faded out like a defective videotape.

"What?" I rubbed my eyes.

"Yes, it is me. So tell me Mr Hari, how does it feel to miss your convocation after you make all this effort to get into IIT." That was Ryan's cocky voice all right.

"What the...what time is it?" I craned my neck to look at the alarm clock. It said seven a.m, clearly in contrast to the sun outside.

"Looks like your clock has also had enough of this place. It is past eleven. Both of us slept through our convocation," Ryan said wryly.

I got out of bed and went outside to the balcony; the hostel was empty.

Damn, I had slept through graduation day. Worse, Cherian had not really cried.

"Fuck!" I said, borrowing Ryan's vocabulary. "Fuck. Does that mean they'll not give us the degree?"

"Of course they will. Just means we weren't there when the rest of the class shook hands with Cherian and parents applauded."

I wondered if it made sense to brush my teeth or eat at Sasi's first.

"Sasi's?" Ryan read my mind.

Man, four years of freaking craziness to get a degree, and when the time came to collect, Ryan and I sat in our pajamas circling our paranthas with dabs of butter. I really don't deserve this degree!

"Hari, you know Dad said he wants to invest in the lubricant project. He is in touch with Prof Veera," Ryan said as Sasi looked at us slyly. Even he knew we should have been at the convocation.

"That is great."

"It's crap. I told them I don't want their money," Ryan said.

"Are you an idiot?"

"And then guess what they said? They said they thought I would be okay because of that letter," Ryan said.

"What letter?" I said, struggling to keep a straight face.

"This letter," Ryan said and took out a fat envelope, "and guess what I noticed on the cover?"

Yep, there it was. The thirty bucks of postage that I put on it was stamped all over.

"So you wrote to them?" I said, still appearing as casual as I could.

"Okay Mr Hari, will you give it up. You made all the effort of typing the damn thing, could you at least have been careful while writing the address? This scrawny handwriting of yours is a dead giveaway," Ryan said.

"What?" I said. Crap, I should have thought of that.

Ryan got up and mock punched me several times over. "You ass, when did you become so senti?" he said as I wriggled my way out of his punches. We burst out laughing. I looked into his eyes. He wasn't mad, maybe even a bit glad. But that changed fast into a serious expression. Yes, Ryan will never admit to wanting this.

"You shouldn't have," he said.

"Oh well, I must have been drunk that day. And I do think your parents are nice. Anyway, it is a good project. Your dad will probably make money out of it." The big picture, that's what I should focus on, not spoil things with paltry confidences on letter-writing.

"I am sure he will. Prof Veera accepted his funding."

"Prof Veera knows what he is doing," I said wisely. "When the hell will Alok come back? Do you think we missed much?"

"All convos are the same. Cherian gives medals to nine pointers. Five-pointers collect their degrees in the background like extras," Ryan shrugged.

I saw a silhouette limping towards us from a distance.

"Alok!" I shouted.

"You fuckers! Chomping paranthas while the country got another batch of engineers," Alok said.

"Whatever Fatso, you want one or not?" Ryan said, making the rare gesture of offering his plate.

"Of course I do. After all that Cherianspeak for an hour," Alok said, putting out his tongue to indicate extreme exhaustion.

"Where are the parents?" Ryan said.

"Invited to the faculty club for lunch. I came back looking for you," Alok said.

"Did Cherian talk a lot? You know I was dreaming of him," I said.

"Really? And I thought you only dreamt of his daughter wearing nothing," Ryan teased.

"Shut up." I turned to Alok. "So what did he say?"

"Nothing. Just the same IITians-are-the-best crap. Though he did mention one thing," Alok said.

"What?" Ryan and I cried in unison.

"That we need to look at the system. Sometimes the pressure is too much. Something about lesser tests and more projects etc. Didn't really follow it – I was dozing off a bit you know," Alok said "You suck man," Ryan said, subsiding back into his seat.

"Yeah right. At least I made it on my last day of IIT," Alok said virtuously.

Last day, Alok's words resonated in my mind. Man, how we had waited for this to get over. And finally it had. Maybe not in style, maybe not with standing ovations or medals, but in our pajamas and eating paranthas at a street-side vendor, we had made it. Yes, the three of us were IIT graduates. Not the ones that would make it to the cover of *Time* magazine, but at least we could be called survivors. "Yes, it was over!" I tried telling myself – but at one level, it felt sad.

"It really is over then, eh?" Ryan echoed my thoughts.

"Yes it is. Time to enter the real world – as they said at the convo," Alok said, showing off.

I wish I had never met Neha. Separating from her would hurt.

"Have you talked to Neha?" Ryan asked, uncannily reading my mind.

"I will. We are meeting tonight," I said casually.

"Does Cherian know?" Alok said

"I don't think so," I said. He may have relented here and there, but me and Neha together was still a no-no.

"And what about us?" Ryan said.

We looked at each other. Hell, this was going to be hard. Why is it that when the bad things about IIT come to an end, the good things end as well. It sucks to leave the hostel, to not be able to see your friends every day.

"We'll be friends. For fucking forever and ever," I vowed filmily and got up to give a group hug.

"Enough guys, this is a decent establishment," Ryan said and we sat back, laughing an embarrassed laugh.

That was the last time we were together at IIT. After that, our lives changed. But I don't really want to get into all that. This is an IIT book after all.

And I didn't know what would happen between Neha and me. I mean I could tell you now what happened, but I don't really want to go into all that either.

Yes, that night we met and said we loved each other and other sappy stuff. And we talked about practical things like how to stay in touch And we promised to keep meeting forever and ever.

But forever is a long time you know, even longer than the four years at IIT. A lot can happen between now and forever, and it will – it is just not something we have to talk about in this book. The convocation was over. Our bags were packed, and that was the last time the three of us were together in IIT.

Alok started his job in Delhi, and with no Ryan and me to bother him, totally immersed himself in it. As a result, his software company sent him to the US for six months. The US assignment earned him a dollar stipend that in one stroke wiped out his family woes. A spanking new car arrived at the Guptas, and I was tempted to consider marrying his sister. Alok's father got a full-time nurse, and his mother is considering leaving her job to do private tuitions. I think she needs to keep a job just to keep sane, but who listens to me?

Ryan worked with Prof Veera, and with all that cash from his dad, is investing in a factory about two hours from Delhi. Local villagers from nearby have been hired for construction, including some women. Sick bastard that he is, he often goes there to check them out. I think he fancies someone called Roopkunwar more than the others — and I think there is a disaster waiting to happen.

I went off to Bombay and, like most responsibilities in my life, hated it. I can't live in cramped cities, and I can't stay away from Neha. In the first three months, half of my salary went in rent for a pigeonhole in the Siberian end of town. The other half went mostly in phone calls to Neha.

God, I missed her — her hair, her laugh, her eyes, her holding my hand and everything else. Sure, I missed Ryan and Alok as well, but it was not the same. I pined for Neha.

She finished her fashion design course and had an offer to work for a local designer. I think she is trying to find something here in Bombay. It should work out, given this city is so fashion crazy.

Meanwhile, next month I am going to Delhi for Alok's didi's wedding. All of us will be there — Alok, Ryan, Neha and me. And that is what is keeping me going for now. You know, it is strange, I might have passed out of IIT, but in some ways, my soul is still there. Maybe in the hostel corridors, or at Sasi's, or at the insti roof...